Fava

John Hazen

The final approval for this literary material is granted by the author.

First printing

ISBN: 978-1-61296-300-6

PUBLISHED BY BLACK ROSE WRITING

www.blackrosewriting.com

Printed in the United States of America

Fava is printed in Cambria

To Lynn, my wife, my one & only.

Fava

1

"Gil, tonight's PowerMax drawing will be an estimated $750 million, the largest jackpot in history!

"I'm standing outside Flores Grocery Store at the corner of Amsterdam Avenue and 165th Street. I've never seen anything like it. The line of people waiting to buy their PowerMax tickets stretches around the block.

"There've already been a few scuffles as people have tried to cut in line. There are similar lines at every lottery outlet in the city, and probably throughout the state and the country as well."

I exaggerated somewhat. Yes, there were waiting times at various locations that sold lottery tickets but they were manageable. For some unknown reason, Flores was the only lottery distributor in this part of the city for a seven-block radius. The queue would therefore be extremely long here as compared to areas where PowerMax tickets could be purchased on nearly every block. I'd purposely chosen to shoot at this unimpressive bodega because the number of people would provide a good visual.

I had Jonas, my cameraman, pan away from me and down the line stretching as far as the lens could see. Darkness was already falling in early-spring New York and a number of people in the line raised a hand up to shield their eyes from the intense light mounted on Jonas's camera.

I headed over to a young dark-skinned woman who was waiting patiently for her turn to enter the small grocery. Jonas followed me.

"Excuse me miss, would you mind saying a few words?"

The young woman shyly nodded her head.

"What is your name?"

"Hilda Llanos," she mumbled.

"So, Hilda, do you think today is your lucky day? Are you going to be the one to win?"

The girl simply nodded and then demurely lowered her head back down. I had just a few minutes earlier chatted with Hilda and she was lively and vivacious. She seemed like an ideal candidate for an interview. Once the camera pointed in her direction, however, she became this shy wallflower.

My initial instinct had been to do a taped piece over which I could do a voice-over, but then I reconsidered. Live segments add a little something extra to any report. The cardinal rule about live broadcasts, however, is you must have the ability to instantaneously adapt. Seeing that Ms. Llanos was a complete dud, I moved on to the man next in line to her. I hadn't interviewed him, so this was a crapshoot.

"And your name, sir?"

"Hector Villanueva, and yes, I'm certain I'm going to win." The 30ish slightly built man with short-cropped hair and a goatee smiled confidently into the camera. I was feeling greatly relieved.

"I feel it in my bones. I'm wearing my lucky underwear today."

"We'll just have to take your word on that one, Mr. Villanueva. What's the first thing you'll do with your 750 million dollars?"

"For one thing, I'd buy a nice diamond ring and ask you to marry me."

"If you had 750 million, I might take you up on it!"

I turned back to the camera.

"The PowerMax game, which is played in 33 states, has not had a winner in over three months. Before arriving here I interviewed Dr. Maxwell Farrier, who teaches statistics at Columbia University."

The scene the viewer was watching shifted to a prerecorded interview I had with Dr. Farrier in his office earlier in the day. The gray-haired and bearded Farrier was seated in his book-strewn office. He was wearing khakis, a brown cardigan and light blue shirt, the unofficial uniform of his profession. All he needed was a pipe to complete the tableau.

"Dr. Farrier, they often say that a person has as much chance of winning one of these lottery jackpots as getting hit by a bolt of lightning."

Farrier interrupted.

"No, actually a person has a better chance of being struck by two bolts of lightning than he or she does of winning the PowerMax."

"So, it's not all that unusual that not one person has hit the jackpot over the course of three months?"

"It's obviously not an impossibility since here we are. But as the weeks have rolled on, the purse has steadily increased and so have the number of people who play, hoping to strike it big.

"It would be extremely rare that any game of chance could go this long without a winner, especially as the jackpot grows. As the weeks have gone on, practically everyone in the country is playing this game. I and my colleagues in the field of statistics are analyzing this closely. There are too many variables for us to come up with the precise odds but over the past couple of weeks, we believe it was more likely that someone would win it than the fact that someone somewhere wouldn't."

The scene shifted back to me on the street in front of the bodega.

"Well, Gil, there you have it. The drawing is at ten tonight. I hope you've already bought your tickets."

I heard the voice of anchorman Gil Patrick through my earpiece. Overall, Gil's a good guy but like most anchors, he can occasionally get a little full of himself.

"Yes indeed, Francine, I bought my lucky tickets yesterday. I stood in line for 15 minutes," Gil noted with a level of exasperation that he, a New York anchorman, had to suffer the indignity of standing in line for anything. "If you don't see me tomorrow, you'll know why."

"And right back at you, Gil. This is Francine Vega, Action 6 News, reporting live outside Flores Grocery at the corner of Amsterdam and 165th Street."

I've always had aspirations of doing more than puff pieces on the lottery but my mother brought me up with an ethic that you had to pay your dues. I only wished she'd finally been able to stop cleaning other people's toilets and enjoy life. Unfortunately, ovarian cancer took her way too young. It's been three years now since she died and damn, I miss her so much.

Instead, she had to settle for living vicariously through me. She put me through private schools and then NYU, saw me graduate with honors and then get my first reporting job here with Channel 6. My mother said that her greatest joy in the hospital was when she could tell the nurses who came to attend to her that that was her daughter on the TV. She nearly took a nurse's arm off when she tried to change the channel during the news.

After interviewing Dr. Farrier and before shooting the segment in front of Flores Grocery Store, I had an appointment with the New York State lottery commission's communications director, Wendy Abernathy. On the off chance that a New Yorker won the coveted prize, I wanted to have already gathered additional information for a follow-up piece. It was just background stuff so I didn't ask Jonas to accompany me since no footage would be required.

When I arrived at the commission's offices, which was on the ninth floor of a building in the Wall Street area of downtown New York, a serious-looking young blond woman escorted me from the downstairs lobby to Ms. Abernathy's office. Since 9/11, escorts for visitors to and from their final destinations had become commonplace at all government and most private offices.

My interview with Abernathy took about twenty minutes. While cordial, she didn't provide me with a lot of new information I didn't already know. When it was concluded, I fully expected to be escorted back out. Instead, she indicated she had some phone calls to make and, since her secretary was on break, she asked me if I wouldn't mind showing myself out. I said of course not and, after we shook hands, I proceeded toward the exit.

As I was walking down the aisle I glanced in each cubicle I passed until I found exactly what I was looking for. Reading the name on the outside of the cube, I spoke up.

"Excuse me, Mr. Epstein?"

An overweight fifty-plus year old bureaucrat with a graying comb-over looked up from his computer screen. Mr. Epstein straightened up in his chair, sucked in his gut, tucked in his shirttail, smoothed back his unkempt hair and took off his wireframe glasses.

"Please, call me Howard."

"Why certainly, Howard," I cheerily intoned, "My name is Francine Vega."

"Yes, I recognize you from the six o'clock news. You're much prettier in person."

"Why thank you, Howard. It's very kind of you to say such a thing. You know what they say about that vicious camera. These are certainly exciting times for the Lottery Commission. The whole place must be abuzz about the big jackpot."

Howard Epstein struck a nonchalant pose to give the impression that such jackpots were commonplace.

"It's a nationwide game. We're only one of 33 states that carries PowerMax. The winner will probably be out in Dubuque or some such place."

"I've been to Dubuque; they don't deserve a winner. What do you do here at the lottery commission, Howard?"

"I monitor compliance all around the State. I make sure no outlets are trying to game the system."

Howard puffed himself up with his own importance.

"That's quite a responsibility they've put on you, isn't it?"

Howard nodded gravely.

"If a New Yorker were to come forward to claim the prize," I continued, "I bet you'd know about it before anyone else on that computer of yours, wouldn't you?"

"I'd know within minutes if not seconds."

"It would be extremely unfair to my competitors but I was wondering if it would be too much to ask you to give me a call if a New Yorker were to come forward. Of course, I wouldn't want you to do anything that would get you in trouble."

Knowing what the answer would be, I had one of my cards all ready to hand to him.

"It would be my pleasure, Ms. Vega."

"Please, Francine. I already feel like we're old friends."

"Me too, Francine."

I shook hands with Howard and, to seal the deal, I put my other hand over his, holding on for just a moment longer than was necessary. After handing him my card, I headed to the door.

Howard was probably correct; the winner would probably be from Dubuque, a place I'd never come within five hundred miles of. But, as the old lottery slogan goes: Hey, you never know.

When the PowerMax numbers were drawn later that night and it was announced that one winning ticket had indeed been sold at a Manhattan convenience store, I knew it was only a matter of time before Howard Epstein would call me. It was hardly a Watergate-size scoop, but I could not be choosy. A scoop on any story was always looked upon favorably.

I did not despair when a week passed and I hadn't received the call. Lottery winners had a year to claim their winnings. Very often, big jackpot winners would wait weeks or months before coming forward so that they'd have time to confer with accountants and lawyers on how best to handle their newfound luck. They may also move away and change their phone numbers so that they could avoid the inevitable hounding by the media and those who'd want to "assist" in managing the fortune.

At one o'clock in the afternoon my cell phone rang.

"Hello, Francine?"

"Yes, this is Howard, isn't it?"

I wanted to make a point that I remembered Howard Epstein just from hearing his voice.

"Why yes, it is. The winner just came in. His name is Alan

Westbrook. He lives at 367 East Third Street in Alphabet City. His social security number is here but you know I can't give you that. That's all I have. Oh wait. It says here his middle name is Starbuck. I guess his parents loved their coffee."

"Howard, you are such a dear to call me like this. I do hope you won't get in trouble; I'm sure your bosses will want to make an exclusive splash with this."

"They'll never know it was me that leaked it. Anyway, I've got enough years in to retire so there's not much they can do. Glad I could help you. Oh, one last thing, the official announcement is going to be tomorrow evening at 8:00."

"Thank you, Howard."

As I hung up, I made a mental note to send something special to Howard as a token of my esteem and thanks. He struck me as a vodka drinker. But first I had to find out all I could about Alan Starbuck Westbrook. I'd camp out at 367 East Third Street and wait for him to appear. However, I didn't know what the man looked like. I had to do some research. Searching though my contacts, I located the name Hiram Fennessey and hit dial.

Hiram Fennessey was another of my middle-aged bureaucratic conquests. He worked at the Department of Motor Vehicles and had been instrumental in giving me insight into a story on the antiquated computers DMV was using. That was a year and a half ago; I hoped he still remembered me.

"Hello, Hiram? This is Francine Vega."

"Francine! It's wonderful to hear from you. I never did get a chance to thank you for the 12 year old scotch you sent me. It certainly was a lot smoother than the stuff I'm used to drinking."

"Glad you enjoyed it, Hiram. It was the least I could do for all the help you gave me. I was wondering if you could help me again."

"You name it, Francine. Fire away."

"I was wondering if you had anything on an Alan Starbuck Westbrook. He lives at 367 East Third Street, between Avenues C and D. I need a photo if you have one."

"Well, let me see what I have here."

I could hear Hiram's fingers clicking away on his computer. A few seconds later, he came back on the line.

"Well, I have a gentleman by that name but not at that address. Kind of a unique middle name so I suppose it may be the same guy. Says here he had a driver's license that expired in '03 and he didn't renew. At the time he lived on East 72nd Street. If it's the same guy, it's quite a comedown to Alphabet City."

"Is there a picture on file?"

"Yep, although it's kind of old now."

"Think you can email it to me?"

"For you, doll, of course. I still have your card with the email address on it. Coming to you shortly."

"Hiram, you're the doll. Watch out for another bottle of scotch coming your way."

"Not necessary, but surely appreciated. Take care."

"You too, Hiram."

My next step was to see if there was anything on the Internet about Alan Starbuck Westbrook. I typed his name into the search engine. A string of entries appeared on the screen. I clicked on the first and started reading about a man who graduated summa cum laude from Princeton and then went on to get simultaneous degrees from Harvard Law and Business Schools. He then clerked for a Supreme Court Justice and was speculated to be of the caliber attorney to someday be considered for a judgeship. The article was written in 1998 at which time he was a top attorney working at the Pentagon.

I clicked on several other websites and read similar entries but the most recent one I could find was from the year 2001. After that, nothing. This Alan Starbuck Westbrook who lived in an apartment on East Third could not be the same one described here, could it? How many Alan Starbuck Westbrooks could there be?

By this time, Hiram's email had appeared on my computer. I printed it out and called my erstwhile cameraman, Jonas Clarke, telling him to meet me in front of 367 East Third Street.

I arrived at the building at around three. The apartment buildings on the block seemed well-kept enough, but not the one in which Mr. Westbrook lived. It was even more dingy than I'd imagined it would be. The lock on the front door looked like it had been jimmied more than once. Graffiti adorned the front and extended into the vestibule. The building had the appearance of just barely a step above a single room occupancy hotel in which an indigent person would reside.

I leaned against a lamppost, trying to look as nonchalant as I could. Fifteen minutes later, Jonas walked up the street, video camera in hand. His appearance always put a smile on my face. Many people's first impression of him—Jonas was the biggest black man I've ever known—was fear and trepidation but all you had to do was to see his beaming smile and get a sampling of his wonderfully wry sense of humor to know that he was a great human being.

"You're always draggin' me to the best parts of town, Frannie."

Jonas motioned down the block to a storefront in front of which fifteen to twenty motorcycles sat. This was obviously a local chapter of Hell's Angels or some other such fine organization. I remember hearing something about a community effort to get them evicted from the neighborhood, but there was nothing the city could do.

"Ah, quit yer bitchin' Jonas. You're such a wuss. You know I'll protect you."

The image of me, all five foot five inches in heels doing battle to protect my six foot four, two hundred eighty pound cameraman brought a smile to Jonas' face.

"It's just a good thing I love your Latin ass to pieces. Otherwise I wouldn't let you drag me away from the safe confines of my apartment where I'd be surfing the web searching for other Latinas who actually put out."

"Jonas, you know I'd be way too much woman for you. You wouldn't know what to do if I ever did let you have your way with me. You need someone who can cook you up some nice fried fish and collard greens and cornbread. That certainly isn't me."

"Yah, that sure would be nice. But a guy can dream, can't he? Anyway, what the hell we doin' here?"

"The lottery winner lives here. I'm hoping to get an exclusive."

"That's it?"

I couldn't hide my hurt look.

"Jonas, I need any scoop I can get, even if it's only some poor schlub who hit it big."

I knew it was a ridiculous nothing story that I was wasting a whole lot of time on, but it wasn't as if scores of substantial pieces were being directed my way. I'd had a few meaty stories over the four years I'd been with Action 6 News, but generally those were steered to the more established reporters. I had to make the most out of anything I could. My eyes were welling up as Jonas put an arm around me to cheer me up.

"A scoop, huh? Using your sources again I see. You're a damn good reporter, Frannie. You connect with people. Sometime soon those idiots in suits are going to come to their senses and give you something good to run with. And need I remind you that you won NY Trends' poll for the City's Hottest Reporter two years running?"

"Thanks Jonas. I love you, too. And next year I'm going to demand they expand the pool to include cameramen so you can beat me out for that damn prize!"

Jonas laughed.

"Damn straight I'd win. Hands down!"

"Absolutely."

"So, did you try seeing if this guy's home? If I just won the big one, I certainly wouldn't be at work today. Then again, I probably wouldn't be hangin' around a dump like this either."

"The mailboxes aren't marked. I asked one woman who exited whether she knew Mr. Westbrook and she said no. I tried looking him up to see if his phone was listed but nothing came up. I guess we'll have to wait."

"Whatever you say, darlin'. I'm all yours."

Jonas and I started our vigil. Luckily it was a pleasant sunny spring day. We spent the first hour taping several takes of my opening remarks. As the subsequent hours wore on, I increasingly thought how stupid I was to be sitting here on the off chance that this man would walk up to me. It wasn't as if I was waiting for George Clooney or some other superstar. Jonas was right when he asked: *That's it?*

At around 7:30 we were about to give up and head home when around the corner came a man dressed in white pants and t-shirt and a khaki army jacket. He was of medium build, in his early forties with a roundish, somewhat handsome face and short dirty blond hair. Even though the picture Hiram had sent was years old, I recognized him instantly. I called out as Jonas hoisted the camera on to his shoulder.

"Mr. Westbrook?"

"Yes."

"I was wondering if we could have a word with you. I'm Francine Vega from Action 6 News. I've received word that you are the sole winner of the PowerMax lottery jackpot. Is that true?"

"Yes."

"Would you like to tell our viewers a little something about yourself?"

"No."

"Can I gather from your uniform that you work in a hospital?"

"No, a diner."

"I don't suppose you'll have to work there anymore, will you?"

"I dunno. I haven't decided yet."

"I bet your family must be excited about your good luck."

"No family, just me."

The interview went on like this for another ten minutes as I tried to coax a little enthusiasm out of Alan Westbrook. For his part, Westbrook was civil and seemed in no great rush to end the interview but he answered only in monotone words and short phrases. He certainly did not appear to be a man who was soon to collect $450 million, the amount he'd receive after taxes for his cash option. I sighed as I decided to wrap up with a couple final questions.

"I see that your middle name is Starbuck. Were your parents coffee drinkers?"

"No, it's out of Moby Dick. My twin brother's middle name was Queequeg."

I noticed the first glimmer of any emotion from Westbrook when he mentioned his brother. Thinking that perhaps I could salvage this interview, I pursued this line.

"You said 'was' his middle name. Does that mean your brother is dead?"

"Yes."

It was back to the monotone.

"Well, thank you for your time Mr. Westbrook. One last question: Is there any one particular thing you plan to do with your fortune?"

Thus far, Alan Westbrook had been facing me, perfunctorily but courteously conversing with me. With this question he turned and looked directly into Jonas' camera.

"Yes, at last I am going to avenge my brother's death."

With that he turned and walked into the building. The coldness with which he delivered this line sent a shiver down my spine. I watched him all the way through the vestibule and into the building. He checked his mailbox. I made a note that he put his key into the second from the right on the bottom row.

2

After taping a few takes of my closing, Jonas and I walked back to the subway. Neither of us said anything for a few minutes. Finally, Jonas spoke up.

"Was that one weird dude or what?"

"What about that final statement? What was that all about?"

While Westbrook's responses up to his last sentence may have been as if from an automaton, they were non-threatening. His final statement, however, was definitely sending a message to someone or something. $450 million could deliver quite a message.

We headed downtown to lower Manhattan, not too far from where the World Trade Center used to be. The streets were pretty deserted but luckily the convenience store where the winning ticket was sold was still open. I spoke with the proprietor, a Pakistani man named Abdulla, who advised me that I was the fifth reporter to interview him, but none had been by in a week. I didn't let on that I knew who the winner was. Because he had been interviewed so many times, he had his answers down pat. I could use a few seconds of his interview to pad the piece, but nothing more.

Jonas handed the tape cassette over to me.

"You think you have enough here to put a decent piece together?"

"Through the power of editing, I'll make Mr. Alan Starbuck Westbrook as suave and debonair as Cary Grant. Thanks for helping me on this, Jonas."

"Anything for you, love."

I returned to the studio and inserted the tape into an editing station. I had to pull together a one-minute piece and then sell it to my editors so that it would run by no later than the evening news the next day, prior to the Lottery Commission's announcement. I had several obstacles to overcome. First, I wasn't authorized to do the piece. Station management claimed to applaud initiative, but they'd often reprimand staff when they free-lanced and demonstrated such initiative. Second, I only had one unofficial source—a self-important and semi-disgruntled bureaucrat at the lottery commission—that Westbrook was the winner. There had been no official announcement as of yet. I did have Westbrook himself confirming he was the winner, but there was obviously something off with him mentally. The commission's official announcement would not take place until the evening at 8:00. Rumors were circulating that the winner had in fact come forward, but the commission was playing it very close to the vest.

The one thing I had in my favor was Westbrook's closing threat made directly into the camera; it was chilling and left no doubt as to the seriousness of his threat. Jonas had captured it perfectly. I didn't think our editorial managers could resist running the piece if for no other reason than to play that line. This was great TV.

Despite being under the gun to finish and polish the piece, I couldn't resist taking a few minutes to go online to do more research on Alan Starbuck Westbrook. But everything I gathered on the Internet was at odds with the actual person I'd interviewed. The Internet presented a brilliant Ivy League-educated Defense Department attorney who had clerked for a Supreme Court Justice. The guy I met, however, washed dishes in a New York City coffee shop. My DMV contact had spoken of a man who had once lived in an up-scale Upper East Side apartment, yet the man I interviewed lived in a cramped roach-infested studio. This couldn't be the same man, could it?

I then plugged 'Queequeg Westbrook' into the search engine to see if there was anything I could gather on the brother. Perhaps through this information I could get confirmation that I had indeed interviewed the correct Alan Westbrook. Nothing came up. Then I put in 'Q. Westbrook' and within seconds a September 15, 2001 Washington Herald obituary was on her screen that read:

Major Frederick Q. Westbrook was laid to rest with full military honors at Arlington National Cemetery this morning. Major Westbrook was killed instantly when the hijacked plane crashed into the Pentagon on the morning of September 11. Major Westbrook worked in the Army Office of Strategic Support. He is a recipient of the Silver Star and two Purple Heart medals awarded for his service during the Gulf War. He is survived by his brother, Alan, a civilian who also works at the Pentagon.

I had information on the brother: he died on 9/11. I briefly toyed with the idea of inserting a voiceover with this fact but time was running out for me to complete the piece. I still had some selling to do. In addition, the logical place to insert this bio on the brother would be at the end, after Westbrook's vow of revenge but I wanted the dramatic effect of closing the piece with the haunting image of Westbrook's face delivering that ominous line.

I crossed my fingers and walked the tape in to Frank McDermott, the station's News Director. Ten minutes later Frank came into my cube.

"Nice stuff, Francine. You're absolutely sure of the source?"

I nodded. Frank considered for a few moments.

"I generally demand a second source to corroborate the story but I figured what the hell. We'll take a chance and air it at 6."

Inside I was giving myself high fives saying, "Yes!"

McDermott smiled. I knew he sincerely hoped I would make it big someday. He said that I had the talent and drive but he also despaired I was too nice to really be a success. He wanted to see more of a killer instinct in me.

Because he liked and trusted me, Frank was taking a chance. The Lottery Commission would neither confirm nor deny that

Alan Westbrook had in fact won the jackpot. Their announcement was to be at 8:00. Scoops on any story, even a minor one regarding a lottery winner, were hard to come by, especially for a network that consistently finished fourth out of four in New York. The worst thing that could happen was that I'd been misled and somebody else had actually won. It would be tough on me if that were the case and the station ended up with even more egg on their face than usual, but it would hardly be a catastrophe. The chance was definitely worth taking.

Like me, Frank said he felt a chill at the coldness of Westbrook's closing line: "I will avenge my brother." I closed the piece with that line, leaving its ominous tone hanging in the air. Frank said it was a masterful touch.

"Any idea what happened to his brother?"

"I think he was killed on 9/11, at the Pentagon."

"What? That's who this wacko is looking use his $450 million to avenge? Shouldn't we get that into the piece?"

"I still need to substantiate it; I only have an obit I found on the Internet. Nothing else."

I didn't mention that I still had lingering doubts about Alan Starbuck Westbrook himself. I had no idea what happened to this man between the time he was riding high and now, living in nearly homeless conditions.

Frank thought it over.

"Okay, it would have been a nice touch but time is of the essence. Let's go with what we have here. The brother could be worth following up on, especially given the creepy tone he used. I certainly wouldn't want to be the one he's after."

The minute the story ran, the emails and calls started pouring in. Who was Alan Westbrook? What did this guy mean? Who was his brother and what happened to him? What revenge was he going to take? As planned, the piece ran about an hour and a half before the official announcement by the lottery commission. The Commission, I understand, was a little put out at having the wind taken out of their sails.

Reporters, including me, attended the presentation and tried to follow up with Alan Westbrook but he said nothing. He accepted his check, shook a few hands and awkwardly smiled for the cameras. At one point, I could swear he made eye contact with me as his lips curled into a brief smile. But the smile disappeared as quickly as it appeared and he departed the stage. The cadre of reporters trailed along behind, shouting out their inquiries but all to no avail.

The City swallowed Alan Westbrook, rendering him invisible yet again. Within twenty-four hours, Alan Westbrook, his newfound fortune and his ominous threat were yesterday's news to everybody in the world.

The only person for whom he was not old news was me.

3

The day after Alan Westbrook received his check at the Lottery Commission office, I returned to his apartment building. The front entry and vestibule doors had both been propped open, probably for someone moving in or out. I walked in and glanced at the mailboxes on the wall to the left. I noted the box into which Westbrook had inserted his key, 4E, and started up the stairs.

Telling myself I needed to get to the gym more often as I trudged up the stairs, a few minutes later I was in front of 4E. The door was slightly ajar.

"Mr. Westbrook?" I called in as I knocked.

No answer.

"Mr. Westbrook? It's Francine Vega from Action 6 News. We spoke the other day."

Still quiet.

I tentatively pushed the door open, stuck my head in and called out one last time. Hearing nothing, I opened the door the rest of the way and walked in. The tiny one-room apartment, euphemistically labeled a studio, had all the appearances of a hasty departure. Dirty dishes were piled in the sink, day-old newspapers were strewn on a small coffee table, and drawers in the room's sole bureau were all open to varying degrees. The one miniscule closet near the bed displayed only a collection of cheap wire hangers with no clothes hanging on them.

Surveying the entire apartment took less than a minute at which point I noticed a small white envelope on the kitchen counter next to the sink. My name was scribbled on the front. I didn't know why, but seeing my name sent a shiver down my spine similar to the one when Westbrook made his threat. Not wanting to hang around any longer than I had to, I picked up the envelope and put it in my bag before exiting.

On the ground floor entryway, a short mustachioed Hispanic man in overalls was on a ladder replacing a light bulb.

"Excuse me," I called out.

The man looked down and smiled.

"Si, seniorita."

My mother came to America from the Cuba in the 1970s speaking only Spanish but she proudly and immediately embarked on a mission to learn English. By the time I was born, she'd mastered enough English so that that language, not Spanish, was the predominant language spoken in our house. Although when she was angry or upset or excited, she'd naturally revert to Spanish.

It wasn't that I didn't know Spanish but my Spanish-speaking abilities never got to be what one would call proficient. Mama was determined that I be American through and through and that meant speaking—and thinking in—English.

Since it was obvious I was Hispanic, the workman on the ladder naturally spouted his mother tongue to me. I responded in English.

"Do you know Alan Westbrook in Apartment 4E?"

"Si, he leave this morning."

"Do you know if he is coming back?"

"No, he no return. He good man and pay me two month rent when leave. He give me computer, say he get new better one. I say this one very good, good enough for my son to take to school!"

"Thank you," I replied as I exited. I hailed a cab and headed back to the office. Once at my desk, I tore open the envelope and read the note inside.

Dear Ms. Vega:

Based on our short meeting, I found you to be a very determined and conscientious reporter. I also figured you to be a fair person who would tell my story, and tell it straight. Therefore, the purpose of this note is to provide you with an explanation of what I am about to do so that the world will make no mistake about my intentions.

As the world well knows, on September 11, 2001, the followers of Islam perpetrated the most heinous crime in history. Since that time, the United States has spent trillions of dollars fighting several unwinnable wars and taking other measures that would purportedly keep this country safe. These moves have been, in my view, cosmetic and have not addressed the root cause of much of the world's strife. I intend to use my newfound fortune to correct this mistake.

Whenever I would watch the news on your station or other outlets, I could not help but to notice a constant theme running through many of the stories of worldwide conflict: the involvement of Muslims. Many of these perpetrators of crime would claim that they were justified because they were killing in Allah's name. Many went so far as to say that the Koran specifically sanctioned their actions.

So long as this false religion is allowed to exist and hold sway over so many people—who in turn devastate the lives of other people—the world will not be safe. I am therefore devoting my entire $450 million to destroying Islam, to remove one of its pillars, even if it means destroying myself in the process.

I will keep you posted as my plans develop.
Respectfully yours,
Alan S. Westbrook

Destroy Islam? What could Westbrook mean by this? What was he planning to do? What did he hope to accomplish by sharing information about his intentions with me? What should I do with this information? These questions and more bounced around my head.

I gazed out the window of the station's midtown office, trying to decide what my next steps should be. Being on the thirtieth floor with a northern exposure, I could look over the skyline of New York and see a hundred blocks or more, past Central Park and up into Harlem. If I focused my stare, I swear I could make out the block on which I grew up. I could imagine my mother in our apartment, forcing me to study algebra while other kids played on the street below. I wasn't overly crazy about my mother at that point in time, but I'd trade anything for just one more of those moments.

I needed to show this letter to somebody and discuss its implications and meaning. I walked into Frank's office. He read the letter slowly.

"Destroy Islam? How does one go about destroying a religion?" he asked.

"I haven't a clue. What should we do with this?"

"I think you have to start digging, Francine. We need to know more about this guy and his brother. You don't have any idea where he went to, do you?"

"No, he could be out of the country by now. What should we do?"

"Well, this letter has Homeland Security implications but my last dealing with those guys left such a bad taste in my mouth I say screw 'em. You got friendly with someone in State last year on that parking ticket issue, didn't you?"

"Yeah, that would be a good place to start."

What was his name? I went back to my desk and pulled out the file. McKenzie, that's it. I got my phone and scrolled through my contact list until I found Edward McKenzie. He worked for the State Department, specializing in American-Arab relations. I'd interviewed him a few years back on a piece on New York City's growing frustration over millions of dollars in unpaid parking tickets owed by diplomats from Arab countries.

McKenzie was an okay guy who seemed to have good insight on our relations with the Arab countries and cultures. He was a bit of a blowhard but he seemed especially conversant on the comings and goings of Arab dignitaries in New York. I was a little put off by the overriding impression during their interview that he would gladly take me to bed at a moment's notice despite having numerous pictures of his wife and three kids on his desk. Unfortunately, I'd gotten used to men like that over the years.

I pressed his number to call him. A female voice answered.

"Edward McKenzie, please. This is Francine Vega from Action 6 News"

"I'll see if he's available"

Ten seconds later McKenzie came on the line.

"Francine, it's wonderful to hear from you. I see you on the news now and then. To what do I owe the pleasure of this call?"

"Mr. McKenzie, I'm following up on the piece I did about the PowerMax lottery winner last week. There's something I'd like to show you. It may have implications about Arab-American relations."

"Call me Edward, please. I saw your interview with the winner. That's one weird dude. I don't think the guy blinked once the entire time you interviewed him. I'd be glad to meet with you. You have me intrigued as to how I could assist you. How about getting together over coffee tomorrow morning? There's a coffee shop near the UN on 32nd Street. It's called the Majestic. I'll meet you there around seven. Work for you?"

"See you then."

The next morning, Edward was in a booth at the Majestic Coffee Shop when I arrived. After exchanging pleasantries and ordering a coffee and a sesame bagel, I handed him Westbrook's letter.

"Extraordinary!" he exclaimed, "How does one propose to go about destroying an entire religion?"

"I have no idea. I was hoping you could provide some insight."

"I have no idea either. You probably need to talk to someone who is more of an expert on Islam than I certainly am. There's a man affiliated with our office I speak with regularly on issues relating to the religion. He's out of the country right now but will be back in New York on Friday. I'll contact him and see if he can see you then."

"I'd greatly appreciate anything you could do, Edward."

"Don't mention it."

First thing Friday, I received a call from Farad Sahari. Sahari officially worked for the United Nations as an Arab-English interpreter but he was really on the payroll as an analyst for the Central Intelligence Agency on loan to the State Department. He was born in Jordan but was now an American citizen.

"Ms. Vega, it's a pleasure to talk with you," he began, "I see you all the time on the news. How can I help you?"

Being a minor local celebrity did have the advantage of opening a few doors, I thought to myself.

"Mr. Sahari, thank you so much for calling me. I was wondering if we could meet sometime soon. I don't know if Mr. McKenzie told you about the letter I received."

"Yes, he did mention it and I am very curious. It so happens I'm free this evening. Perhaps you could join me for dinner? There's a wonderful Moroccan restaurant in the West Village that I'm partial to. I could meet you there around 7:00?"

I quietly sighed. Another man on the make. Even though I was always leery about getting together with men I didn't know in unfamiliar settings, I needed his insight. I agreed to meet him for dinner.

As I approached the restaurant, it occurred to me that I didn't think to ask him what he looked like. Well, hopefully he'd recognize me.

As I stepped into the restaurant, the most gorgeous man I'd ever seen in my life sitting at a table to my right rose from his seat and called out.

"Miss Vega, over here."

I felt a little embarrassed as all eyes in the restaurant shifted to me. I could imagine the various patrons telling their respective spouses when they got home: 'You know who I saw in the restaurant? That reporter from Channel 6 News. I can't think of her name but you know her. Pretty, Hispanic. Yeah, that's the one.'

I walked over to the table to greet Mr. Sahari. He got even better looking the closer I got. About six foot two. Obviously takes care of himself. Dark complexion, hair and eyes. Neatly trimmed mustache. A pronounced cleft in his chin. A stylish gray suit, crisp white shirt and red patterned tie.

We shook hands and then he held my seat for me. A gentleman, I noted to myself. I'd only been there a few moments when an earnest, smiling waiter named Earl appeared to take our drink orders.

"I'd like a sea breeze," I responded. After Sahari ordered a Coke, I realized my potential faux pas.

"I'm sorry. That was unthinking of me to order alcohol while with you."

"No problem whatsoever. It's my choice not to order alcohol but I'm not going to impose my beliefs on my companions. If I did that, I'd be a very lonely man here in New York, wouldn't I?"

He smiled; I could feel myself melting. We got our drinks and placed our dinner orders.

"So, we have a man who intends to destroy Islam, do we?" Sahari breezily asked.

"That's what he says he intends to do but he's rather scant on the details. He also told me when I interviewed him that he was going to use his new-found fortune to avenge his brother, who I've since discovered was killed on 9/11."

"How much did he win?"

"He netted over $450 million after taxes."

"That could buy a lot of vengeance, couldn't it?"

"I guess my basic question is: How can somebody destroy Islam or even think they can? My knowledge of Islam is for the most part non-existent. I know it's frowned upon to drink alcohol and Muslims are supposed to pray five times a day but beyond that, zilch."

Sahari smiled again. I imagined that educating the masses on the basics of Islam was a regular part of his routine.

"We're not all that different from Christians and Jews. Same God. Same Ten Commandments. Same do as to others. We even believe that when the world ends it will be Jesus, not Mohammed, who comes back to earth. We just feel that Allah made a more perfect revelation of himself—and what he wants of us—through Islam than he had previously.

"In terms of destroying Islam, I can't conceive of any way to do such a thing. Islam is a collection of ideas and ideals. It's a matter of faith. How does one destroy that?

"I'm sure you can't imagine one man destroying Christianity, can you? The Nazis tried to destroy Judaism, one person at a time, but they were obviously unsuccessful. Even $450 million is not enough money to do what he is claiming. Now, he has the means to hurt and kill a lot of innocent people along the way with that much money, but I hardly foresee Islam toppling down because of one madman."

As he was finishing that sentence, our food arrived. He'd ordered a chicken and prune tagine while I had couscous with spicy mergez sausage. As we ate our meals, Alan Westbrook faded to the background while we talked about ourselves. In many ways our lives had followed similar tracks. We were the offspring of immigrant parents, he from Jordan, and me from Cuba. We each had it drummed into our heads practically from birth that we needed to learn perfect English in order to succeed in our new home. Both of us had intense drives to succeed.

I had such a good time talking with Farad that it wasn't until I glanced at my watch that I realized we'd been there for over three hours. The restaurant was ready to close and I had to be up early for an assignment on a looming transit strike.

Farad would not hear of me paying my share of the tab and walked me out to wait for a cab. While we stood waiting, for the first time there was an uncomfortable silence between us. Finally he spoke.

"Ms. Vega,"

"Francine, please"

"Francine, would you object if I were to call on you again? Perhaps we could have dinner again? I know we are so different in many ways, but I feel so much in common as well."

"I'd like that very much, Mr. Sahari. I feel the same way."

He just gave me a look and I corrected myself.

"Farad."

"That's better."

As I crawled into bed that night, I knew I was going to have trouble falling asleep. I couldn't stop thinking about Farad. I also couldn't stop thinking about how insane the whole thing was. I was very intent on developing my career at this point in my life. I couldn't get involved with anyone, let alone with someone so completely different from me in so many ways. The religious differences alone presented a seemingly insurmountable gulf between us.

I tried to pass it off as just an enjoyable evening with an interesting and gorgeous person, but my mind quickly raced to the romantic possibilities that lay in front of me. Eventually, I drifted off into a peaceful sleep, hugging my pillow.

I was jolted out of my blissful reveries as a cacophony erupted from my phone. As a reporter, I had to be on call at all hours and thus had the volume on my telephone set to the maximum, most annoying ring possible to ensure that I wouldn't sleep through a call.

I glanced at the clock. It was 2:17.

"Hello," I mumbled into the receiver.

"Francine, it's Farad."

"Farad?" I mumbled back, not making the connection immediately.

"Farad Sahari, from last night."

"Of course, Farad. When I said it would be alright for you to call me back sometime, I didn't think it would be so soon in the middle of the night."

"I'm sorry to have awakened you, Francine. It's just that I couldn't sleep after our conversation. I kept wracking my brain: destroy Islam? destroy Islam? What could he mean? Then I reread the copy of his letter you gave me and this time it jumped out at me. He mentioned taking down a pillar. I think I know what he wants to do. Can you meet me at Edward McKenzie's office at 10:00? He should hear what I'm thinking as well."

"Okay, I'll see you there."

First thing next morning I was at City Hall, waiting for a statement from the Mayor on whether any progress had been made the previous night on negotiations with the unions that represented transit workers. He was scheduled to come before the press at 8:15. 8:15 passed, then 8:30, then 9:00. I was getting anxious because I was supposed to be up at the U.N. at 10:00 to meet with McKenzie. To be honest, I was eager to see Farad again. However, this press conference was my actual job for this morning; discussing Islam was only a follow-up on a previous story so I could hardly leave before the Mayor made his statement.

At 9:07 the Mayor strode out to the microphones, made a terse announcement that the talks had broken down that night. He abruptly turned around and left without answering a single question. He obviously was fuming and was in no mood to respond to a barrage of inane inquiries from reporters. I was certainly not going to try and convince him to stay. Luckily, I'd run into a deputy mayor on the way in who gave me enough background to do my piece so I also made a hasty withdrawal. I flagged a cab and worked my way up to McKenzie's office.

Farad was sitting in the waiting room when I arrived. He got up and gave me a big hug, which I returned in full.

"McKenzie's not here yet. He's due any minute. Hopefully he'll be able to squeeze us in. His receptionist was moderately optimistic."

I told him about waiting nearly an hour for the mayor to show up.

"Patiently waiting comes with the territory of being a reporter."

So wait we did. At around 10:45 the door opened and Edward McKenzie walked in.

"Farad, Ms. Vega. We didn't have an appointment, did we?"

"No Edward," Farad responded, "but it's important we talk."

"I'm late for a meeting already but I can give you a few minutes. Come on in."

We all walked into his office. McKenzie looked at us and waited for us to talk. Farad spoke first.

"Edward, I think I know what Westbrook wants to do, how he thinks he can destroy Islam."

"I'm all ears, Farad."

"I think he wants to use his fortune to destroy Mecca, probably to wipe it off the face of the earth."

McKenzie looked first at Farad, then at me, then back again. He started to laugh like we had just told him a joke.

"You're kidding, right?"

"No, I'm afraid I'm not."

"That's preposterous! What would lead you to such a conclusion?"

"The tenets of much of Islam hold that there are five pillars upholding the religion. Prayer, charity, acceptance of Mohammed as the true prophet, and fasting are four of these pillars. There's nothing he can do about those. The fifth one, however, is something I could see someone insanely saying could be knocked down."

McKenzie glanced at his watch; obviously wishing Farad would get to the point.

"The fifth pillar is the hajj, the mandatory trip every Muslim must make to Mecca at least once in his life if physically and financially able. I believe Westbrook's got it into his mind to obliterate this city—and in turn Islam would crumble."

"This is all fascinating, Farad, it really is. But first of all there's nothing we can do about it based only on your speculation. Second, I find it inconceivable that a private citizen would have the wherewithal to carry something like this off, lottery winnings or not."

"He's a private citizen who used to work at the Pentagon," I pointed out.

"Be that as it may, it's still idle speculation at this point. I'd love to stay and hear more but I'm really late and if you'll excuse me I'll have to say goodbye. Let me know if anything more on this comes up."

With that, he got up and left, leaving us alone in his office. We in turn showed ourselves out.

We shared a cab back to my office. Farad would drop me off and then continue on to the Upper West Side for a meeting at the Arab-American Friendship League, where he chaired one of their ecumenical committees. For the first couple of minutes during our taxi ride neither of us said anything. He broke the silence.

"That went well, didn't it?"

All I could do in response was give him a wan smile.

"I suppose we jumped the gun," he continued. "It's just that it was the only theory that seemed to fit and, once it popped into my mind, the more frightening the possibility became."

He paused for a second.

"I haven't made my pilgrimage yet. It's always one of those things that I'll get around to some day when I'm not as busy. Just the thought that I might not ever have that chance told me that I had to pursue the lead, no matter how outlandish it may be."

I reached over and took his hand. He appreciated the gesture.

"We need to get more information about Alan Westbrook," I remarked. "He's still such a mystery. We know he worked at the Pentagon. That would be the place to start asking some questions."

"Isn't Alan Westbrook old news for your station? They're going to want you to cover new things, especially with a possible transit strike."

"I'll make the attempt to do it officially but if I can't, I'll take a leave of absence for a month. I have the time; I haven't taken a vacation in my four years at the station."

"Thank you, Francine."

He still looked worried, but he seemed somewhat better knowing I was going to keep pursuing this story. What exactly I'd find out was a mystery to me, but I was glad it made him feel some relief.

The cab pulled in front of my building and he reached over to shake my hand. I surprised him by leaning over and kissing him on the cheek before I got out.

I knew Frank would be supportive of me continuing my investigation, but his higher-ups were going to give him a hard time about me devoting time to a story they considered completed, and a minor piece at that. My job description was to report on stories that were handed me as they developed, not to go investigating open questions on past pieces. The city had a looming transit strike that was going to require all hands on deck. I had to think over carefully my approach in swaying him to let me do this.

It was a Friday when Farad and I met with McKenzie so I decided to take the weekend to think over my approach and then talk with Frank on Tuesday, since Monday was a holiday.

I screwed up my courage and walked towards his office. Before I got there, he called out for me.

"What's up, Frank?"

"Sit down. Wait until you see this. You're not going to believe it."

I sat in one of the chairs in front of his desk. He sat in the other chair and angled his computer around so we could both see the screen.

"One of our interns, Nadine I think her name is, is a YouTube devotee. She was surfing around and found this. She knew you were working on something involving Islam so she brought it to my attention."

A few clicks later the title *Pastor Advocates Destroying Mecca* displayed at the top of the screen was. The video soon clicked to life, displaying a fortyish somewhat chubby minister with thinning hair already in full throttle of a passionate sermon. He was wearing a moss green robe. Then he paused. You could feel the anticipation of the hushed congregation as they awaited his next utterance. I noted to myself how professional everything was.

There were three cameras providing different angles. The lighting was perfect. The video was obviously edited by someone who knew his stuff. Every aspect of the video perfectly complemented his delivery.

As if on cue, he continued his sermon. However, instead of the passion and force we saw just seconds ago he now continued in an earnest, contemplative manner. Previously he'd spread his gaze over his entire congregation; now he focused straight on the center camera, which zoomed in on his face.

"My friends, I do not think I have ever spoken to you before on a matter of such grave importance as I do today. The very future of our nation, our church and our very lives hang in the balance. I beg you to hear me out."

The preacher paused again. He obviously knew how to milk the drama out of any situation.

"For some time now, it has not been fashionable to acknowledge that the devil is real, that he lives among us, planting seeds of hate and evil wherever and whenever he can.

"The devil is just a myth, and we're too modern, too advanced, to believe in such an outdated medieval myth, we tell ourselves.

"Every couple of years, a new motion picture graces our screens to ruminate on the work of the devil as he inhabits a child or other being, hoping to bring about the end of the world. We flock to these movies to be scared and entertained. The advances in the use of special effects make these movies even scarier and more entertaining. But then we go about our lives, pushing the devil to the furthest most reaches of our minds. Or maybe we're just confident that, like in the films, good will ultimately rise up and defeat this foul, evil being.

"What I'm about to tell you may shock some of you: the devil is real. We see it nearly every day on our TVs and computers. It is constantly in the news. He has deeply affected our lives for a decade now and he won't stop until we defeat him or until we as a people are defeated and destroyed, our very way of life ground into the dirt under his sandaled feet.

"Who is this devil? How does he represent himself on this earth?

"He has come to us in the most innocuous and insidious manner possible. He is cloaked in the mantle of decency and respectability, but he is there all the same.

"He eats away at the moral and ethical fabric of the entire earth, chipping away and preparing for the ultimate blow. He is waiting for his jihad.

"Yes, my friends, I said jihad."

He paused a few seconds.

"The devil is Islam."

He paused again.

"The purported leaders of this so-called religion tell us that Islam is a peaceful, loving religion. Yet all we see day after day is violence, hatred and death perpetrated in the name of Allah.

"We all saw the horrific footage from Afghanistan last week on our televisions. It is quickly becoming an iconic image etched on our minds up there with the kiss in Times Square, the lone man standing in front of the tank in Tiananmen Square and the shooting of the Vietnamese prisoner. It is a picture of a lovely young woman, her face wracked with grief as she holds the lifeless, bloodied body of her four-year old son.

"She is inconsolable as she looks up to heaven, supposedly to Allah, for comfort and strength. But none is forthcoming. Allah will never help her because he does not want to help her. He wants to inflict even more pain on her, if that is at all possible. The devil is like that.

"As this pain is inflicted on a follower of Allah; you can imagine the suffering this devil would love to mete out to us nonbelievers, us infidels.

"Who among us can ever forget the billowing smoke rising from the twin towers, the Pentagon and the fields of Pennsylvania? The acrid aroma that seared our nostrils was a sweet perfume to Allah. He would love to inhale a hundred, a thousand, a million times more smoke like that.

"Yes, the devil lives here on earth, my brothers and sisters. He lives in Islam and he is an abomination, an affront to all the good Christian people in this country and throughout the world. We need to fight this evil wherever we can find it. We must stamp it out once and for all.

"Last year, many of you made the crusade twenty miles east to Wainridge, where an Islamic Center was being planned. Because of your good work, the followers of Islam decided to move elsewhere to spread their poison.

"I commend you all for your efforts, but we must continue to be extra diligent. We cannot put down our guard. The purveyors of evil will be back. We need to fight them and beat them once and for all.

"I was recently made aware of an ingenious and yet simple plan to beat the devil at his own game. There are the five pillars of Islam. Like pillars in architecture, they bear the weight of carrying this religion, of keeping it raised on high. Knock one of these pillars down, and the religion—I use this term very loosely here, mind you—will collapse under its own weight.

"We can't do anything about four of these pillars: prayer, fasting, charity and acknowledgment of Mohammed as God's true prophet. The fifth, however, presents us with possibilities. It's called the hajj, the pilgrimage to Mecca. Every follower of Islam is required to make this pilgrimage once in his or her lifetime.

"The plan that I speak of is so simple, so elegant, that I am shocked that no one ever thought of it before. It asks the questions: What if Mecca was no more? If Mecca ceased to exist, a hajj would not be possible, would it? Why don't we erase Mecca from the face of the earth, just like God wiped away Sodom and Gomorrah?

"Like the story of Samson in the Old Testament—or at least the Victor Mature and Heddy Lamar version of the story—once the pillar is torn down, the religion will topple. The devil will be defeated.

"Now, I see the look of horror on many of your faces. 'Won't innocent people be killed?' you ask. 'Are you really condoning violence, Reverend?'

"We often speak of the New Testament God as a kinder, gentler deity, but I tell you, He has some fire in him yet!

"Unfortunately, some people may be killed, but I believe adequate forewarning can be given to protect the innocent. They will be given ample opportunity to come over to the light. But even if a few innocent people are tragically killed, a more fundamental benefit is that billions of souls will be saved. The devil will be defeated.

"In the coming days, as this plan gets more fully revealed you will probably hear that the government will disavow this fine idea. "We are better than that," the government will tell us.

"If anything, our leaders should lead the charge to accomplish his holy task, not be hindering it.

"And so, my friends, I am hoping to start a groundswell right here and right now. Like the famous movie line: I'm mad as hell and I won't take it anymore. I beseech you to join me in this holy crusade."

With his final line, the organist launched into the classic hymn *Onward Christian Soldiers*. I could hear the congregation sing the hymn with gusto and passion. Frank hit the pause button on his computer. The screen froze with the smiling face of the pastor beaming as he looked out over his flock.

"That wacko who won the lottery, didn't your Muslim friend come up with a theory that he wants to use his fortune to blow up Mecca?" Frank asked.

"Yes, that's his theory. Who is this preacher?"

"His name's McKenzie. He's pastor of some backwater church upstate."

"That explains it. He must be related to my contact in the State Department, the one who laughed Farad and me out of his office for coming up with such a ludicrous theory. Well, he must have thought enough of it to tell it to his brother or whoever he is."

"Well, why don't you grab Jonas and head up there? Little town of Wayland, about a three-hour drive. Jonas has a car, doesn't he?"

Like many native New Yorkers, although I had a driver's license, I didn't own a car and never had. I instead relied on the subways, buses and just plain walking to get around the city. Jonas did have one, though it was an old clunker.

"Yeah, he does."

"If he can't drive you, use my car. I'd like to get you up there ASAP before other reporters latch onto it."

Jonas and I piled into his beat up 1989 Dodge Aries and headed north.

"When you ever going to get rid of this heap?" I asked.

"Till she stops rolling, I 'spect. You'll probably see footage of a massive backup on the FDR some morning after she up and dies on me in the left lane."

"I probably should have told Frank that your car was in the shop. He would have lent us his brand new Beemer. Wouldn't you rather be in that instead of this old POS?"

"Now, now. No disrespect. She can hear you. She's been a good friend all these years. She'll get us where we need to go, which is where again?"

"Wayland, about three hours up the Thruway and hang a left for a bit."

"And what on earth do we want to go there for?"

Jonas was obviously imagining how well a six foot four black man and a Hispanic woman were going to be able to blend into some hick upstate town.

"Some preacher spouting stuff related to our friend Starbuck. Stuff about blowing up Mecca."

"Oh yeah, that theory you and your Arab friend came up with."

"Yup, that's it."

"Speaking of your Arab friend–what's his name again?"

"Farad Sahari."

"Speaking of him, how's it going?"

"What do you mean?"

"C'mon Frannie. It's me. You're obviously interested in this guy."

I smiled.

"Jonas, you're in the wrong line of work. You should be a matchmaker."

"An evasion, which I'll take to mean that you want this guy. Just remember how different your two worlds are. Don't want you getting hurt, little darlin'."

I didn't know where the relationship, if you could call it that, was heading either. I was fully aware of how far apart our worlds were, but I knew that something was happening that I couldn't resist. Nor did I want to resist it. I suspected the same of Farad.

The ride up to Wayland took about two and a half hours. It was one of those quaint, working/middle class communities tucked into the Catskills. It looked better off compared to similar towns where factories up and left decades before. As we drove down Main Street, it was easy to see that Jonas was correct: we were the proverbial sore thumbs in this small white town.

We located the church with relative ease; it was a block and a half from the middle of town. The parsonage, a modest white clapboard house in which Reverend McKenzie and his family resided, was next door. I knocked on the front door. I decided that it would probably be better for Jonas to remain in the car until I got the lay of the land. Jonas readily agreed.

"Hello, can I help you?" the Reverend cheerfully asked.

"Reverend McKenzie, my name is Francine Vega. I'm a reporter for Action 6 News out of New York. I was wondering if I could speak with you about your recent sermon. I saw a piece on the Internet about it."

"That would be wonderful. I was wondering how long it would take for TV crews to come knocking on my door. Is that your cameraman in the car there? Invite him in."

"I asked him to stay in the car so it didn't look like we were ambushing you."

"Ambush away. Ambush away."

I motioned for Jonas to join us and to bring his camera. We

walked in and got ourselves settled. Reverend McKenzie asked if we'd like anything to drink or eat. Jonas asked for a bottle of water if it wasn't too much trouble. While Jonas was getting set up, I struck up a conversation to put the Reverend at ease, although I didn't think he needed a lot of preparation. He was relishing this moment and was a natural.

"Thank you for giving me your time, Reverend."

"Please, call me Malcolm."

"Okay, Malcolm. I do have one initial question before we get started here. Are you related to Edward McKenzie, who works in the State Department?"

"Yes, he's my brother. We've been told that we look so much alike, although I can't see it. I'm much, much better looking."

No, I was not going to have much trouble with this interview. I made a mental note that I could not expect that any further conversations I may have with Edward McKenzie would be kept confidential.

Jonas indicated that he was ready and the interview began.

"I'm here with Reverend Malcolm McKenzie, pastor of the Wayland United Methodist Church"

"and the Somerset United Methodist Church in the adjoining town," he interjected.

"to discuss a controversial sermon he gave this past Sunday. Reverend, why don't you summarize for us what you said during this sermon."

"Certainly, I spoke about the need to eradicate Islam. This so-called religion is an abomination in the eyes of God and an affront to all that is good and pure in the civilized world. After 9/11 I have been especially distressed over the increased importance Islam has been exerting in the world, even here in the United States. For all too long we have treated the adherents of Islam with kid gloves, trusting that these backward societies would someday make progress towards modernity and democracy. We have only been kidding ourselves. I believe we should take off those gloves and put this religion where it belongs: extinct like the religions of ancient Egypt, Greece and Rome."

"Can you describe how you think an entire religion can be destroyed?"

"It's actually quite simple. Islam has five pillars on which the religion rests. Like pillars in architecture, they bear the weight of carrying this religion, of keeping it raised on high. Knock one of these pillars down, and the religion—I use this term very loosely here, mind you—will collapse under its own weight.

"We can't do anything about four of these pillars: prayer, fasting, charity and acknowledgment of Mohammed as God's true prophet. The fifth, however, presents us with possibilities. It's called the hajj, the pilgrimage to Mecca. Every follower of Islam is required to make this pilgrimage once in his or her lifetime."

I noticed that these words were verbatim from his sermon, which in turn mimicked what Farad had said. He was just like a politician who has a basic stump speech to be delivered over and over again at different locations to different audiences.

"You really think that would topple the entire religion?"

"Well, no other religion I can think of demands that its adherents go to a specific place. It's nice if a Catholic can make it to Rome. A Jew wants to see the Wailing Wall and a Hindu has a strong desire to bathe in the Ganges once in their lives, but as far as I know, none of these trips are obligatory. Unless Muslims have some sort of health or financial excuse, they're required to go to Mecca. So, if we remove Mecca from the equation, the religion itself is in trouble. It's quite an elegant solution, I believe."

"But how do you think destroying Mecca can be done?"

"We both know the answer to that, don't we? A well-placed weapon of mass destruction would do the job very nicely. I think the government should take on this holy endeavor, but if they don't, private citizens should take it on. Our military should do it. This would be such a better use of our tax dollars than many of the things they go towards now."

"You can't be promoting using an atomic bomb or other weapon of mass destruction to kill thousands if not millions of innocent people, are you?"

"Ample warning can be given so that people can clear the area in time."

"This is all crazy, you realize, don't you?"

"Not in the least. It's time we woke up and answered an eye for an eye."

"But you're a preacher, a man of the cloth. What happened to turn the other cheek?"

"We've run out of cheeks. As the old saying goes, fool me once, shame on you; fool me twice, shame on me. At some point, the Christian world has to stand up for what is right. We have to defend ourselves."

As he said this, McKenzie pulled a pen and a small spiral-bound notebook out of his jacket pocket, scribbled something down. He immediately put the pen and notebook back in his pocket even before I could ask her next question.

"Do you think the American public will stand for this?"

"A few years ago, an enterprising high school student developed a modest web site for our churches. Each week he records our services and loads them onto the website so that anyone who missed the service can get the Word at home. Through donations and whatnot, we've improved the production value of our broadcasts but generally our site gets at most 50 hits per week. However, two days after my sermon was posted, our server crashed! We got over 300,000 hits! We've since transferred the footage to YouTube and it's now up in the millions. My inbox is similarly bursting with emails from people supporting me. Many contain donations to advance the cause.

"My sermon has, as they say, gone viral. I'm assuming that's how you found out about little ol' me, isn't it?"

I dumbly nodded.

"Oh no, Miss Vega, the people won't stand in the way. In fact, they are hungry for justice to finally be meted out. Oil or no oil that the Saudis may have, I see a groundswell here that will ultimately force the government to act, and act decisively."

After that, I could ask only a few perfunctory questions as I wrapped up the interview. As we headed back to the City, Jonas asked the question on both of our minds.

"Frannie, do you really think the American people are that bloodthirsty?"

"I don't know, Jonas, I don't know. I do know that this preacher has megalomania written all over him. He absolutely loves attention. He won't stop until he's giving orders to the President himself."

Personally, I was leery about giving Reverend McKenzie the New York airtime he obviously craved. Frank agreed with me but we both knew this was news. I tried to do my piece objectively, without sensationalizing the story or making the preacher into a messianic hero. The piece ran that night as a follow-up to my lottery piece. I'd hoped that this would be the end of the story.

4

I woke up the following morning and immediately turned on the news, as was my habit. I have three televisions in my apartment and would turn each of them on to different stations. Anyone walking in would ask me how I could stand the cacophony, but to me it was like an orchestra playing a modern discordant symphony. One station would be the string section, another was percussion, while the third was woodwinds. My ears and brains would shift back and forth from station to station, trying to catch facts and story-lines that might be pertinent to my current duties or might provide me with a seed for a future piece.

On this day, however, there was no discordance, no cacophony. Instead, the stations were all in perfect harmony as each station was providing commentary and footage on the story of the morning. Just hours previously, firebombs and explosives were sent into the American Embassy in Riyadh, the Saudi Arabian capital. Once the building was ablaze, the inhabitants, including the Ambassador, started to flee. That's when gunmen from rooftops on nearby buildings started to open fire. Footage showed the local police idly standing by.

Latest reports were that six people had been killed. There was no word yet on the fate of the Ambassador. Finally, local authorities exerted control and the firing stopped. At this point the crowd, or more precisely mob, had slowly grown to a size where it could occupy the entire square in front of the embassy. The chants had started, which the reporter translated as 'Death to the Great Satan.' There were not yet any televised burnings of the American flag, but that would undoubtedly come soon.

While no official reason had been given as to what sparked the attack, everyone knew the cause: the YouTube video of Reverend McKenzie's sermon had indeed gone viral. It had made its way to the Arab world.

The reporters and anchors noted that the State Department had lodged an official protest with the Saudis and had demanded greater protection from the local government. It was only at this point, the anchors theorized, that the army was sent in to tamp down the protest and violence. The State Department was nervously monitoring reaction in other Arab countries and had put its embassies and consulates on highest alert.

The Saudis for their part had demanded that the American government denounce the video in no uncertain terms. They were even suggesting that the video be taken down and that the Internet be censored to keep such expressions from popping up again.

The White House issued an immediate statement denouncing the substance of the video, saying that its message had no place in the civilized world. Because Reverend McKenzie was promoting violence and a vicious act of war, the President indicated he would look into whether any laws were broken. However, he also made it clear that freedom of speech was a cornerstone of American democracy and that we had no plans to take any steps that would censor the Internet or squelch our basic freedoms.

Over the next few days, the riotous atmosphere in the Arab countries died down as Reverend McKenzie and his message of hate faded into the background. I saw Farad steadily over the course of these days and his mood mirrored that of his homeland as he went from quiet and introspective to more of his usual self.

I was at my desk working up some questions I would ask at the upcoming press conference with the transit union president. Previously, he'd predicted that if there weren't any further development in their talks with the City in the next twenty-four hours, his members would defy the law, the mayor and everyone else and walk off their jobs effective 7:30 AM two days hence. In other words, subway trains would be abandoned at the first station they pulled into at or shortly after 7:30. Preferably from the union's point of view, the trains would be full of commuters at that moment in time.

I was typing away on my computer when I heard my phone buzz. Someone was sending me a text message. I hoped it was Farad.

I was disappointed but intrigued when I looked at the display and saw a number with a 672 area code that I didn't recognize. I started to read the message.

> Ms. Vega, You're good. I expected you to eventually figure out my intentions but I didn't think you'd get there so quickly. I was very surprised to see that somehow a preacher had been let in on my little secret, but that's perfect. If the public is behind it, maybe I won't have to do a thing. If the Arab world continues to act like they did over the past week, the American public will flood to my way of thinking. In any case, my plan is coming together. I'll be in touch. ASW

I quickly punched area code 672 into my computer's search engine to see if I could get an idea at least where Westbrook was texting me from. My jaw must have hit the floor when the answer came up: Antarctica!

I had my doubts that Alan Westbrook was snuggling with a bunch of penguins down in Antarctica. Somehow he was routing his phone through that area code. There was a lot more to the down-and-out man I interviewed than I realized. I was anxious to find out what his plan was.

If Farad was correct and Westbrook was looking to use his fortune to destroy Mecca, he could not do this alone. My best guess was that he would reignite the old contacts he had in the Pentagon where he had worked prior to 9/11. Someone there would definitely be able to carry this off. I needed to get down to the Pentagon.

"I can't afford to let you go, Francine," Frank told me in no uncertain terms after I showed him the text. "Barring some unforeseen miracle, the transit workers are set to walk off the job tonight. The Mayor is threatening to ask that the Governor bring in the National Guard. Blogs are threatening violence by vigilante groups against striking workers if they stop the trains and buses from operating. There's just too much to cover. The text message is compelling but I can't let you go to investigate this story right now. It'll have to wait."

I knew he was right. This strike was going to suck us dry. Every reporter, cameraman, editor and everybody else at the station would be on call 24/7. I'd just have to put on hold looking into something that had the potential to erupt into World War III to cover this transit strike.

"Okay Frank, what's my next assignment?" I sighed.

The sides finally stopped their blustering and came back together for talks. Eventually cooler heads prevailed as they came back to the table and hammered out an agreement in relatively short order. The strike never happened and within three days there was a signed agreement. No National Guard was needed. Nobody was beaten up. My assignment during that time was to cover the union. The spokesman was a very nice guy named George who loved to show pictures of his kids to the reporters.

Mecca, Westbrook, McKenzie—they all faded into the background during this time. The one person I couldn't get out of my mind though was Farad. Once I finally had some time to myself I hurried to speed dial. I could hear the phone ring on the other end.

"Hello."

"Farad, it's Francine. Can you see me?"

"Anything new?"

"Yes, but it's also, it's just, well, I just wanted to see you. That's all."

"And I'd like to see you as well, Francine."

"Majestic Coffee Shop, two o'clock tomorrow afternoon?"

"I'll see you there."

Farad and I picked up again where we'd left off. While the passions of the Middle East were cooling, ours was only intensifying.

I'd just returned from my lunchtime rendezvous with Farad when Frank called me into his office.

"Our friend, Reverend McKenzie, is back in the news. Fifteen minutes of fame is not enough for this guy."

"Still putting forward the destroy Mecca mantra?"

"Yes, but on a much bigger stage. He's gotten a massive following. His sermons are going national, and not just on YouTube. He's becoming a modern day Father Coughlin."

I looked at Frank, waiting for the other part of this story.

"This guy is on a full-throttle power trip. He believes he's on a mission from God to help eradicate the scourge of Islam. He's heading down this Sunday to Georgia to speak at one of those megachurches."

"He is?"

"Yes, you've heard of Reverend George Warriner, one of the biggest televangelists there is. He's got his own cable network. He's going to have McKenzie come to his church, or rather stadium, and preach to 10,000 there and millions on TV. Warriner contacted all the networks. They want national media coverage."

"But what about the situation in the Middle East? This is just going to reignite everything all over again. Can't anyone stop him?"

"My guess is that the Feds are trying, but they need some legal excuse to shut him down. He's moving too quickly for them. Plus, the Feds don't want to be seen as buckling to a foreign government and stifling free speech. Unfortunately,"

Frank paused for a few seconds, figuring out how to break the news to me.

"Francine, network is taking this over. I pleaded with them to keep you on as the primary reporter, but they want to hand this over to what they said is a more seasoned journalist."

To emphasize the point, he made air quotation marks. I could hardly wait to hear who this "seasoned reporter" was.

"Maria Wallace will be covering the story from now on. I'm sorry Francine. There was nothing I could do. Maria would like to meet with you tomorrow to go over your notes and footage to help her prepare."

"But Frank, it's my story. That's first and foremost. But even more to the point, Maria Wallace is an air-headed idiot. And you know I'm being kind here."

I was surprised at the vehemence of my protestation.

"I know, I know," was all he could say.

I sulked out and headed back to my work area. Maria Wallace! Maria Wallace?

Maria was with the New York affiliate when I first started here. Though I'd met her only a few times, I'd developed an intense dislike for her.

I'm not above using my looks to get a story. I've charmed more than my share of middle-aged men to get some tidbit that would enhance a story or give me a fresh lead. I may be flattering myself, but I like to think I also have other tools such as smarts, drive and intuition that make me a decent reporter. Looks and sex appeal are all Maria has.

She's very tall, six feet or more, with long blond hair, perfect skin and pouty lips. She's made for the camera. My guess is that being a journalist was not exactly what she wanted to do with her life but her acting abilities were limited so Hollywood was out and here she was.

She was promoted to the national network a few months after I started. Word around the station was that sex was involved. Now, I know things like that cattily get said about most any female who rises up the ranks. It usually makes my blood boil when I hear this because I generally attribute it to sour grapes and sexism, but in Maria's case I can't discount it. Beyond her ability to make love to the camera and in turn have the camera respond with an orgasm (which I do admit is a talent), there is not much there.

Her laziness and inattention to detail when it came to research were legendary. My favorite was when she was interviewing Les Bentley. He was a movie star of some note a few years back whose fondness for cocaine has since landed him in jail. Anyway, Les had come to New York to perform on Broadway. Maria got to interview him for our station's Spotlight on NYC segment.

"So, is this your first time in New York?" Maria asked.

"Um, no. I was born in Manhattan and lived here until I was seventeen."

"Are you going to see the sights while you're here?"

"I saw them all when I was a kid."

"I've often talked with folks from the West Coast, even from the big cities out there who get overwhelmed the first time they step foot in New York. Are you one of those people?"

"No, as I said, I'm from New York originally and lived here a good part of my life. I don't find it overwhelming at all."

And so on and so forth. She had a set of ill-informed and inane questions she was going to plow through regardless of the answers she received. The actor did his best but I don't remember him ever getting to talk about the play he was acting in. When she wasn't inquiring about his "first" visit to New York, Maria focused on the excitement of living in L.A. It was a short time later that the station executives swore never to have her do a live interview on the air again. To this day, anytime you see her on TV, she's taped.

Now she was taking over this story, my story. I'd cordially meet with her but I'd be damned if I give her my notes or anything other than the most superficial information that was in the public already. As long as I kept a smile on my face and sounded sincere, I doubted she'd know the difference.

On the one hand, it bothered my ego that this was being taken from me and handed over to someone like Maria Wallace, but on the other hand I didn't care one way or another. Reverend McKenzie had told me everything he was going to say. He would simply be delivering the same lines on a bigger stage. The only thing I'd be curious about was who else was there to hear his message of divine justice. I'd like to get a chance to interview any politicians, celebrities and dignitaries who may also be in attendance.

I had to decide what I would share with Maria and what I would withhold. The trick was that I had to give her enough so that it didn't appear I was holding back. I decided to go with quantity over quality; I'd swamp her with reams of paper. I'd provide her with printout after printout off the web, stuff that was public news already but stuff that she'd have been too lazy or dumb to research on her own.

For some reason, she wanted to discuss this over lunch and she'd meet me at Bisque, one of the trendiest restaurants in all of New York. She told me upfront that it would be on her expense report, which I appreciated. If I wanted to eat in a restaurant like that, I'd have had to go through layer upon layer of approvals but all she had to do was pick up the phone—or rather have her assistant pick up the phone—and make a reservation. It's one of the perks of being national rather than local, even if the local is New York.

As was my habit, I arrived at the restaurant precisely on time. The hostess sat me and twenty minutes later Maria flounced in. She made a big show when she came over to me and kissed me on the cheek in greeting.

I had a large accordion file stuffed with printouts and hastily scratched out notes of the most unimportant recollections I could muster. The look of revulsion on her face at the sight of the file immediately reminded me why I detested Maria and could not ever in my mind put her name and the word "journalist" in the same sentence. Any reporters worth their salt would have appreciated the background as they dived into a story. Instead, Maria only wanted a two page, double-spaced memo of talking points that she could memorize. If it were anybody else, I would have prepared such a memo in addition to the background, but I didn't feel she was worth the effort.

To her credit, she adjusted her facial expression and graciously accepted the folder as she sat down.

"Francine, it's wonderful to see you again. How long has it been?" she asked.

"Way too long, Maria," I lied.

"How are things at my old stomping ground? There are times when I really miss local news."

Like hell you do, I thought.

"Oh, same as they ever were. Lots of shootings, scandals and transit strikes to keep us busy."

Our lunch continued on in this manner for an hour or so. Maria would feel the occasional need to remind me that she was with the network while I labored with a lowly affiliate, albeit the flagship New York one. She asked a few questions about the reverend but not the obvious ones such as: Why did you go to interview him in the first place about his sermon promoting destruction of Mecca?

Instead she asked superficial questions about the minister, what he seemed like, his marital status, etc. I did not volunteer anything about Westbrook or Farad.

I wished her luck down in Georgia at the rally. She made a response to the effect that she didn't need luck; her talent would carry her along. I just smiled in response.

I hailed a cab and was at the coffee shop ten minutes early. Farad was waiting outside. I could feel my heart skip a beat when I saw him. Judging by the smile on his face when he saw me, I thought he might be experiencing a similar reaction.

We hugged and kissed on both cheeks and then walked into the coffee shop.

"Farad, he contacted me."

"Westbrook?"

"Yes."

I showed him the text; Farad read it silently.

"I am so very sorry that I guessed correctly. 'Things are

proceeding,' " Farad read out loud, "What do you think he means by that?"

"I don't know if it means he's close to getting a device or whether he'd planned to use me all along to get the word out. Perhaps he had some grand scheme that in the end the U.S. will do his dirty work, and I've been his accomplice."

"In just a few short days this story has generated such headlines. He certainly is getting the American public riled up."

"You mean I have."

"We've all played our part, Francine. I assume you're going to be heading to Georgia soon to cover Reverend McKenzie's talk."

"No, I've been taken off the story. It's being covered by one of the network reporters, Maria Wallace."

"That idiot!"

"You know her?"

"She did a piece on Arab-American relations a few years back. She interviewed me. She didn't know the first thing about Arab culture and here she is doing this piece. She got everything wrong. I'm surprised she didn't cause an international incident on her own."

"I don't know anything about Arabs either, Farad."

"Yes, but you admit it and are willing to learn. She walked in like she knew everything and had the story already written in her mind. She just needed me to give her a couple of quotes to pepper her story to make it sound somewhat authentic. Francine, I don't know why but I think it would be a grave mistake for you to give up on this."

"It's not my choice to make."

"Well, then continue doing it on the side. I doubt you're going to share this text with her, are you?"

"I was supposed to give her my notes and fill her in on everything I've done up to now but I only gave her the bare minimum, the things that are public record. That was enough to make her happy."

"Believe me, she'll only hear what she wants to hear anyway. In the meantime, we'll continue working behind the scenes."

"Thank you Farad. It's nice to hear someone believes in me."

Again, his radiant smile and piercing pitch black eyes weakened my knees.

"Listen," he continued, "I understand the Reverend's sermon is going to be covered live on Christian Broadcasting. Why don't you come over to my place and we can watch it together? I'll whip together a dinner for us and then we can put it on. It might be a late evening, so perhaps you'll want to stay over. I have a spare bedroom."

I was secretly hoping he didn't have a spare bedroom.

"That sounds like a plan, Farad."

"Good, here's my address. Come over around 6:30."

Farad lived in a massive apartment on Fifth Avenue overlooking Central Park. He had modern furnishings and every conceivable device and convenience known to man. Reverend McKenzie would be rendered nearly life size on Farad's enormous plasma television that took up the majority of one wall.

The dinner he "whipped up" turned out to be a braised lamb that was so tender it obviously had slow cooked all day. I couldn't get enough of it. Farad talked about how he used to help his mother in the kitchen growing up. While his father didn't think this was an especially manly endeavor, neither did he stop him. The result was that Farad was one of the best cooks around; certainly far better than any man I ever knew.

We then repaired to the media room to watch the big event. I initially sat in one of the chairs off to the side while Farad sat on the black leather sectional couch. After a few minutes I realized I didn't have a proper angle to see the screen and moved over on the couch beside him. The show began.

The broadcast opened with an empty stage, or rather pulpit, of the Resurrection Cathedral filling the screen. The stage was huge; it would be the envy of any Broadway theater. There was a Lucite podium holding a microphone and a twenty-foot high silver cross suspended ten feet above the stage. An organ played inspirational music as the tension mounted. Hanging across the back of the stage was a huge banner stating: NO CHEEKS LEFT!

I recalled McKenzie jotting something down when I asked him about turning the other cheek. He had latched onto that as his slogan. This made me feel even guiltier. I not only had given him his inspiration through his brother, I gave him his rallying cry as well!

I looked over and Farad. He was visibly shaken anticipating the event. I tried to lighten the mood.

"What a stupid slogan," I ventured.

"I feel that many of my people will die."

"Farad, it's just a passing madness. Things like this come and go. It's a flavor of the day. Soon McKenzie will fade back into oblivion."

Given the Arab reaction to the YouTube version of his sermon, I didn't convince myself, let alone Farad.

"That's exactly what a lot of Germans said in the late 1920s, only it didn't fade away. There's meanness in this country that didn't used to be here. People are scared about many things and when people are scared, they lash out at those who are different from them."

I wanted to console him but the words did not come; I agreed with his sentiment. So, instead of words I took action. I leaned over and kissed him tenderly on the lips.

"I've wanted to do that ever since I first saw you."

"Likewise."

We looked into each other's eyes. Farad hit the RECORD button then got up, took my hand and led me into his bedroom. Needless to say, none of the spare rooms got used that night.

Three hours later we wandered back out to the media room to watch the spectacle and also to see if there'd been any immediate reaction in the Arab world.

Farad went to the recorded show and resumed where we had been. The camera was still on the empty stage. The crowd was buzzing in anticipation. Suddenly, the organ music ceased, as did the crowd noise. Then a single trumpet burst forth a fanfare. The camera slowly pivoted from the cross, podium and banner to the far left entrance to the stage.

Seconds later, an imposing man with a shock of unruly white hair and full beard strode from behind the curtain towards the main microphone. The crowd went wild as Reverend Warriner made his entrance, waving and smiling broadly to his adoring public. Then three additional cameras came into play as the shots alternated from two different angles providing close-ups of the Reverend, to broad shots of the stage and his entrance to candid shots of members of the congregation either in utter rapture that rendered them speechless or in exuberant cheering and shouting of Hallelujahs at being in the presence of the great preacher.

Warriner accepted the tribute for three full minutes at which point he raised his arms up in a beseeching manner, closed his eyes and bowed his head. The hall suddenly became silent as if a magic spell had descended on the 10,000 in attendance.

The preacher stood there like this in total silence for another minute. Almost in a whisper he began to pray.

"Our heavenly Father, the world is in peril like no other time in its history. The powers of Satan have risen up, cloaked in the guise of respectable religion, and are choking the air out of the civilized world. We've prayed for your guidance and you have answered our prayers. You have sent us a prophet, your mouthpiece, to tell us what needs to be done. It is a hard lesson we need to teach, a bitter medicine we must swallow. But if we ignore this lesson or pour this medicine down the sink, we will perish. Make no mistake about it, we and our way of life will perish if we do not act, and act now."

Warriner then opened his eyes and looked out upon the throng of people. He paused for effect.

"My brothers and sisters, sometimes things happen in your life that are so momentous you have to sit down and say: Wow.

"The other day, one of our church elders brought to my attention a sermon delivered by a preacher in a small church in upstate New York. Luckily this sermon was saved for posterity on the church's website.

"It was a rather short sermon. Now, you all know how I can get all wrapped up in what I'm saying. I lose all track of time when I am up here delivering God's message to you. Luckily, not too many of you drift off as I'm rambling on."

The crowd chuckled a bit at the preacher's attempt at self-deprecation.

"But anyway, I heard this sermon, looked up to heaven and said: Wow. I immediately got on the phone. I had to talk with this man. He answered the phone and within two minutes I was so impressed with this man of God that I had to get him down here to share his message with you.

"And so, without further ado—and also so I don't inadvertently steal any of his thunder—let me introduce to you the Reverend Malcolm McKenzie!"

With this the organ poured forth Onward Christian Soldiers as McKenzie confidently strode onto the stage. Buoyed with nothing more than support from Reverend Warriner and the knowledge that this New York minister had personally put the Middle East into a frenzy, the crowd went wild.

As with his introducer, McKenzie remained silent for a minute or so, acknowledging the crowd but obviously fully aware of the location of the cameras. At last he began.

"Thank you, thank you all. I can attest to the world right here and now that southern hospitality is alive and well."

The crowd burst into cheers.

"Why, in the two days I've been down here, I swear I've put on five pounds from all the fried chicken, barbequed ribs and peach cobbler you have bestowed on me."

The people roared with laughter.

"I will never forget the welcome I've received; I hope I am able to give you something in return.

"You are all probably looking at the words hanging behind me, trying to figure out their meaning. NO CHEEKS LEFT? You ask.

Probably some high fallutin' New York expression this carpetbagger is trying to ram down our throats, I bet some of you are saying to yourselves. Well, let me explain myself before we get too far down that road.

"A couple of days ago, a reporter from a New York City television station came up to interview me. If you think I look out of my element down here among you good folks, well you should have seen this slick city reporter trying to fit in my little town."

The crowd went wild again.

"I'm surprised he didn't note that I'm Hispanic to complete the stereotype," I remarked, "and that I was there with a huge Black man!"

"I had a nice chat with this woman but at one point she asked me if the approach I advocated was not truly in the Christian spirit. I told her we could only turn the other cheek so many times. I am here today to tell the world that we've had it; we have no more cheeks left to offer to our enemies.

"But I'm perhaps getting ahead of myself here. Let me back up some.

"Like many of you, I felt a piece of my soul torn away when we were attacked on 9/11. I did not personally know or was related to anybody killed in these brutal and Godless attacks; yet I felt a kinship with each and every American who died on that infamous day.

"But being a man of God, I felt it my duty to offer messages of peace and hope in the months and years that followed. And so I did, but try as I might I could never bring myself to forgive the perpetrators of these horrific crimes. Perhaps it is a failing of mine, but with each new assault that is inflicted upon us by the follows of Islam, I felt more and more angry and helpless.

"I would cry to the Lord for an answer, for retribution if it is his will, to end this madness. And then it was made known to me that there was a way. And that way was to destroy Islam.

"You may ask: How can you destroy a religion? Well, I have several answers for you. First, Islam cannot in all good consciousness call itself a religion, a true expression of God here on earth. It is the work of Satan, pure and simple. Satan would like you to believe that it is a religion of peace and love. But what do we ever see emanating from Islam? Hate and violence. Most of the civilized world gave up stoning of women for adultery about 2,000 years ago. Yet what do we constantly hear out of the Middle East? We hear story after story about Moslem women who are stoned to death after they have the effrontery of getting themselves raped. I wish someone would explain to me where God can be found in any of that.

"The devout Muslim will tell you that Allah made his most perfect revelation to the world through Mohammed. Yet we all know that you can't get any more perfect than the revelation He made through his son, Jesus Christ. At best, Islam is superfluous; at worst it is an abomination, the work of the devil. We need to wipe it from the face of the earth.

"Still, you all ask whether it could be possible to eradicate an entire religion. Not if it's a true religion, one that is contained here."

McKenzie pats himself a few times on the chest, over the heart.

"A religion that can be found here can never be destroyed. As good Christians, we want to travel to our holiest places. We'd love to walk in the same places that Jesus once walked: Bethlehem, Nazareth, and Jerusalem. But there is nothing that tells us we have to go there in order to be proper bona fide Christians. Even the Jews dream of going to the Wailing Wall in Jerusalem, but if they don't they are still good Jews.

"But what about Islam? Well, there are five what they call pillars of the religion. The first is to pray five times a day. The second is to periodically fast to cleanse the soul. The third is to support charities. The fourth is to believe that Allah revealed himself to the prophet Mohammed.

"It is the fifth pillar on which this satanic worship rests that makes it the most vulnerable. It is the Hajj."

The rest of his polemic was essentially a rehash of his YouTube sermon. He did end it, however, with a ploy to involve and excite his audience.

"Does God want us to keep turning our cheek?"

At this, McKenzie put a hand up to his ear and the crowd responded with a resounding "No!"

"I am a man of peace. I worship the God of love, but a man and a country can be pushed only so far. Do you believe God wants us to continually be subjected to crimes perpetrated by the disciples of Satan?"

Again, the hand goes to the ear and the "No!" this time is earth shattering.

"Our God is one of mercy, love and compassion. He would accept these people back into his fold if they would only come to him. But God himself can be pushed only so far. Do you think God himself has any more cheeks to turn?"

This time he doesn't have to do the hand-to-ear trick. The crowd is fully into it now and again responds "No!"

"The time for action is now! I know of a very simple plan: destroy Mecca. Undoubtedly, our government and others will try to stop this ingenious initiative. They will say that this will bring about World War III. But you and I know that is a pile of crap, if you will pardon me for resorting to the vulgar for a second here. The government should be assisting this holy endeavor in every way possible. They should be saying to themselves: Why didn't I think of that?"

As McKenzie progressed, his delivery got louder and more impassioned. It was obvious the crowd was at a fever pitch. Now he scaled back and modulated his tone.

"There's an old saying, my friends, that nice guys finish last. Well, just look at our recent history. When we try to "respect other cultures" we get our asses kicked. On the other hand, when we do our job and proceed with the rightful assumption that we are in fact better, the world is better off.

"My father would tell of his experiences in the South Pacific during World War II. We had a take-no-prisoners, unconditional surrender, attitude and look what happened. Not only did Japan fall but they came back to be a strong, proud country and one of our closest allies. The same can happen in the Middle East.

"We've already had our modern day Pearl Harbor, so what are we waiting for. We can't, nor should we, turn back."

He paused, looking straight into the camera.

"What do you say? Are you with me?"

It started as a low rumbling from one section of the auditorium, but soon the volume of a discernible chant rose up and filled the hall. "No Cheeks Left! No Cheeks Left!"

The volume increased as Reverend Warriner walked over to Reverend McKenzie and they stood there, raising their arms in victory. It reached a final crescendo when Congressman Wade "Pete" Connors—Georgia's new darling of the right, a former Navy Seal and a man being touted as having presidential timber—strutted out to congratulate the two preachers.

Onward Christian Soldiers blared once again over the loudspeakers as Farad clicked the remote to a 24-hour news channel. Three talking heads were discussing the sermon and its repercussions.

"Already we've had threatened reprisals from every Muslim country on earth. They've all indicated that there is no way they can guarantee the safety of U.S. personnel in their countries."

"There's got to be some way the government can shut up this lunatic." I noted. "Free speech is one thing but the Supreme Court has consistently said that you can't yell fire in a crowded theater when there is no fire. This reverend has singlehandedly put the world to the brink of war. He should have been stopped before he ever set foot on that stage."

"Well, we haven't quite gotten to the point where we prosecute someone in advance of their actions. If he's broken some law, he'll be prosecuted. But I'm not sure if he actually has broken a law. First, the freedom of speech protections are pretty broad. Second, he's a man of the cloth, so everything he says is cloaked in religious protection. There are a lot of gray areas here."

"His gray areas may cost a lot of American lives."

"And Muslim lives, too."

"Of course, but all I'm saying is that this guy must be more sensitive to the fact that his words may endanger his fellow citizens."

Farad switched to another station, which was more of a straight news format. Footage was being beamed in of demonstrations in Jordon and Libya. Reports of violence were pouring in from everywhere. It was after midnight in New York so Europe, which was five or more hours ahead, was just starting to wake up and already there were Arab protests around the American embassies in Paris, London and Brussels.

Finally, Farad turned off the television completely.

"Francine, you have to find Westbrook and stop him."

"Me? We really need to get the authorities involved. This is an FBI and CIA matter."

"What do we have? My intuition, a megalomaniac preacher and an oblique text from a wacko. Arab uprisings notwithstanding, without more concrete proof you'll get the same reactions we got from McKenzie in State."

He was right but I was getting scared. I was way in over my head. I leaned over and nestled into his arms. He stroked my hair, staring off into space. Eventually, we drifted off to sleep.

The next day, every morning news program led with a destroy Mecca story. Foreign governments, especially the Arab countries, expressed their outrage even more vehemently and demanded that the President and members of Congress publicly denounce Reverend McKenzie and his message. The Saudi King went so far as to deliver what could be considered a veiled declaration of war. Various radical Islamic organizations announced that jihad was the only answer and that justice would be swift and decisive.

Airports were put on high alert. Security was enhanced at public monuments and gathering sites around the country. Websites and chat rooms sprang up out of nowhere to discuss this new, bold idea. Congressional websites crashed as nearly everyone was emailing his or her opinion to respective Members of Congress.

For their part, many public officials (except Congressman Connors, of course) publicly said they abhorred violence and many, including the President, specifically denounced McKenzie and his message.

5

As much as I would have liked to make Westbrook/Mecca my full-time job, I did have actual assignments to work on. Much more mundane stories—a shooting of a ten year-old girl in Brooklyn, salmonella contamination in chicken, an unjust and illegal foreclosure of a wounded veteran's home—came my way. As usual, I immersed myself in these jobs and lost track of the world.

Unfortunately, Farad also dived back into his work. I hadn't heard from him—not a call, not a text, nothing—since the night of McKenzie's sermon. His conference on improving Arab-American relations was more important than ever before. But still, it would have been nice to get a note or a text or a call telling me he missed me and was thinking of me.

I tried contacting him, but all my messages went unanswered. One day I even went back to his apartment but there was no answer. The doorman said he hadn't seen or heard from him in weeks. I was beginning to think he finally thought it over and decided our differences were too great to overcome. He was probably right. I would have preferred he told me this face to face rather than to just have him disappear like this.

I settled back into my daily routine. After three weeks, I started to wonder why I had gotten myself so worked over the Mecca story. Reverend McKenzie had finagled himself thirty minutes of fame instead of fifteen but he was finally in the rear view mirror.

After the FBI very publicly arrested him and filed terrorist plot charges against him, the Middle East situation calmed down somewhat. The agency was heavily criticized in the media for moving against the preacher's freedoms of speech and religion. Everyone knew the charges wouldn't stick. Still, though, the action was enough to satisfy many of the world's Muslim leaders and the violence subsided.

This whole episode was obviously nothing but I had let it get the better of me. As a journalist, I needed to maintain better control over my emotions and remain impartial. Lesson learned for the future.

The same could be said of my schoolgirl crush on Farad. It was an exciting fling with a suave, debonair, worldly, intelligent and handsome man, but that's all it was. I had to move on.

I'd just returned to the office from doing a story on a controversial art show depicting Jesus as a pimp at the Museum of Interpretive Art. I was ready to start cutting my piece when Frank called for me, asking me to come into his office.

I walked in and saw two scrupulously clean-cut men in dark suits and boring ties sitting there quietly.

"Francine, these men are from the FBI."

In unison, they rose and extended their cards to me.

"My name is Special Agent William Allen and this is Agent Bernard Willoughby."

I shook their hands.

"FBI?"

"Yes, ma'am."

Allen turned to Frank.

"Can you leave us alone for a few minutes? We need to speak with Miss Vega confidentially. Thank you."

This was obviously not a request. Frank gathered up some papers he was working on and headed out of his office.

"Francine, I'll be right out here if you need anything."

Frank could be such a dear. He obviously would be no match for these highly trained agents, but he wanted to make it clear to them that if anything were to happen, he was ready to rush in.

"Thanks Frank." I hesitantly responded.

Once he left and closed the door behind him, the agents asked me to sit down. Since Frank was a certified slob and had papers piled high on every chair around his small conference table, I sat down in his chair behind his desk while the agents assumed their places in the two chairs on the other side of the desk. This all was taking on a surreal aspect to it.

"Ms. Vega," Special Agent Allen started, "Do you know a Mr. Farad Sahari?"

"Yes."

I decided to keep my answers as short as possible, answering only the questions asked and no more.

"How well do you know him?"

"Somewhat. I interviewed him on a story I was working on. We had dinner together and we saw each other a few times after that and spoke a few other times. Why do you ask?"

They ignored my question. Agent Willoughby asked the next question.

"Did you sleep with him?"

"I don't think that's any of your business."

"Please answer the question, Miss Vega." Allen was obviously the leader of this pack.

"Not before you give me some idea what this is about."

Again, they ignored my protestation.

"Are you familiar with the Arab-American Friendship League?"

"Only that Farad does some work for them and has been busy planning a conference they are hosting."

"When was the last time you saw or spoke with Mr. Sahari?"

"Three weeks ago."

"What were the subjects of your conversations with Mr. Sahari?"

These guys were really starting to piss me off. I occasionally glanced out the window out into the main office and saw Frank sitting there, watching us intently. This time when I looked out, however, he had gone. He picked a hell of a time to run to the bathroom.

"I would like to have one of the station's lawyers here, if you don't mind."

"Ms. Vega. You do know you can be charged with hindering an investigation if you withhold evidence, don't you?" Willoughby asked.

"I haven't withheld anything. I've only requested that an attorney be present. Also, you haven't told me you were investigating anything. As far as I can tell, you only are interested in who I am sleeping with."

"Shall we continue with the questioning?"

Allen was trying to at least be civil.

Seeing that they were going to ignore my request for an attorney, I reached into my bag and pulled out my recorder. I switched it on and placed it in front of me.

"What are you doing?" he asked.

"Since you've told me I could be charged with a crime but have denied my request for legal counsel, I thought it would be wise to record the rest of our conversation."

"Turn that off."

"No."

When Allen reached over to grab the machine, I pulled it back. So Willoughby grabbed my wrist instead. Within seconds, the door flew open and Frank rushed in, Jonas following closely behind.

"Get the hell out of my office!" Frank bellowed.

The two agents looked at Frank, then at Jonas and then at each other.

"Thank you for your time," Allen said as the two agents rose to exit, "I'm sure we'll be talking again, Ms. Vega. Gentlemen."

They departed. Frank stared at their backs all the way to the elevator.

"Nice touch, Frank, running for reinforcements. Thank you, Jonas."

Jonas smiled and then excused himself, claiming he had work to do. Frank took the chair vacated by Special Agent Allen, letting me remain in his chair.

"So, what was going on? Were they asking about Westbrook?"

"No, Farad Sahari."

"Sahari? What did they say he'd done?"

"They never said. They kept asking about how well I knew him, even whether I'd ever slept with him. When I told them it was none of their business, they started to threaten me with prosecution. That's when I asked to have one our lawyers present. When they ignored my request, I pulled out my recorder. Then they started to get physical and you rushed in."

"How well *do* you know Sahari?"

"You want to know whether I've slept with him, too?"

"No, I'm just saying that you've only known this guy a few weeks. How much do you really know about him? You said you hadn't heard from him in over three weeks. For all you know, he and his little organization could be putting the final touches on some terrorist plot."

I said nothing in response. I really didn't know Farad at all, did I? What had he been up to all this time? Why did he cut off all contact with me? Could I have been blinded by infatuation that easily? Finally I responded.

"No, Frank, I guess I don't know him at all."

"I'm sorry, Francine."

At that moment Jonas reappeared holding two envelopes, a large manila one and a standard letter-sized white one. The manila envelope was opened, the other unopened.

"Frannie, when I got back to my desk this was waiting for me. I looked at the envelope and saw it was postmarked Paris."

"Paris, as in France?" I asked.

"None other. I don't know anyone in Paris so I was a little leery, but what the hell, I opened it and inside was this second envelope addressed to you."

We looked at each other, big question marks in our eyes. I reached over and started to open the letter. Frank stopped me.

"You think that's smart? With all the anthrax and ricin scares over the past decade? I wouldn't put it past some wacko to send a booby trap to a reporter he didn't like."

I considered his concerns for a second.

"Seems like a rather elaborate set-up for a booby trap, sending it through Jonas like this. Anyway, who would I report this to, the FBI? I'm sure they'd like to come back for another crack at me. If you want, I'll open it outside."

"No, that's okay. I'm just becoming a conspiracy theorist in my old age."

I ripped open the envelope and started to read.

> *Dear Francine,*
>
> *I apologize that I have not been able to contact you earlier but I had to leave the country rather unexpectedly and hastily. Through some of my contacts, I discovered that I have become the subject of a federal investigation. In the next few days you may hear some horrendous things attributed to me and to the Arab-American Friendship League. None of it will be true. In fact, quite the opposite is the case. I believe I am on the trail of Alan Westbrook. Colonel Jacob Lawson is assisting him.*

"Lawson?" Frank interrupted.

"You know him?" I asked.

"I know of him. He's one of the most powerful men in Washington, if not the world. He's a key liaison between the National Security Council, the Pentagon, NATO and every other military organization in the world. No significant military decision is made without his input. He's worked under three Presidents. He's a first class ruthless prick who knows where every body is buried. And he's buried more than a few bodies himself. He's stayed a colonel because he prefers it that way; he can fly under the radar better than a general could."

"If he's that powerful, how come I've never heard of him?"

"You haven't heard of him because he doesn't want you to hear of him. He's a behind the scenes guy all the way, a puller of strings and master chess player. He's not one you'll see in front of Congressional committees but he'll have had a hand in everything that will be told to those committees."

"How do you know so much about him?"

"You remember when I came here from network three years ago?"

"Yeah."

"It wasn't by choice. Who purposely goes in that direction as a career choice? No, I was sent here both to protect me and to keep me in line. You remember Frank Merrill?"

"The White House reporter who hanged himself a few years back?"

"The same. He was my friend and colleague. We were the two Franks. About five years ago he stumbled on some classified documents implicating Lawson in all sorts of nefarious dealings, Iran-Contra types of intrigues. I use the word 'stumbled' euphemistically. Someone, probably one of Lawson's legions of enemies, had left a box of these documents on his doorstep. Well, Frank was one of the best investigative reporters I've ever known and he started to dig and to put pieces together. That's when the notes started to arrive. Every couple of days a new note would be found. Sometimes it would be on his windshield, sometimes in his morning newspaper. They would just be one word, something like 'wife' or 'daughter' or 'son.' The message was clear: End this investigation... or else.

"Frank wasn't the type who could be pushed around, though. He kept on asking questions, digging for the truth about Lawson. Then it happened. His daughter, Ashley, was crossing the street. She was a beautiful girl. Sixteen years old, just a lovely person. A white van ran the stop sign, blew through the cross walk and killed her instantly. The van was found about a mile away, stolen plates, no fingerprints or any other trace.

"Well, Frank went into swift decline after that. He knew Lawson was behind it, making good on his threat. He had no proof except for the one-word notes, which anybody could have sent. His wife blamed him for not backing down and soon filed for divorce. Eventually, he burned all his tapes and notes, sending pictures of the ashes to Lawson to protect his son and his former wife. Then he hanged himself, although I wouldn't be surprised if Lawson somehow arranged that as well.

"I'd read everything Frank had pulled together or written on Lawson. We talked about this for months. I was his sounding board. I knew too much but I don't think Lawson ever became aware of me. The company, to its credit, shipped me here to try and keep me out of his clutches."

Frank fell silent.

"I'm so sorry, Frank," I offered, "that obviously was difficult for you to dredge up."

"Why don't you finish Sahari's letter?"

I read on.

I need your assistance. An international watch has been placed on me through Interpol. They know where I am and I have two agents posted outside my door twenty-four hours a day, monitoring my every movement. Luckily, I have a friend, a French official, whom I have known for many years who is helping me without raising suspicions. But in his official capacity, he can only do so much to help track down Westbrook. I need you to come to Paris for a few days. I will totally understand if you can't. Please call my friend, Captain Jean Marc L'Eglise, at 1-33-45-45-23-23 to let him know what you can and cannot do.

In the next couple of days, some bad things may happen and the blame will be laid at my feet. You must believe me that I have nothing to do with any of this. Please.

I look forward to hearing from you.
With Love,
Farad

Now, all three of us fell silent. I looked at Frank and then Jonas and then back at Frank.

"What should I do?" I asked to nobody in particular.

"If Lawson is involved," Frank responded, "this can get plenty dangerous. In addition, as I asked before: What do you really know about Sahari? Couldn't he be guilty of whatever they're accusing him?"

"I really don't know, Frank," I wearily responded, "but something in my gut tells me he's not; that's he's one of the good guys here."

"In other words, you're saying that you're heading to Paris, no matter what I think. Am I right?"

"Yeah, I guess you are. I just feel I have to go. I've got plenty of vacation time accumulated."

"No."

"No what?"

I really didn't want to get into a fight with Frank over this. I wanted to leave on good terms, but I had to leave.

"No, you're not taking this trip on vacation time. This is a work assignment. We'll pay your way. And Jonas is going with you."

"Are you sure, Frank?"

"Damn straight. I've been waiting years for someone to go after Lawson. I've seen you in action, Francine. If anyone can get the goods on this bastard, it'll be you. I just want you to promise you'll watch your back at all times."

Before I could say a word, Jonas spoke up.

"I'll always have your back, Frannie."

6

We caught a six fifteen plane out of JFK. It was a seven-hour flight into Orly, just outside Paris, getting us there at around ten in the morning. I was glad Frank agreed to pick up the tab for this trip. Company policy was that, if the trip involved international travel, we'd fly business class. Much as I loved Jonas, the idea of him wedging his huge frame into a coach seat beside me for that long a time was not very appealing.

I'd never been to Paris before. I'd wanted to go there on my honeymoon but Eddie really wanted to go to London so I acquiesced. I certainly didn't enjoy London and probably wouldn't have enjoyed Paris either as I came to the frightening realization on the flight over that marrying Eddie was a big mistake.

I'd gone out with him for two years before we got engaged. He was fun and intelligent and personable but I should have read the clues that this was perhaps not my ideal match.

First off, while he had a well-paying job with a liberal political think tank when I met him, he spoke vaguely about a checkered prior employment history. Second, during the time we dated, he never had one drink. Not one. My mother thought that suspicious. It wasn't until the flight that he admitted—but only after he'd downed three vodka and tonics—that he was an alcoholic. The thought of flying petrified him and it was enough to throw him completely off the wagon. From then on, all the bad habits he had kept in check during the time he knew me came out one after another. As a result, our marriage only lasted a year and a half, although to this day I have to admit that a part of me still loves the guy.

Jonas had been to Paris a couple of times with his then live-in girlfriend, Eunice. His eyes literally lit up when Frank suggested he accompany me on this trip.

"Oh, you're going to absolutely love Paris," he declared, "I guarantee it. I'll show you some of the out-of-the-way places tourists rarely get to visit.

"All those stories about the snobby French people are somewhat true, but that only adds to their allure, at least in my book. I'm sad to say that Paris has become a little more Americanized over the years—fast food joints and all that—but it's still quite a place. If you stay away from the tourist spots, the food is far better than anything you can get anywhere in New York."

Knowing how much of an ardent New Yorker Jonas was, this was some compliment. I've seen Jonas almost come to blows with people who insulted his hometown in any way.

We chatted about Paris and this and that, sipping wine while we talked. I was gradually falling asleep when about four hours into the flight the lights in the cabin unexpectedly came alive. It was so sudden I expected some sort of announcement to be made. Instead, I looked back into coach and saw two men rise simultaneously out of their seats. They were both rather scruffy looking with five o'clock shadows. Both were of medium height, one was a dirty blond, the other a brunette. Both wore wearing casual beige pants and white button down shirts.

The blond man headed to the front of the plane through business section into first class; the brunette headed to the rear of the plane. I looked back and forth as they progressively and systematically moved toward the middle.

"What's that all about?" I whispered to Jonas, nudging him awake. The way they choreographed their rising up out of their seats and their marches to the ends of the planes made me nervous that we might be watching terrorists in action.

"Marshals," he wearily responded, "I heard them chatting with one of the flight attendants in the waiting area."

The two Marshals systematically looked at each passenger as they made their ways to the center. Since most were asleep, I'm not sure what they'd be able to determine by this type of inspection. When the blond one got to me, I looked up at him and we locked eyes for a second before he moved on.

Once they completed this exercise, they nodded to each other and then silently returned to their seats, but they didn't sit down. The blond one pulled some papers out of his bag. They went down a list of some sort; most likely it was the passenger list. They stopped on a particular item at which point they both looked in my direction. They couldn't help but see me staring back at them. They came my way.

"Ms. Vega?" the blond man inquired, "Could you come with us please?"

"What's this about?" I responded in a soft voice.

"We'll discuss that in a few moments."

Jonas got up to let me out and was going to accompany me but I indicated he should remain, that I'd be okay. The marshals and I walked back to the kitchen area in the back of the plane. A flight attendant was there, taking a break. The blond man showed her his badge and asked if we might be alone for a few minutes.

"Ms. Vega," the blond agent began, "We are air marshals. I'm Brian Kowalski and this is Wendell Wilkins. We'd like to ask you a few questions."

"Okay," I tentatively responded.

"What is the purpose of your trip?"

"I'm traveling on business."

"Are you traveling with anyone?"

"Jonas Clarke."

"What is the nature of your business?"

"I'm a journalist."

I could tell they were getting frustrated with my non-expansive answers. As a reporter, I could tell when people agreed to be interviewed but really didn't want to tell you anything. They would answer just the question and only the question. This had several advantages for them. First, it would tend to frustrate the interviewer, perhaps convincing him or her to shut the whole thing down prematurely. Second, it didn't open up any avenues for additional questions. Sometimes a person I interviewed would open up additional questions in my mind because their answers were too complete or expansive.

"Mr. Clarke is also a journalist?"

"No."

"What does he do?"

"He's a cameraman."

"Who are you planning to see on this trip?"

"Jean Marc L'Eglise"

"And who is he?"

"A captain in the French National Police."

"And what are you seeing him about?"

"A story I'm working on in New York?"

"What is the nature of that story?"

"It's on immigration from France to the US."

I don't know where that came from but it sounded plausible and there was no way they could check on it.

"Do you know a man name Farad Sahari?"

Now we were getting down to business. I obviously must be entered into a database as a person of interest related to Farad. Since the FBI already knew about my relationship with Farad, it would do no good to tell these men otherwise.

"Yes, that seems to be common knowledge."

"Do you know where Mr. Sahari is at this point in time?"

"No, I don't."

"Are you familiar with the Arab-American Friendship League?"

"I know of it but am not familiar with its workings."

"Does Mr. Sahari work for them?"

"He indicated as much."

The marshals either decided they weren't going to get anything more out of me or figured there would be a better time and a better place for this interview. In any case, they thanked me for answering my questions and handed me their cards, advising me to call them if I had any further information. Since they didn't ever tell me the reason I was being interrogated, it would be difficult to know if I had any information that would be useful to them. I went back to my seat.

I certainly couldn't sleep after that. My mind was racing. What caused them to search the plane in the first place? What were they looking for? What was my connection to any of this? How was Farad involved?

I turned on the in-flight entertainment, hoping to find a news channel to catch up. Finding the 24-hour news channel that was owned by my network, it all became crystal clear. On the screen, smoke billowed from what used to be an SUV. Behind it, the front of an office building had been blown off, revealing desks, cabinets and other items that could be found in an ordinary office, except these weren't offices anymore. Rather, they were now cubbyholes that opened out to the street below. The title across the bottom of the screen was: Terrorist Bombing in Topeka.

In a macabre touch, the camera zoomed in on a picture of a little girl—she was probably only about 6 or 7—hanging on the back wall of one of these offices. I plugged in my earphones to get some information. A reporter was giving a recap.

"At approximately 8:30 this evening, a powerful explosion rocked downtown Topeka. The explosive appeared to have been planted in a white Ford Explorer. Reminiscent of Oklahoma City, the explosion sheared off the face of Exeter Life Insurance building. Because of the late hour, no company employees or customers appeared to be in the building. However, cleaning and maintenance crews were believed to be working. The number of people killed or wounded has not yet been released although unconfirmed reports indicate that at least three people have been killed.

"Forty-five minutes after the blast, our New York affiliate received a call from a man claiming to represent a radical organization known as the Arab-American Friendship League taking credit for the bombing. Officials are investigating this organization whose website cites the

*official mission as being, and I quote: To build bridges of
understanding and common ground between the Arab
community throughout the world and the United States of
America.*

*"For more on the Arab-American Friendship League, I'll
send it back to New York. This is Leslie Levant reporting live
from Topeka, Kansas."*

I wanted to listen to the report on the Arab-American
Friendship League, on Farad's organization, but I was too stunned
to hear what was being said. What was Farad Sahari into? I didn't
know the man one little bit, did I?

His note to me did indicate that something was going to
happen for which the League was to be blamed and that I
shouldn't believe it. But a terrorist attack? Was Farad telling me
that an attack of this type would be carried out solely to discredit
his organization? Or was he simply trying to deceive me, perhaps
getting me to unwittingly be his accomplice?

No wonder the marshals singled me out. After the bombing, I'd
imagine their first order of business was to try and ensure that
the plane was safe. Their first objective would be to attempt to
spot a would-be terrorist amongst all of the sleeping passengers.
Their next step would be to review the passenger list to see if
anyone jumped out at them. After my unsatisfactory interview
with the FBI agents, my name undoubtedly was placed on a watch
list. I don't know why it wasn't flagged at the airport but I
supposed they're more vigilant regarding people coming into the
country rather than going out. I couldn't worry about that now.

When we landed, the marshals eyed me as we deplaned. When
we reached immigration and customs at Orly, they were speaking
with French officials, each of whom would occasionally look over
at me standing in line. I expected any minute for someone to come
over and ask me to accompany them to some windowless room
for hours of interrogation under a bare light bulb, but in the end
no one came for me. My passport was stamped and I proceeded

on to collect my luggage and out of the airport.

Jonas and I took a cab to a hotel not far from the *Arc de Triomphe*. Despite being a bundle of nerves over what I was walking into, I couldn't help but be excited as the taxi weaved its way through Paris. At one point we turned a corner on a broad boulevard and there it was, the *Tour Eiffel*. It was as magnificent as all the tour books said it was. A few minutes later we were in a mass of automobiles maneuvering the circle around the Arc. My heart was beating as fast as I've ever felt it.

Jonas had a satisfied look on his face as if he'd returned home after being away for a long time. In just the short time I'd been there, I could understand his feeling. The cab made one last turn off a main thoroughfare down a somewhat narrow side street and then pulled in front of our hotel.

Even though the station was paying for our trip, I didn't feel right staying at one of the upper scale hotels such as the Ritz or the George V. Jonas recommended a small three star hotel, *l'Etoile*, that he had stayed at previously. It was just perfect. There were around 20 rooms, each with its own bathroom. It was clean and well-maintained. That was all I needed.

I called the number Farad had given me. It was Captain L'Eglise's direct line and he picked up on the second ring. He said he'd meet us at the hotel the following morning at around 9:00. Jonas and I had the rest of this day to ourselves. We slept for an hour after which we headed out to see at least one sight and then have dinner. Jonas remembered a quaint little Basque restaurant in the Marais, which was on the other end of town. He said not to worry; the Metro subway system was a thing of beauty and efficiency.

The meal was as delicious as Jonas had described it. I had a sort of escargot soup with the most delicious broth I had ever tasted. Then I had the duck confit, which was so tender I never used my knife once. We followed this with a Basque cheese and then a slice of a hazelnut flavored cake. Of course, we split a bottle of wine. By the end of the meal I'd almost forgotten what I had come to Paris for, but I knew that before long it would be back to work.

After that, we went to a late night jazz club in the *Sainte Germain* neighborhood of Paris. A wonderful quartet performed. A 30ish pretty woman with a great voice sang. An older, distinguished gray haired man who I subsequently learned was her father played piano. The drummer was a longhaired hippie type. The last musician was a youngish man with dark hair and a roundish face played the bass. Or more precisely, he made love to the bass. We split a bottle of rosé wine and could have very easily stayed through another, but we had a busy day coming up.

Sharply at nine the next morning my phone rang. It was the front desk announcing that a Monsieur Jean Marc L'Eglise had requested to see me. I told the clerk to let him up to my room. A few minutes later, I opened the door to a thin dark haired 40ish man, stylishly dressed in black slacks and a gray pullover cashmere sweater.

"Miss Vega? Allow me to introduce myself. I am Captain Jean Marc L'Eglise of the French National Police. It is a pleasure to meet you."

"The pleasure is mine, Captain L'Eglise. Won't you come in?"

"Please, call me Jean Marc. Perhaps we could go to the brasserie next door and have a cup of coffee. Would that be acceptable to you?"

"Yes, it would."

I sensed that Captain L'Eglise would not feel it proper to enter a single woman's hotel room. Everything about him screamed Old World manners and etiquette. While I always loved New Yorkers and their direct ways of doing everything, it was nice to encounter a gentleman of this sort.

Since our hotel did not provide room service, I'd already been down to this brasserie about an hour and a half earlier to get some coffee. At that time it was bustling with people stopping for a cup before heading off to work. Now, there were only a few patrons lingering over the morning newspaper. The front page of one of the papers had a picture of the smoldering SUV in Topeka. Terrorism anywhere made news but when it happened in America after 9/11, it made the headlines everywhere in the world.

L'Eglise and I occupied a booth in a far corner of the restaurant. We both ordered an *espresso* and a *pain au chocolat*.

I'd considered asking Jonas to join us so that he could keep up with all that was being said but then I decided against it. First, I thought my first chat with the Captain should be confidential and frank. I imagined that he knew something about me from Farad. Introducing a new person, no matter how much I attested for him, might inhibit his comments. Second, we were meeting in a public place and, until I got a better lay of the land, I thought it better to be as inconspicuous as possible, especially after my experience on the plane. It was impossible for anyone to miss or ignore a six foot four black man. It would just be better to fill him in later.

Jean Marc waited until the coffee and pastries were delivered before he started talking.

"Mademoiselle Vega, Farad has told me all about you."

"Please, call me Francine. Farad and I have only known each other a few weeks so he couldn't know that much about me." I paused for a few seconds. "Nor could I know that much about him either."

"Well, I do know Farad, and I can tell he cares very much about you. If fact, in all the years I have known Farad I have never heard him talk about a woman as much as he does you."

"How long have you known Farad?"

"About twenty years. He came to live with my family for a year as an exchange student. We became like brothers and have been close ever since then."

"Is Farad still in Paris?"

"Yes, he is."

"Can I see him?"

"I do not think that would be wise right now. As you probably know, he is being pursued for questioning regarding the explosion in Topeka, Kansas. I want to assure you that he was not responsible in any way for that explosion. His organization had no role in it also."

"He's alright?"

"Yes, he is quite safe. We move him to new location periodically so authorities do not find him."

"Who are the "we" you talk about? Which authorities are you keeping him from? Aren't you part of the "authorities?"

"It is safer that I do not tell you who else is involved. The main agency looking for him is your Central Intelligence Agency. And, yes, I am part of the authorities looking for Farad, but I am also Farad's close friend. That is why my hands are tied in helping him. That is why we need you. Will you help us? Before you answer, I do have to warn you that this may get dangerous. The explosion in Topeka is only taste of how dangerous this may be. There may be times when it will seem like you are work against your own government."

Although I had no desire to get involved in anything dangerous, I inexplicably found myself responding, "Yes, I'll help."

"Good. Farad said you would say yes. Now, let me tell you what I know and then we can discuss what you can do to help."

I could not believe I was about to go down this road. In essence, I was about to become a spy, to work undercover to foil any number of plots and intrigues. And I was placing my trust in a man I'd only met a few weeks ago and another man I'd met a few short minutes ago. And yet I was more than willing to do this, not only as a journalist but because something was telling me this was the right thing to do.

Jean Marc told me that Westbrook was in fact in Paris. Colonel Lawson had joined him there just two days ago. Jean Marc had the men under close surveillance.

"Jean Marc, do you believe that Westbrook can carry out his plan?"

"I don't know, but Farad believes he can. In any case, I know Colonel Lawson can. Lawson is well known in our circles. He has a reputation for knowing as much as anyone about arms trafficking throughout the world. With the amount of money Westbrook has, the two of them can be a very dangerous pair. We will watch them as closely as we can, but if they choose to leave France, there is not much we can do. They have not committed any crimes. They have not said they intend to perform any criminal acts. Right now we are acting on Farad's intuition alone. I would trust that intuition with my life, but it is not enough to take anybody into custody."

"Do you believe there is a connection between Westbrook and Lawson and the explosion in Topeka?"

"Farad believes they are responsible for the explosion, if not directly then indirectly perhaps."

"How so?"

"When you first start to look into possibility that someone may want to destroy Mecca, word leaked to a minister who contained it in one of his sermons, correct?"

"Yes."

"And his sermon was replayed over and over again on the Internet, correct?"

"Yes, it got thousands if not millions of hits."

"But, like most every Internet sensation, the excitement died as people go about their lives. Even the national broadcast had only a short life. They need a way to create new enthusiasm for it. So they detonate a bomb and then plant the seed that an Islamic organization is behind bomb. Back in the States, there are many calls for retribution."

"Other than Farad's word, how do you know it wasn't an Islamic terrorist organization behind the explosion?"

"Well, other than the fact that Farad's word is good enough for me, let's look at the facts. First, Topeka?"

"It sure would be unexpected and probably would catch everyone off guard. Numerous plots get foiled in New York and other large cities that we never hear about because the constant threat is so great that day to day precautions are taken."

"Perhaps, but the bomb did not explode until nighttime. If a terrorist organization were behind it, wouldn't they do it during a time period when they could take the most lives?"

"Maybe their timing mechanism wasn't working properly."

"Again, perhaps. But it has been my experience that after an event such as this, there is a waiting period before the group responsible makes itself known. That way the terrorist organization drags out the terror, make people think something else may be ready to blow. In this case, the call was made to the television station within minutes, to announce that Farad's organization was responsible."

I was about to offer my argument refuting his latest justification that the Arab-American Friendship League may not be responsible for the explosion when he held up his hand.

"All I say is that there is doubt about the call to claim responsibility. That is where we would like you to help. We are afraid that the officials in America may stop looking now that they have a convenient and believable party taking responsibility, what you would call scapegoat. We like you to ask questions. I believe the call came in to your television station."

"Yes, the call came in to our station in New York. I know someone I can talk to."

"Good. That is start. Once you believe that Farad's organization had nothing to do with this, which you will, we'll trust your reporter training and instincts—which Farad says are substantial —to uncover the truth."

"I'll do my best."

"I know you will. I will remain in touch with you. When do you return to the States?"

"Tomorrow morning."

"Then you will be my guest tonight for dinner, you and your traveling companion. Jonas is his name, correct?"

"Yes, Jonas." I wondered how he knew about Jonas, whom I had not mentioned. It made me wonder how much he already knew about me.

"Then tomorrow I will drive you to the airport. I will be able to get you around the lines on this end but I am afraid you are on your own with your Department of Homeland Security once you arrive back home."

"After already being question twice by federal officials, I'd expect to be detained for questioning, but there's not much I can tell them so it should be alright."

"Good, I'll pick you and Mr. Clarke up at your hotel at 8:00. If you would like to write a letter to Farad, give it to me then and I will make sure he gets it. Does that sound okay to you?"

"Yes, I'll see you then."

"Oh, one last thing. We need a plausible story to tell officials if they ask why you are here to see me."

"I told the marshals that I was here to talk to you about immigration from France to New York. I have no idea why that popped into my head."

"Why, that's brilliant. A few years ago, I served on a special joint task force with New York Police on illegal immigration of Arabs from France into New York. This evening I will bring you some files that you can show them. I will have copies in my desk at work in case they want to verify your story. I am not sure if anyone at my office is aware of my relationship with Farad, but just in case, this presents a plausible cover."

Jonas was just waking and pulling himself together when I returned to the hotel.

"Hey doll, where ya been?"

"I was meeting with Captain Jean Marc L'Eglise, Farad's friend"

Jonas looked hurt I didn't include him.

"I should have asked you along but I'd never met this guy and I wanted him to speak freely. I didn't think he knew you were with me. Turns out he knew all about you and he's invited us both to dinner tonight."

With that news, Jonas brightened up.

As promised, Jean Marc arrived in front of the hotel at 8:00 sharp. We then proceeded to *La Tour d'Argent*, an exclusive restaurant on the banks of the Seine. Despite losing a couple of Michelin stars over the past decade, it was still considered one of the classiest eateries in the world. From the time Jean Marc pulled the car up in front of the restaurant to when we were seated in our seats on the fourth floor overlooking a brilliantly lit Notre Dame cathedral, we'd encountered five separate escorts, and we still were to meet our waiter and the sommelier.

I could only imagine that getting reservations for this place must be done months in advance. It made me wonder how Jean Marc was able to get a prime table for three on less than a day's notice. I wasn't going to ask.

The meal was superb. Jean Marc suggested I order the pressed duck, the restaurant's specialty. He explained that the dish was first served to a Prince of England (he couldn't remember which one) in 1919 and that they kept count of each one served since then. At the end of the meal I was presented with a card that indicated I had consumed the 1,187,536th such duck.

We split two bottles of wine—one Champagne and one Bordeaux—between the three of us. Jean Marc did most of the talking, regaling us with stories about his service in the French National Police, his two sons, Claude and Bertrand, and his times with Farad. I was sad when it came time to get up to leave.

We took the elevator down to the ground floor and had just exited to the street when I found myself dragged down to the pavement. Jonas threw his bulk on top of me. I tried to yell at him to get off but I couldn't; he'd knocked all the wind out of me. It wouldn't have mattered if I could shout. He wouldn't have been able to hear me as the rapid fire of a machine gun obliterated the night calm.

I was able to peer out from under Jonas just enough to see Jean Marc grab his throat and then his chest before he finally succumbed and slumped to the ground. The next thing I heard was the revving of the motorcycle engine as it sped off. Jonas rolled off of me.

"Frannie, you okay?"

"Yes...no...I don't know."

Jean Marc was lying face up on the sidewalk, his eyes lifelessly staring up at the streetlight. The 'don't walk' figure flashed incessantly above him, giving half his face a periodic reddish hue.

"Jonas, what happened?"

"We were almost gunned down. I'm pretty sure Jean Marc's dead. Sorry if I hurt you, Frannie. I saw the guy on the back of the bike pull out a gun—looked like an Uzi—and I just threw myself on you."

"Jonas, thank you for saving my life."

We could hear the sirens now, getting louder as they approached. For a split second I considered telling Jonas that we should get out of there but I just as quickly reconsidered. We had no reason to run. Where could we go anyhow?

Before long there were scores of policemen and detectives swarming the entire neighborhood around *la Tour d'Argent*. I was taken to the local precinct; I lost track of where Jonas was. I was placed in an interrogation room where I remained for about fifteen minutes. The door opened and a middle-aged gentleman with a neatly trimmed graying mustache walked in. He looked more like a stereotypical American detective than what I would imagine a French inspector to look like.

"Good evening Miss Vega, my name is Inspector Paul Murat. I'd like to ask you a few questions about the events of the past hour, if you don't mind.

"Certainly, Inspector."

"How long have you known Captain L'Eglise?"

"We only met this morning?"

"And yet takes you to *la Tour d'Argent*? Or did you take him?"

"He took us. I guess we really hit it off when we talked this morning."

"What did you talk about?"

"I'm a reporter for a New York television station. I'm doing a piece on illegal immigration of Arabs into New York. Captain L'Eglise was recommended as a source of information on this subject since he serves—or rather served—on a special joint task force with New York Police."

I was glad that Jean Marc had provided this cover. Otherwise I'd have been fumbling for an explanation that did not involve Farad.

"Who recommended him?"

"I don't know. The lead came from my station's research department. I have some files Captain L'Eglise gave to me if you'd like to see them."

The Inspector stared at me doubtfully but did not pursue this line of questioning further.

"You said there were two men on the scooter, is that correct?"

"I actually didn't see the scooter or the men. My friend Jonas pushed me to the ground and covered me. I only knew it was a motorcycle from the noise it made when it pulled away."

"Ah yes, that's correct. Your friend Mr. Clarke told us that, not you."

"Where is Jonas?"

"He was taken to the hospital?"

I bolted straight up out of my chair.

"The hospital!" I screamed.

"He's quite alright. He is having a bullet removed from his arm. Nothing vital was hit."

I sat back down. My mind was totally numb. Jean Marc L'Eglise, a man I'd only just met but had come to like, was dead. Jonas was at the hospital having a bullet removed from his arm, a bullet he received saving my life. I was lying, or at least not telling the whole story, to the police investigating Jean Marc's murder. I had no idea where Farad was. I was having severe doubts about what kind of man he really was. For all I knew, he could have been behind the shooting, not counting on Jonas to be so nimble and save my life. The inspector brought me back to the real world.

"Madame Vega, did Captain L'Eglise discuss with you any of the cases he is currently working on?"

"He mentioned something about a case of extortion and perhaps murder for hire by an underworld figure but he didn't mention any names or details of the case. Other than that, he didn't really talk about his current cases."

Murat jotted something down on his pad.

"An underworld figure. That would make sense. Jean Marc was always handed the toughest—and often most dangerous—cases. He'd often been told to be careful but he always would brush aside this advice. Is there anything more you can remember?"

"No, I told you and the officers on the scene everything I know," I responded wearily.

"Very well, I understand you are scheduled to fly back to New York tomorrow," the Inspector looked at his watch and noticed that it was 1:30 in the morning, "I mean later today. I would ask that you stay in Paris a day or two more while this investigation is still fresh. Your friend will need some time to heal before he should fly."

"We can stay another day or two. If there's anything we can do to help, please let us know. I really liked Captain L'Eglise."

The Inspector smiled a sad smile and sighed. "So did I, Madame."

He stood up and shook my hand, but before he turned to leave he spoke up.

"Oh, I almost forgot. We have been contacted by your State Department."

He pulled out a single sheet from the folder he had with him, my folder. I could see the FBI logo on the top of the sheet.

"It says here that you have recently become a person of interest for your Federal Bureau of Investigation. Would you care to tell me about this?"

"I've been questioned twice about an acquaintance of mine who they suspect may be linked to a terrorist group."

"How well do you know this person?"

"As I just said, he's an acquaintance, nothing more."

"Do you think there may be any connection between this person and Detective L'Eglise's murder?"

"I don't know."

The inspector regarded me closely one last time and then said

I could go.

I went back to the hotel to wait for Jonas. They didn't tell me the name of the hospital he'd been taken to. I thought it better to wait for him here anyway. It would be my luck to get to the hospital only to find that he'd been released minutes earlier.

I checked at the front desk and luckily the hotel was not fully booked for the next couple of days and I told the clerk Jonas and I would be staying on for a few more days.

I sat down in the lobby and started my vigil. The next thing I knew, someone was gently shaking me awake. I looked up and Jonas was hovering over me, his bandaged right arm in a sling.

"Hey doll, what you doin' down here?"

Without responding, I jumped up and gave him a big hug, inadvertently bumping into his wounded arm. He winced but he didn't say a word or cry out.

"Sorry," I said as I slowly backed away. In response, he pulled me back to him with his good arm and gave me a giant bear hug.

"Only a scratch."

I doubted that but I didn't want to dwell on his wound. I looked out the window and could see the early dawn starting to light the Paris streets.

"What time is it?

"5:00 or so. They were done with me quite awhile ago but they liked my sparkling urban wit and kept me around to keep them entertained."

We chatted like this for a few minutes, Jonas trying to make light of the fact that he could easily be dead right now. We were about to head up to our rooms to get a bit more rest and to clean up when I asked him the question most on my mind.

"Jonas, did you tell them anything about Farad Sahari?"

"Nope, didn't even mention his name."

"That's good. This thing's complicated enough without adding his name to the equation. I promised the police we'd stay around another couple of days in case anything new comes up."

"Boy, would I love to get back to New York right now but it's probably better to hang around for a bit. If nothing else, these pain killers are going to wear off soon and I don't think I'll be in any shape to travel for a day or two."

We waited around the next two days but heard nothing more from the police. Finally, Inspector Murat called me and said it was okay to leave. He indicated that the investigation was focusing on Jean Marc's underworld drug case.

I'd already changed the tickets and we were ready to go. Jonas' arm was feeling somewhat better by that time. The police hadn't sent any advance word to detain us so we went through the security and immigration checkpoints with no incident. The same was true on the other end at JFK. A middle-aged TSA agent looked at me, smiled and stamped my passport without question. When I smiled sweetly back at him, he was so enamored he didn't bother passing the passport through the scanner.

7

An eerie silence greeted me as I walked through the door into the newsroom. Nobody knew quite what to say. I smiled and said hello to everybody as I walked towards Frank's office.

"How you holding up, Francine?"

"I'm fine. I wish everyone would stop asking me that. It's not the first time I've ever seen a dead person. In fact, it's not the first time I've ever seen somebody killed."

"It's not?"

"When I was ten, a crack dealer set up shop in a first floor apartment in our building. My mother led the campaign to get him out of there. She tried everything. The cops wouldn't lift a finger; they didn't have evidence enough to arrest the guy, or so they said. Mom was convinced somebody was on the take so she went over their heads to City Hall. She got to be quite a pain in everybody's butt, but she was so beloved in the community they wouldn't dare touch her for fear of an uprising.

"One day my Mom had just picked me up from school. We were about to head into our building when she met one of the tenants, Hector Alvarez, who was walking out. Hector was a really nice man. Three kids, hard-working. He always loved to tease me on this and that.

"Mom and Hector were chatting in front when a black Pontiac raced up and a man in the passenger seat pulled out a pistol and shot Hector in the chest. My mother tried her best to stop the bleeding but the damage was too great. He was dead within minutes.

"The cops never caught the shooter but Mom knew exactly who was behind it. He was sending a message to her: Back off or you or your daughter could be next. Instead, it made my mother even more determined. She organized the tenants and opened a bank account into which all the rent would be paid instead of paying it to the landlord. She told the landlord and the cops that the rent would be paid in full once the drug dealer was evicted, arrested, dead or any combination thereof.

"Well, to make a long story short, my mother was successful but it wasn't until a newspaperman, Francisco Rosario, took up her cause. He's actually the one who made me want to get into reporting.

"To this day, I have the image of Hector dying on our stoop. Now I have the image of Captain L'Eglise dying right in front of me as well."

Neither of us could say much after that so we sat in awkward silence for a minute or so until a commotion started out in the bullpen outside Frank's office. It started as one person clapping, and then two and then everybody in the whole office were on their feet, applauding and cheering. We looked out Frank's window. Jonas was standing there, still with his arm in a sling, humbly accepting their acknowledgments Frank and I walked out and I gave Jonas a big hug and a kiss.

After a few minutes, everyone got back to work and Frank, Jonas and I walked back into Frank's office.

"So," Frank began, "other than the obvious tragedy and heroics, did you learn anything while you were in Paris? Did you ever get to see Sahari to get his side of the story?"

"Farad's in hiding. Captain L'Eglise was acting as his go-between. He gave me some names and numbers to follow up in the States. He assured me that Farad had nothing to do with Topeka. He was certain that Westbrook was working with Colonel Lawson. He said that Lawson had been seen in Paris as recently as last Tuesday, but they have no idea where he presently is. Farad and others seemed to believe they might be getting closer to obtaining an illicit nuclear device. That's about it."

I hesitated.

"What?" Frank asked.

"Jean Marc—I mean Captain L'Eglise—knew Farad Sahari

since childhood and vouched for him up and down, but I'm having my doubts. Who else but Sahari knew we'd be coming out of that restaurant when we did?

"L'Eglise was an experienced policeman. And because he was so careful, I can't imagine him telling anybody he didn't absolutely trust where he was going and with whom he was meeting.

"The only other person who knew I was going to the restaurant that night was you. I told you I was going there when I filled you in that day. I seriously doubt you put out an order to have me killed. That leaves Farad."

"And?"

"And, if Farad cared as much about me as he professed, I'd have thought he'd try to contact me through some other channel, especially after his friend was killed. It makes me wonder, that's all."

Jonas spoke up.

"Let's not jump to any conclusions here. Personally, I think Sahari is who he told you he is."

Jonas had never professed an opinion about Farad Sahari one way or the other so this surprised me.

"What makes you think so?"

"Nothin' special. Just my gut," then he smiled, "and it's a pretty big gut, so you better listen to it."

"Okay, I guess so," I remarked unconvincingly, either to myself or to the two men.

"So, what's been happening around here, Frank?"

"A rash of car-jackings, a scandal swirling around Councilman Myers, a lost cat from Colorado who ended up in Midtown Manhattan; you know, the usual. If you're up to it, I'd like you to sit in on the monthly press conference the Joint Terrorism Task Force is holding this afternoon. Usually Jim Leonard covers this. It's generally a boring rehash of latest anti-terror initiatives, new federal money, bureaucratic things like that. I'd like you to sit in and see if there is anything new on our friends at the Arab-American Friendship League. They've been playing their investigation pretty close to the vest. Why don't you see if you can coax anything out of them?"

"Will do."

To make sure there were no ill feelings I went up to Jim to tell him Frank wanted me to cover the press conference. Jim was an old-timer at the station. I liked him. Everything about him defined the word nonchalant. He was so laid back you sometimes wondered if he had a pulse. But once you started talking to him, he had a sharp and sardonic wit. He was the type who could zing you without you even knowing it.

When I asked him if it was okay that I go in his place to the conference, his first response was: "Permanently, I hope."

"No, I'm afraid not, Jim, just this one time."

"Well, my only advice is to drink plenty of coffee before you go. Why they do these things monthly, I have no idea, but I've been covering them for nearly seven years now. I was looking to get rid of this assignment after six months but haven't been able to shake it. I guess they hold these things so they can tell everybody how transparent they are but then, month after month, they purposely tell us absolutely nothing. If any of us asks a question, the standard response is either: 'You'll have to contact headquarters' or 'I'll have to get back to you on that.' But they never do get back. I'd stop going but it would be just my luck that the one time I miss, some major announcement would be made."

"I guess I can interpret this to mean you're not upset I'm going in your place."

Jim smiled.

"Not in the least. But I do appreciate you taking the time to ask me before heading off."

A few hours later I signed in for the press conference. There were six other reporters there, beat reporter types who all seemed bored out of their skulls. Jim Leonard would have fit in perfectly with this group. As the newcomer breaking into their little fraternity, they all eyed me rather suspiciously.

From Frank and Jim's descriptions, I wasn't expecting too

much at this event. A group of three middle-aged men and one somewhat younger man, probably in his mid-thirties, walked out; the three elder officials went to the podium while the younger man stood off to the side, leaning against the wall. One of the three, Allen Watts, spoke first. Watts was the press spokesman for the Anti-Terrorism Unit of the City's Police Department. He was to be the emcee for the affair. The other two gentlemen—Rick Bailey for the U.S. Department of Homeland Security and Conrad Elkins who worked for some comparable State agency whose acronym I missed—were there to field questions pertinent to their particular agency.

As Frank had predicted, they went through a litany of announcements about a new federal grant for transit security, planning for a mock terrorist drill scheduled for the following spring, an enhanced presence on City buses and other such things. After they concluded, they asked if there were any questions but almost immediately started to walk away from the podium as if they knew from experience that there would be none forthcoming. I raised my hand and called out. They stopped short and returned.

"Yes, young lady," Watts asked, "Do you have a question?"

"Yes, I'm Francine Vega from Action 6 News. I was wondering if there has been any further information related to the investigation of the Arab-American Friendship League's possible role in the bombing in Topeka?"

The federal guy, Bailey, spoke up. His manner was extremely curt.

"That investigation is being conducted by Homeland Security and the FBI out of Topeka. You will have to ask them for that information."

"Yes, I understand the main part of the investigation would naturally be handled out there but, since the League is a New York-based organization, it would be just as natural for there to be a component of the investigation conducted here, wouldn't it?"

"We have no information to share with you at this point in

time as it is an ongoing investigation."

I was not going to be that easily deterred. Knowing that I was not going to receive any responses to my inquiries, I still thought the questions needed to be asked.

"Have the leaders of the League been brought in for questioning? Have there been any arrests? It was my station that received the call allegedly made by the group when they claimed responsibility for the bombing yet, to my knowledge, no law enforcement authorities have interviewed anyone at the station to follow-up. I spoke with the receptionist who took the call and she said that after making the initial report, she has not heard anything from anybody. Can you explain why there has been so little follow-up?"

The three men were all fidgeting and seething. They were unprepared for this line of questioning and wanted to get out of that room as fast as possible. The fourth man who had stood off to the side, on the other hand, had a bemused look on his face. The City spokesman then said that I would have to contact headquarters if I wished to continue this line of questioning. The three then scurried off the stage. The fourth man remained, however, still leaning against the wall with that same grin on his face. I walked over to him.

"You seemed amused by your colleagues' discomfort," I said.

"Oh, very much so. This is the first of these events I ever attended and I was warned they were deathly affairs but you made it eminently enjoyable."

"It was my first as well. And if those guys have any say, it will probably be my last."

He laughed.

"It looks like we were here for the same reason, because of the Topeka bombing."

"And you are?"

"Oh, where are my manners. I'm Special Agent Alistair Conable. It's a pleasure to meet you Ms. Vega. I believe you have already made the acquaintance of two of my associates, Special

Agent Allen and Agent Willoughby."

I felt my body involuntarily tighten at the mention of their names. Conable continued.

"I read the reports and I have to apologize for their, let's call it exuberance. They're good men but they sometimes get so focused on their task at hand that they forget there's a person on the other end of an interrogation."

"Apology accepted. I must say I've never met an Alistair before. There's not too many of you on this side of the pond, I daresay."

"Both my parents are English Professors and they had ambitions that I would become a titan in the literary world. Needless to say, they were sorely disappointed when I chose law enforcement as a career path. It took time, but they've finally come around. I'm fully confident I'm their favorite child once again."

"Oh really? How many siblings do you have?

"None."

It was my turn to laugh.

"Shall we go somewhere for a cup of coffee," he asked, "and compare notes on our favorite Arab advocacy group?"

We went to a Starbucks (which I thought appropriate) around the corner and sat on a sofa to talk about the Arab-American Friendship League. He started.

"We've been investigating the League for some time now. We do believe there is something shady about them, their connections and their operations but there's never been anything we could pin on them or specifically cite them for. If it's any consolation, we're pretty sure your friend, Sahari, is not part of anything nefarious. It very well may be that he's only been exposed to the benevolent, philanthropic part of the organization and may truly believe he's doing good things. Although I must say that skipping the country is hardly a way to demonstrate your innocence."

"And where do you think I fit into all this?"

"You're a reporter trying to do her job, no more, no less."

"Your men seemed to believe otherwise."

"No, they didn't believe one thing or another. They were simply doing their jobs and going where the clues and evidence leads. At the time, your relationship with Sahari indicated that we needed to look into you and your life."

"And now? By telling me all this, are you saying I'm cleared?"

"Well, Agent Willoughby still has his suspicions and will probably keep digging. He's a real pit bull, that one. As for me, I'm convinced. As more of a management rather than front line type, I have the luxury of letting my beliefs and feelings color my opinions rather than simply letting the evidence guide me totally."

"And what have you come to believe about me?"

"Well, that you're the epitome of the American dream. Your parents fled Castro and came to America with nothing, not even a word of English in their vocabularies. Your father deserted you and your mother soon after you were born, leaving your mother to raise you single-handedly in the rough and tumble world of Harlem. She not only raised you and kept you off the streets but she made sure you learned English as your primary language. I'd bet you don't even think in Spanish.

"She scrubbed floors and scraped together to not only raise you but to make sure you got a proper education at a private school and assimilated into society. This is where you took over, excelling at everything you did and earning scholarships to get into NYU, graduating with honors. An internship and employment as a reporter—the hottest TV reporter in all of New York if I'm not mistaken—naturally followed.

"It would take either a world class indoctrination and brainwashing or the mother of all infatuations with Sahari for you to do a one eighty on everything you've come to believe over the years to fall in with a bunch of Muslim terrorists."

He stopped. I sat there dumbfounded, amazed that anyone could have learned so much about my life. Neither Jonas nor Frank, the people I was closest to in the world, could recite such a narrative about me. How much more of my life did he know?

"Okay," I said as I began to re-gather my wits about me, "I still don't know why you're sharing so much with me about your investigation."

"It's easy. We can probably help each other. You've obviously got a connection with Sahari that we don't. We need to talk with him. I really don't think he's involved, but he may have some valuable information about the League's goings-on that could be useful to our investigation."

"But I don't know where he is or even how to get in touch with him. The one possible contact that I had with him was killed when I was in Paris."

Conable looked surprised at this revelation.

"Captain L'Eglise knew Sahari?"

"Yes, they were boyhood friends. I'm surprised you didn't know that. He knew Farad was in Europe, probably in Paris, but he couldn't or wouldn't let me know where he was. When L'Eglise was murdered, my link with Farad was broken."

He considered this for a moment.

"But I thought you were in Paris doing a piece on Arab immigration to New York."

"Well, yes, I," I stammered until he headed me off with a smile.

"Don't worry, your secret's safe with me."

I returned his smile. I felt I could trust him but still I did not want to confide in him enough to talk about Westbrook, Lawson and their plot.

"I guess we should both get back to work," he noted, "Please, here's my card. Let's keep in touch."

With that we both went our separate ways.

8

When I got back to the station, Frank called out to me, asking me to come into his office.

"How'd the press conference go?"

"The conference itself was a snoozer, but I had an interesting chat with an FBI agent. He's the boss of the two guys you and Jonas' chased out of here."

"Oh, really?"

"He was much different than those two, he definitely took the honey as opposed to vinegar approach to getting information, which I suppose makes him far more dangerous."

"Well, you watch your back."

"Okay, Frank."

"What are you going to do now?"

"I want to find out more about Lawson. I'm going to have that intern, Shelley, see what she can gather on the Internet about him."

From Frank's description, Lawson would be perfectly capable of mowing down anyone, especially someone as insignificant as me, who got in his way. He'd describe me as "collateral damage" which I understand is the term of choice that a man like him uses to justify murder. He'd rationalize that, if some innocent person gets killed in the pursuit of a larger good, there's a net benefit to America and his actions would be justified.

The only thing I had at the moment was Frank's assessment of Lawson and some of the notes he'd collected on him over the years. While I was certain this was an accurate portrayal of the man, I needed more. I'd have to slog through the station's archives and newspaper reports to see if there was anything on him. Given what Frank had said about Lawson's penchant for being a behind-the-scenes player who manipulated people like they were chess pieces, I fully realized that these sources themselves would give me very little insight. What I was hoping they'd do was to give me some other names as leads. If Lawson were as powerful as Frank intimated, he'd have left in his wake numerous enemies who'd be only too happy to chat with a reporter about their nemesis.

That's where one of our interns, Shelley Wilson, came in. Shelley's a pretty lithe blond who had just graduated from Syracuse. Her father worked in Sales. She was bright, pleasant and eager to do whatever you asked of her.

"Shelley," I called out to her.

"Hi, Francine."

"You in the middle of anything at the moment?"

"Naw, I was just cataloguing some footage for Frank."

"Good, I need your help on a story I'm working on."

"Is it related to the shooting in Paris? I was awfully sorry to hear about that."

"Thanks but no. There's some background research I'd like you to work on. It's tied to the 'destroy Mecca' story I'm sure you heard about."

Her eyes lit up at the thought of doing some real investigative work rather than carting around tapes or performing routine and tedious updates of our databases. It brought me back to my days as an intern and the way I'd look forward to doing something real and substantive.

"I want to find out everything there is to know about Colonel Jacob Lawson," I told her. "He works at the Pentagon in the Army's Office of Strategic Coordination. What I need is not only general background stuff but I need names of people I can talk to about him. I need you to use your computer and social network skills—which I know to be estimable—to ferret out people who have been screwed over by this guy over the years. From what I understand, he's left quite a wake of such people. The trick is that you have to do this without him becoming the wiser. I don't want him knowing that we're looking into him. Do you think you can do this?"

"Oh yes. You better believe I can!"

Her palpable enthusiasm was infectious. She ran off to her computer.

I had to sit down and do some of my own research on the Arab-American Friendship League. Thus far, I took it as a matter of faith, believing Farad's assurances that neither he nor his organization had terrorist leanings. But what did I really know about him or the group? Special Agent Conable certainly had a number of misgivings about the organization. I had to stop thinking with my heart and start being a journalist again.

I'd just returned from Shelley's cube when I heard Frank call out from his office. I looked up and could see him hanging up the phone as he yelled out.

"Francine, come on in. I want you to go check out a possible story. It's a truly weird one."

I walked in and sat down.

"What is it, Frank?"

"I just got off the line with this woman; Kelley Something-or-other, I have the info here. She lives out in Astoria, Queens. She claims to be the victim of what she's referring to as 'reverse stalking.'

"What on earth does that mean?"

"Well, she's a single mom, struggling to make ends meet. She fell behind on her mortgage and went to the bank to see if she could buy some more time. When she got there, she was advised that not only had the mortgage been brought up to date but had been paid off for the next two years as well. She said a similar thing happened with her car loan, her credit card and her property taxes."

"Why did she call here with this great news?"

"Because she has absolutely no idea who made all of these payments and she was hoping that by getting her story out on the airwaves maybe the Good Samaritan would reveal himself. I'd like you and Jonas to go out there and see if there's any story here or whether it's yet another wacko looking for her fifteen minutes.

We've had a spate of them lately, haven't we?"

Jonas and I drove up to the address Frank gave me. It was a typical Queens neighborhood, something straight out of *All in the Family*. I rang the doorbell. A few seconds later the door opened slightly and a pair of blue eyes peered out.

"Kelley Williams?" I asked.

"Yes, I'm Kelley Williams."

"My name is Francine Vega from Action 6 News. This is Jonas Clarke, my cameraman. I understand you spoke to my boss, Frank McDermott."

"Yes, I recognize you. Please come in."

Ms. Williams looked to be in her upper thirties but had a haggard look far beyond her years. Still, she was a very attractive blond who must have been a knockout in her younger days.

She eyed Jonas somewhat suspiciously as he walked into her house, but she was otherwise cordial to both of us. We sat down on the flowered couch and divan in her cozy living room. Obviously under the impression that we were going to start taping immediately she asked: "Where do you want me?"

"Let's just chat a little first—get to know each other—before we start taping. Okay?"

"Okay."

"Why don't you repeat to me what you told Frank."

"Well, my former husband left me and the kids about two years ago. On his way out of town the bastard stopped by the bank and cleaned out nearly every cent we had. Cops have been trying to track him down ever since to make him pay up for our two kids. I was still working at that point so we had enough to scrape by, but it was tough. I'd delay paying Peter so I could pay Paul, but eventually they both got paid. Then about a year ago my place downsized and I was let go. Nobody was hiring so we went on assistance.

"It didn't take long for the letters to start coming. First it was my maxed-out credit card, then the car loan and finally the mortgage on the house. At first they sent friendly reminders that I may have overlooked a payment and that I should remit the minimum as soon as I could. With each letter, the tone became more threatening with promises of legal action if they did not get their money.

"The car I could probably do without and I could live without a credit card but I'd put too much into this house to lose it. So I got myself all prettied up yesterday, dropped my six year old son off at school and then me and my three year old daughter went off to Astoria Credit and Loan to beg for more time on the mortgage. I was going to drop Lacey off at a neighbor's but I figured having a cute little girl with curly blond hair along couldn't hurt my chances at the bank.

"I stood outside the bank looking in, waiting until Mr. Moore, the bank manager, disappeared. He's a real SOB and I'd have to deal with him eventually but I figured I could work my pitch on one of his underlings. So, finally I walked in and sat down at the desk of the assistant manager, Estelle Franklin. I'd dealt with her before and she seemed nice.

"I explained my plight and she punched up my account on her screen. I expected her to say something like, 'You haven't made a payment in over four months. We're going to need some sort of good faith effort on your part to try and bring this up to date before we can consider doing anything.' Instead, she very simply said, 'According to our records your account is completely up to date. In fact, there's a note in here indicating that monthly payments for the next two years are to be made through an automatic withdrawal.'

" 'What?' I screamed, 'How can that be?' Not that I was complaining, mind you, but I just couldn't believe it. She showed me the screen and it was all there as she said. I asked her who made the payments and whose account that was. She said she wasn't at liberty to tell me; the person wished to remain anonymous.

"I walked out of the bank in a fog. By the time I got back home, the mail had come. On top of the pile was mail from the finance company that has my car loan. I sighed, knowing my good fortune couldn't continue, but when I opened the envelope my eyes nearly bugged out of my head. The statement said the loan had been paid in full. My outstanding balance, which was about $8,000, was now zero.

"Thinking I was on a roll, I called my credit card company. Same thing: I had a $4,500 balance that was mysteriously paid in full. Likewise, they couldn't tell me who made the payment.

"I called the bank back and spoke to Mrs. Franklin again. She repeated that she could not break the confidence of the person who paid my mortgage. I asked her to then look up my savings account. When Max, my ex, skipped town, he left me about twenty dollars. I guess he figured that if he cleared it out totally I'd be sent a statement right away but if some token amount remained the statement would be delayed until the next cycle. Well, Mrs. Franklin looked it up and said the account balance was now over $20,000. Again, a deposit had been made anonymously.

"That's about it. I've wondered if there are any other mysterious gifts waiting for me, but nothing more has popped up."

I waited a few seconds before responding to see if she had anything more to offer. Nothing more was forthcoming.

"Why did you call my station?"

"I really want to know who is doing this to thank him or her. I was at the end of my rope and thoroughly depressed. We were on the verge of becoming homeless. I don't know what I would have done if things continued the way they were.

"This person saved my life and the life of my children. Why would someone do this? I'm really a very private person. I don't have that many friends and certainly don't know anybody who has wealth like this that they can just spread around without getting anything in return."

"Back to my original question," I asked, "why call our station?"

"Well, Ms. Franklin said my anonymous benefactor forwarded a note that if I had any questions, I was to call you."

"Me?"

"Yes, she said he was very specific about calling Francine Vega at Action 6 News. You weren't at your desk when I called so they connected me with Mr. McDermott. Next thing I knew, you were ringing my doorbell."

Now I knew exactly who her knight in shining armor was.

"Miss Williams, do you know an Alan Westbrook?"

"There was an Alan Westbrook in my high school class. He was a nice kid, rather shy. He and his twin brother used to hang around together all the time. Last I heard of him was when he went off to Harvard. He was quite brilliant. He knew his way around computers; he set up the system for the entire high school. His brother was very smart, but Alan was the really brainy one. You know the type. You think it was him?"

"Well, did you know he won the big lottery a few weeks back?"

"That was him? All I knew was that I didn't win so I didn't pay much attention to who did. I've been so depressed lately; I haven't watched the news much. Are you trying to tell me Alan's the one who's made all these payments?"

"I can't say for sure, but it would seem to be the case, especially since he told you to call me. Somehow we've developed a sort of connection."

"Well, I'll be. Doesn't that beat all?"

She seemed very happy to have an answer. The more she thought about Westbrook, the more she remembered he had a crush on her but never approached her or even spoke to her all that much.

I had Jonas shoot me interviewing her. Even though it had a human-interest angle that could appeal to some people, I knew this didn't have much chance of getting on the air. Nor did I really want it to.

9

"Francine!"

"Hi Shelley. What's up?"

"I've got a couple possible contacts for you to find out about Lawson. Reading the posts about this guy, he's some piece of work, isn't he?"

"Yes, he is. You didn't do anything beyond searching on the web, did you?"

In her exuberance, I hoped Shelley had not done something like reaching out to any of these people. In the short time I'd known her, I was impressed with her initiative. I should have emphasized more clearly that she had to be extremely careful. This guy could be dangerous.

"No way, all I did was look at the social network sites and see what people say about this colonel. What I've been reading about him made my skin crawl. I didn't want to get anywhere near him."

"Smart girl. So, whaddya got?"

"Well, the first one is a former Army Captain. His name is Mohammed Hamedi. He won the Medal of Honor for heroics during the first gulf war and was serving in the intelligence services. According to intel I read, he was instrumental in tracking down Saddam. Despite his record of extreme patriotism, he was subsequently forced out of the service. He claims that once Lawson became aware of him, or more precisely his name and ethnic background, his life became a living hell and he soon withdrew from the service. His posts online are especially bitter about Lawson."

"Any idea where he is now?"

"He's an adjunct teaching military tactics at VMI."

"Sounds good. You said you have a couple possible contacts. And the second guy?"

"Not a guy, a woman. Her name's Carol Baumgarten. They

were romantically linked for a couple of years but he unceremoniously broke it off. Boy, a woman scorned and all that. She's started a blog for jilted military wives. Some pretty racy and vitriolic stuff; let me show you."

Shelley punched in the web address for the blog and soon the screen was filled not only with Ms. Baumgarten's rants but scores of other women who found themselves in a similar situation.

"She lives in the DC area?"

"No, actually she moved in with her parents in Stamford, Connecticut."

"Well, I guess I'll start with her."

Shelley gave me the woman's name, phone number and address. I dialed the number. A woman answered.

"Hello."

"Hi, this is Francine Vega from Action 6 News in New York. Is this Carol Baumgarten?"

"Yes, it is."

"Ms. Baumgarten, I'm doing a piece on the military and I'm gathering information on Colonel Jacob Lawson. I understand you may know him."

All I got in response was an icy silence. After a few seconds Ms. Baumgarten issued a terse response.

"Yes, I am acquainted with Colonel Lawson."

"Would you mind if I came out to Stamford to talk with you about him? Everything will be on background. No cameras and no attribution."

Given the level of vitriol in her posts, I thought it important to let her know upfront that I just wanted to talk. Still, I knew it was going to take some convincing to get her to talk to me.

"My blog notwithstanding, it's a period in my life I'd like to put behind me so I'd rather not."

She was about ready to hang up.

"Ms. Baumgarten, I believe Colonel Lawson may be into something bad, something that could be catastrophic for the world and the country. I may be way off base here, but I need your help to determine if I am."

"If you suspect him of something, why don't you go to the police?"

"I don't have enough evidence to go to the authorities. I'm trying to put pieces of a puzzle together. You may have one of those pieces or you may not. All I'm asking is for a half-hour of your time."

Again there was silence, but I could tell she was thinking it over.

"Okay, can you come here at 3:00 this afternoon?"

"I'll see you then."

I had a couple of hours before I headed up to Stamford so I thought I'd spend some time trying to track down Mohammed Hamedi. I got VMI's general number and started there.

After only four transfers and twenty minutes on hold, a deep male voice came on the line.

"Hello, I'm Mohammed Hamedi. How can I help you?"

I went through the same opening I did with Ms. Baumgarten. Instead of having to coax Mr. Hamedi into talking, however, he wouldn't even let me finish my sentence when he was offering to open up on the issue of Colonel Lawson.

"If I can give you anything you need to nail that bastard," he enthusiastically offered, "I am more than ready, willing and able to provide it!"

"Why, that would be most appreciated, Mr. Hamedi."

"Please, call me Mohammed. Rather than having you come all the way to god-forsaken Virginia, I'm going to be up in DC for a conference this weekend starting on Friday. I'll be at the Argonne Hotel on Massachusetts. I could meet you there. It sort of splits the difference. How about I meet you in the lobby, Friday two in the afternoon is between sessions. Would that be okay?"

"Works for me. I'll see you then."

I borrowed Frank's BMW and headed up to Stamford, Connecticut. Carol Baumgarten greeted me at the door of her mother's house. The house was a modest two-story colonial painted a turquoise blue.

Ms. Baumgarten looked to be around fifty. She had short ash blond hair, although I doubted it was her real hair color. I imagined that she had once been quite attractive but had not kept up her appearance over the last couple of years.

She offered me some water, which I accepted, and suggested we sit out on the porch. It was a pleasantly warm day so I told her I thought that an excellent idea.

"So, what's Jake got himself into now?"

Based on the few short minutes I spoke to her on the phone, the question did not surprise me. I'd decided to tell her the truth, or at least part of the truth, to get her to talk.

"I have no evidence but I believe he may be involved in a plot that could potentially lead us to World War III."

She considered this for a few seconds.

"Figures. What can I tell you about the asshole?"

"Well, I guess you can start with why you hate the guy."

"Let's see, where do I begin? Could it be that we saw each other for seven years and then he calmly walks into my office, tells me we're through and then just as calmly turns around and walks back out? Or could it be that shortly before that he talked me out of taking another job that would have resulted in thousands of dollars of increased pay because I would have had to move to another city and he said he couldn't live without me? Or another possibility is that after he broke up with me he was responsible for having my security clearance revoked so I couldn't even keep the job I had. Or perhaps it was his convincing me to get an abortion after I told him I was pregnant with his child.

"I'll let you pick. Any one of these will do."

"In other words, a world-class shit," I observed.

"You really are a first-class reporter to come up with that conclusion."

"Ms. Baumgarten, I don't know why you see me as the enemy. We're really on the same side here. I just came here to ask you a few questions. You can give me all the sarcastic and snide responses you want but I'm going to keep asking the questions until I get the answers I need about this bastard. The stakes are too high for games, but if you want to play games, I'm very patient."

Tears were welling in her eyes.

"Please, please, I'm sorry. I get so bitter when I even think about him and I tend to take my bitterness out on whoever is in the vicinity. I'm sorry."

"I understand. The litany of offenses you just ticked off would be enough to send anybody off the deep end."

She was looking down at her lap on the verge of totally breaking down in tears. I reached over and took her hand.

"Let me guess: a part of you still loves the guy, right?"

She continued to look down but nodded slowly.

"I divorced my husband five years ago," I confided, "It didn't take me long after we were married to come to the conclusion that I made a terrible mistake. He was not the man I could ever think of making a long-term commitment to. My private nickname for him was 'Worthless'. He always had some Ralph Cramden-type scheme that was going to make us rich but then he'd never put any work into it. I'm a very goal-oriented hard worker and I found his attitude and indolence infuriating. Eventually, I'd had enough and left. But to this day, he still has a hold on some part of me."

My attempts at bonding were working as she loosened up a bit and smiled a sad smile.

"I'm better now. You can ask me whatever question you want to now. I'll behave."

We both smiled.

"How did the two of you meet?"

"I was working for a defense contractor, Newman Lewis. I was based out of Dallas but spent a lot of time at our Silver Springs office, just inside the Beltway. My job was to oversee quality control for the equipment we shipped to army bases around the world. Jake was in the office negotiating a contract when we bumped into each other. Literally. I was rushing down the hall, late for a meeting and looking at files I was carrying when I crashed into him, my files spraying all over the place.

"As he was helping me pick up the files we happened to look into each other's eyes. It was, you know, one of those moments. It wasn't long after that I was able to engineer a transfer to the DC area, mostly to be with him more."

"I'm told he's been quite the mover and shaker for the military over the years. Have you seen him in action this way?"

"Oh yes, many times. I've seen Major Generals quiver in his presence. He always gets what he wants."

"It's interesting that he's this important and feared guy but before this I never heard of him. In fact, I'd hazard a guess that if you walked down the street and asked ten people if they'd ever heard of him, nine or maybe even ten would say no, they never had."

"He always felt he was more effective acting below the radar. J. Edgar Hoover got to be well known but most of the fear he imparted was due to his behind-the-scenes actions."

"He liked being feared?"

"He thrived on it."

"When we first started talking and I mentioned that he may be involved in something that could possibly lead to World War III, you didn't seem the least bit surprised. Is this because of his megalomania?"

"No, not at all. I believe he would be involved in something of this sort out of patriotism."

"Patriotism?"

"Yes, or at least his skewed version of it. He used to rail about how we were wimps and needed to stand up to those bastards in the Middle East, South America, you name it. He felt America had gotten soft and complacent. He'd definitely support some dramatic gesture that would return us to our former glory."

"Even if it meant a world war?"

"Even if it meant a world war."

We both were silent for a few seconds as this statement sunk in.

"Would Colonel Lawson have the capability to obtain a nuclear weapon?"

"I don't know; but if anybody could, it would be he."

"Have you ever met an Alan Westbrook?"

"Bucky? Boy, I haven't heard anything about him in over a decade."

"Bucky?"

"That was Jake's nickname for him; it was based on his middle name being Starbuck. He was a real nice guy but he went bonkers after his brother was killed. We tried to help him through but there was nothing we could do. He dropped out of sight soon after."

"Remember the big lottery last month?"

"That was him? Well I'll be. I saw the news accounts of it but didn't pay it much mind. We'll I'll be."

"After he won, I think he hooked up with Colonel Lawson again. He and Lawson are working together. Have you heard about this preacher who's been an Internet sensation, Reverend McKenzie?"

"The guy who wants to destroy Mecca?"

"Yes, him. The plan he is referring to in his sermons was concocted by Alan Westbrook."

"And he has Jake helping him."

"I think so, along with $450 million."

"God help us."

There was not much more I could add to that thought.

"Well, thank you very much for your time. You've helped fill in some gaps. If you think of anything else, please don't hesitate to contact me."

I got up to leave but as I did, Ms. Baumgarten grabbed my arm.

"Be very careful, Ms. Vega. If you were someone Jake perceived to be standing in the way of fulfilling his mission—especially if he believed the fate of the nation was on the line—he would take you out without hesitation or remorse. You did say that this interview was to be entirely on background and that I wouldn't be mentioned, correct?"

"Yes, that is correct."

"Good, because he wouldn't have any qualms about killing me either."

10

What was I getting myself into?

That was the question I kept asking myself as I drove back to the city. For each time I asked it, though, I failed to come up with a satisfactory response.

Despite our obvious differences, I wished Farad were here. It felt so wonderful in his arms. His strength and confidence made me strong and confident. But I hadn't heard a word from him in weeks. The better part of me still believed he could not be involved in any terrorist activities; but there was that tiny voice saying he was, and it was getting louder as time went on.

The traffic coming back into the city was horrendous. I was beginning to worry about gas as I crawled down the FDR. But ultimately I made it back with enough gas to spare for an intern to run out and fill the tank.

I got off the elevator and headed back through the office. Something seemed amiss that I couldn't quite put my finger on when I saw them in Frank's office. My two FBI friends were back. What on earth could they want now?

Frank saw me first and tried signaling me to turn around and disappear until they left. However, he was not very adept at this type of communication as the agents picked up his signals and saw me approaching. In any case, I was sick and tired of having federal agents dictate what I did, with whom I met and where I went. I knocked on Frank's door. Frank told me to come in.

"Special Agent Allen, Agent Willoughby," I said to the two men as I shook their hands.

"After our last encounter I'm surprised you made the effort to remember our names."

It was Allen who spoke. I was pleased he was making an attempt to be cordial.

"It's the reporter in me. Attention to detail and all that. Plus, I did have a chance to meet your colleague, Special Agent Conable, and he proved to me that an FBI agent can actually be a human being as well."

Allen smiled and I had to admit that he had a very captivating smile.

"We do have a few more questions we'd like to ask you."

This time it was Willoughby who spoke, and he maintained the dour, official manner.

"Do I need my attorney here?"

Willoughby responded.

"I don't know, do you?"

Before I could issue a retort, Allen interjected.

"No, Ms. Vega, I don't believe you do, but if you'd feel more comfortable having your lawyer here, by all means it's your right."

Willoughby glared at his partner. Allen didn't respond but kept looking at me with that great smile. Willoughby's reaction indicated to me that this wasn't a 'good cop, bad cop' routine they were running here. Allen was simply a nicer person.

After a few moments of reflection, I finally responded.

"No, I guess we can all just have a chat, but I'd like Frank to remain."

Willoughby was about to protest but Allen beat him to the punch.

"The more the merrier."

We all sat down. Allen started in.

"When we last spoke with you about three weeks ago we asked you about your interactions with Farad Sahari. Have you had contact with Mr. Sahari since that time?"

"No, I haven't."

"Do you have any idea where he is?"

"No, but I was under the impression that he was in Europe somewhere."

"You haven't thought it strange that he hasn't contacted you in all this time?"

"Not really. Given the scrutiny that he and his organization have been under since Topeka, I suspected he had to lay low. He probably didn't feel safe after the hysteria. He probably thinks you have my phone bugged. I'm sure I'll hear from him again soon."

Willoughby spoke up.

"You were attacked recently in Paris, weren't you?"

"That seems to be pretty common knowledge."

I liked Willoughby less and less as we progressed.

"You were attacked but were unharmed. However, someone you were with was gunned down, correct?"

"Again, common knowledge. I'd just finished having dinner with Jean Marc L'Eglise. He was a captain in the French National Police. I believe I told you about him when we last spoke."

Allen replied.

"Yes, you did. You said you were doing a follow-up for a story about Arab immigration. That was it, wasn't it?"

"Yes, but you've probably heard from Special Agent Conable that that wasn't entirely the whole story."

At this point, Willoughby pulled out a small notebook.

"No we hadn't, but a different contact told us that Captain L'Eglise not only knew Farad Sahari but they were close boyhood friends."

"Yes, that's true."

"And you didn't use this to re-establish contact with Mr. Sahari?"

"No, I already told you I haven't had contact with Farad in weeks."

"Yes you did say that, didn't you?"

I didn't respond. Willoughby was obviously trying to entrap me. He knew I'd lied about the immigration story. But they couldn't prove it and even if they could, for what purpose? We stared at each other for a few moments. Allen broke the silence.

"Ms. Vega, what if I were to tell you that Sahari returned to this country?"

"You seem to know more about him than I do. Why then are you asking me all these questions?"

Allen fidgeted a bit, as if he were trying to properly phrase what he had to say next. Before he could say anything, Willoughby bulled in.

"The body of Farad Sahari was found this morning. It was in a dumpster by an abandoned industrial site in Queens. He was shot in the chest. We estimate his body had been there about a week. Do you know anything about this?"

I felt all the blood rush from my head.

"Oh no!" I wailed. Tears started to well in my eyes.

Allen was furious with how his partner broke this news, but Willoughby was not going to be deterred.

"No," I stammered, "I don't know anything."

"It just seems that coincidences follow you around, doesn't it Ms. Vega? People seem to end up dead wherever you go."

Allen had enough as he rose.

"I'm very sorry for your loss, Ms. Vega. Let me give you my card once again. If you know anything that could help us track down Mr. Sahari's killer, please give me a call."

"I will. Thank you."

Willoughby wanted to continue the interrogation but Allen could see the distress I was under and cut it short. They left. Frank came around his desk and put his hand on my shoulder.

"I'm sorry, Francine."

"It's true, isn't it? First, Jean Marc and then Farad. A few inches one way or the other, Jonas would be dead, too. And if it weren't for Jonas, I'd be dead. What's going on, Frank?"

"I don't know, Francine, but you're a good reporter, and I believe you're going to find out. Take the rest of the day off to get your head on straight and start fresh tomorrow."

"I think I'll do that. Thanks, Frank."

I left the building and wandered around midtown for a couple hours before heading home.

I got to my apartment and was about to insert the key when I noticed the door was slightly ajar. I heard some rustling inside. Moving off to the side and around a corner, I pulled out my phone and dialed 911.

"911, how can I assist you?"

"There's someone in my apartment. Please send the police."

Just then I heard the door open. I angled an eye to see if I could catch a glimpse of who was emerging and to move quickly if they headed in my direction.

"Never mind, operator. False alarm. Thank you."

I came out from hiding.

"Eddie, what the hell are you doing here?"

My ne'er-do-well ex beamed a huge grin at me.

"Hi, hon. You don't look happy to see me."

Knowing that he was probably here to squeeze some cash out of me (which I knew I'd inevitably give him), I can't say I was thrilled. But then again, a part of my heart would forever have a soft spot for the poor alcoholic schlub. He was so personable and intelligent. The man certainly knew how to tell a story. Before long I'd be laughing so hard that I'd forget every trouble I had in the world. In addition, Eddie was fantastic in bed. I really needed all of this right now. I walked in and closed the door behind me.

True to form, when I woke up the next morning I found myself several thousand dollars poorer but very, very satisfied. I looked over at Eddie sleeping beside me. The rest of the routine would go as follows: I'd get out of bed and make some coffee. I'd bring him a mug to help wake him up. We'd sip our coffee together and then he would make his pitch. He'd changed; he was responsible now; drinking and drugs were demons of his past, he was on the verge of landing a steady job, etc. He'd note how great we were together and suggest that we give it another go.

"Eddie, you know that's not going to happen," I'd patiently explain to him, "I love it when you pop in like this on occasion, but you know as well as I that we can't be together long term."

"Frannie, you seeing anyone?" he'd ask, genuinely wanting to know out of concern for my well-being.

Thinking of Farad I very sadly answered, "No, I'm not seeing anybody right now."

He took my hand.

"That's too bad. You deserve only the best."

I smiled but a tear worked its way down my cheek.

"Thank you Eddie. And thank you for showing up when you did. It was exactly what I needed right now."

"Well, hon, you know my standing offer will always be there if you ever change your mind."

"I know Eddie, but you need to find someone for yourself as well. You deserve it, too."

"You're right, Frannie. Maybe some day."

We both knew that he wouldn't find anyone else, that in his mind I was the only one. What he didn't say was that he knew that no woman worth her salt would want to hook up with a loser like him. I appreciated that he didn't say it out loud, putting me in a position of having to lie and tell him he wasn't a loser or not saying anything, which would acknowledge what we both already knew.

Eddie got dressed and I saw him to the door. I kissed him on the cheek and held his hand.

"You watch out for yourself, Eddie."

"You too, dearest."

He left. I sighed and started to pull myself together to go to work.

Before leaving, I poured myself another mug of coffee and sat down at the computer to check if any important emails had come in overnight. I checked my work email first. There were a couple follow-ups from Frank, but nothing of immediate concern. I then switched to my personal account.

There were a bunch of junk emails that I eliminated, although an eminent Barrister who had a check for 150 million pounds sterling tempted me. I was about to mark another email as spam when the sender's address caught my attention. It was ASW@Queequeg.nz. There was no subject. I nervously clicked on it.

> Francine,
> I hope you don't mind that I'm calling you by your first name. I feel that by now we've gotten somewhat close. I hope you feel the same.
> I am quite chagrined by the killings of Farad Sahari and Captain L'Eglise but their deaths were unavoidable as they were starting to get too close and threatened our holy endeavor. I apologize that your life and that of your cameraman were put in danger. That was not supposed to happen. However, if you continue in your present investigation, I cannot assure your safety. As you are quickly learning, my associate can be rather ruthless. Think of Topeka.
> I'm sure I'll be in touch with you again soon.
> ASW

My very being was filled with dread. Jean Marc was not killed by an underworld figure he was investigating; he was killed because of his friendship with Farad, which led him to become involved with Westbrook and Lawson. They were also involved in Farad's death.

Was I also a target? Was I only alive because of Jonas's quick reactions and mammoth size shielding me? Did I know too much and was already in Lawson's sights?

I needed help. I had to level with the FBI.

I dug Agent Conable's card out of my bag and started to dial his number but then I stopped. Thus far Westbrook had sent me an untraceable letter, texted me from a non-existent number with an Antarctica area code and emailed my personal account from what I was sure was a phantom address. Who knows what kind of taps he could have placed on my phone? For all I knew, someone could be watching me right now.

I called Jonas.

"Hey J, think you can come over my place?"

"You finally came to your senses and finally want me, huh, doll?"

I usually loved Jonas' banter but I was scared.

"Please, Jonas, can you come over right away?"

He could sense the urgency in my voice.

"I'll be over right away, Frannie."

Fifteen minutes later Jonas knocked on my door.

"Frannie, it's me."

I let him in and gave him a big hug.

"You okay? Your voice didn't sound so good."

"Let's go to the coffee shop downstairs."

We took the elevator. The irony didn't escape me that I was going to a Starbucks to ensure that Alan Starbuck Westbrook couldn't overhear me.

"I'm afraid, Jonas. Westbrook is out there. He was involved in both L'Eglise's and Farad's deaths. I think I might be next. Furthermore, the man seems to be everywhere. He has my email and private phone numbers. I wanted to talk to you here because for all I know my place is bugged."

Jonas stared at me disbelievingly.

"Someone could be watching us right now. I need to get in touch with the FBI but I don't want to let them know I'm contacting the FBI. I guess I could go to a phone booth. Are there any of those left?"

"Hold on."

Jonas ran out of the store and went into his car, which was parked in front. He returned within a minute, holding a cell phone.

"Here, make your call on this. It's one of those disposable jobs. Untraceable."

I looked at Jonas questioningly.

"Don't ask."

"Okay, Jonas. Thanks."

I walked outside to call. I dialed Conable's number.

"FBI. Special Agent Allen speaking."

"Special Agent Allen, this is Francine Vega. Is Special Agent Conable around?"

"He's away for a few days. Is there anything I can help you with?"

"He's not reachable?"

"Probably not. He's on a skiing trip."

I had a decision to make. I didn't want to wait but did I really want to deal with Allen? At least the last time I saw him he was quite civil.

"Are you available? I need to talk with you immediately."

"Why certainly, Ms. Vega."

"Can I meet only with you? I don't especially like Agent Willoughby."

"That's no problem. Where do you want to meet?"

A half hour later I was in the coffee shop where I went with Farad. In fact, I was in the very same booth we had occupied. Allen walked in and nodded to me.

"Ms. Vega."

"Thank you for coming to see me, and for coming alone."

Allen smiled.

"Willoughby's a good agent but I think that when he was born the angel in charge of dispensing charm and tact was on vacation. He's definitely an acquired taste."

A waitress sidled over to our table.

"Coffee and a toasted blueberry muffin, please," was Allen's request.

"Sounds good; same for me."

"So, Ms. Vega, what did you need to tell me that was so secretive we had to meet in such an out-of-the-way place? It's hardly near either of our offices."

I gauged him to see whether he was annoyed at the

inconvenience or was simply bantering, perhaps slightly mocking me for what he perceived as a cloak and dagger approach I was taking. I decided it was the latter.

"Special Agent Allen,"

"Please, call me Will."

"Okay, Will, I wanted to get together with you to let you know I haven't been entirely open with you. I haven't lied, but I haven't told you everything. Something happened today that convinced me I need to reach out to you and give you the entire story."

"What happened?"

I handed him the email I'd received. He read it. He reacted when he read Farad's name and when Westbrook took credit for Topeka. Farad's body was only found last evening and the news had not been yet been released to the press. As far as I knew, the FBI had not yet made any attempt to contact Farad's next of kin, not that I was aware he had any, at least not in the States. And this cast doubt on the predominant theory that there was an Arab connection to the Topeka bombing.

I then proceeded to tell him the entire story, starting with my interview of Westbrook after he won the lottery, through Farad's theory about how Westbrook is looking to destroy Mecca and Colonel Lawson's involvement. I told about discussing this with McKenzie in the State Department and how this theory made its way to his brother, Reverend McKenzie. The theory was subsequently confirmed in messages from Westbrook himself.

I told about my trip to Paris to meet with Captain L'Eglise, L'Eglise's connection with Farad and being shot at on the street.

I relayed the interview I had with Colonel Lawson's former girlfriend who confirmed how ruthless Lawson could be.

Allen regarded me closely.

"You'd make a fine FBI Agent, Ms. Vega."

I acknowledged this as perhaps the epitome of a compliment the Special Agent could give. I was also relieved that he didn't seem to doubt or question any part of my story, which even I had to admit was so out there as to be unbelievable.

"Francine. Please call me Francine."

"That's a lot of good work you've done, Francine. Do you really think you're in danger?"

"I don't know, but I wouldn't doubt it. The man has sent me messages through every medium possible. He has my cell phone number and my personal email. He seems to know everything about me.

"I believed the theory put forward by the French authorities that L'Eglise was killed by some underworld figure, but here Westbrook accepts credit for it. Likewise with Farad Sahari. I didn't think his death was common knowledge."

"It isn't. I'm still not thoroughly convinced of his involvement with Topeka. There are too many pieces of evidence that point to Muslim extremists. He could be accepting credit for someone else's work."

"Why would he do that?"

"Who knows? Could be any number of reasons. Maybe he wants to impress you. The guy doesn't seem overly stable and there may be no reason at all. What I'm saying is that it's my job to keep all avenues of inquiry open until they reach a dead end or are disproved."

"I guess that makes sense."

"Do you really think he can carry through on his plan to obtain a nuclear device," Allen asked, "and somehow deliver it to Mecca and then blow it up?"

"I don't know, but he's got $450 million dollars to play with and a wacko military extremist friend who knows as much as anybody how to get his hands on one of these things. It's too much of a risk to pass it off as a hare-brained scheme."

"You're probably right."

"I'm scared but I'm not going to go underground."

"What are you planning on doing next?"

I was touched that the tone of Allen's question betrayed that he was worried about me.

"I'm going to go to DC to talk with a former officer who was screwed by Lawson. The mistress gave me some personal insights into the colonel. Perhaps he can give me some professional insights as well."

"I'd like to go with you if you don't mind."

"Not in the least, but I rather thought you'd try to talk me out of it."

"I probably should. You're a civilian who is probably diving in way over her head. You've already been shot at and have received not-so-veiled death threats. I should tell you to stick to reporting and turn this over to the pros.

"However, you're our only contact with Westbrook right now. His use of an Antarctic area code shows that this guy knows what he's doing. Likewise, his email is out of New Zealand, but I'd rather doubt he's down under consorting with the Maoris. My guess is that email address is also untraceable. He could be anywhere. We need you to continue to be his link.

"Plus, I wasn't kidding when I mentioned how impressed I was with the work you've done thus far. I've seen agents with years under their belts not accomplish as much in months or years that you've done in a few short weeks."

"Why, thank you, Will."

"This guy is obviously going to contact you again. If nothing else, he's got a thing for you."

"Great. My luck with men continues."

Allen laughed.

"When you heading to DC?"

"I'm going to take the train tomorrow. It leaves at 9:00."

"I'll meet you at Penn Station."

11

The four hour train ride from New York to DC was much more pleasant than I imagined it would be. Will and I traded life stories. He was raised in a New Jersey suburb by a saintly mother and an abusive father. His decision to go into law enforcement was in response to his father, as a way to protect himself and his mother.

He excelled at any sport he tried, but his favorite was football, which earned him a full scholarship to Rutgers. Weakening knees, he claimed, is what kept him from going pro.

Figuring the experience would do him good, he enlisted in the Air Force and became a fighter pilot, doing two tours in Iraq. It wasn't until I pressed him that he admitted he received numerous commendations along the way.

The Air Force wanted him to re-up after his second tour but he wanted to settle down. He'd always had a thing for law enforcement and heard the FBI was recruiting so he went to their New York office and spoke to the head there. It was love at first sight on both their parts. He made Special Agent in only two years. He probably could have advanced further but that would have required more desk duty; he liked fieldwork too much for that.

He bragged about his two kids, Albert and Stella, aged seven and four respectively. His wife had passed away from cancer a year and a half ago and it was obvious he missed her terribly. Luckily, he had a terrific nanny, Emma, who lived a couple of blocks away and looked after the kids while he was away.

As Special Agent Conable told me, the FBI had a complete dossier on me, so Will probably knew my life story. Even so, he graciously let me talk about myself, not letting on that he already knew my background.

We talked about whether he should involve other agencies— Homeland Security, CIA—but he thought it best to go solo at this point. Mainly he thought what we had was so speculative, we needed to gather more background first. He didn't say as much, but I also sensed he didn't have a lot of use for those other agencies.

We talked about how we would approach Mohammed Hamedi. Although Will was somewhat uncomfortable about it, we decided it would probably be best that he not identify himself as an FBI agent. It might scare off Mr. Hamedi or make him clam up. Keeping this entirely as an off-the-record press inquiry might make him talk more freely. I'd introduce Will as my producer, figuring that nobody ever quite knows what a producer does anyway.

We arrived at the Argonne Hotel about fifteen minutes early; time enough to get a cup of coffee but not much else and I was starving. I'd slept late and didn't get breakfast and I hated the food they served on trains. I hoped my stomach growling would not be too much of a distraction.

I thought back to the first time I met Farad at the Moroccan restaurant. I had no idea what he looked like but at least that was in a small setting. Picking him out was not that difficult. Now, here I was in a huge hotel lobby with all races and ethnicities milling about.

Luckily, Mr. Hamedi was a regular traveler to New York and he recognized me immediately from my broadcasts.

"Ms. Vega, it's a pleasure to meet you."

"Mr. Hamedi, Thank you so much for taking time out of your day. Let me introduce Will Allen, my producer. I hope you don't mind that he tagged along."

"Of course not. Let's have a seat."

"So, were you close with Colonel Lawson?"

At the mention of the name, Hamedi's face tightened.

"I don't think anybody can get close to Colonel Lawson."

"Did you ever know Alan Westbrook?"

"Ah yes, Mr. Westbrook. I must amend my previous statement. He and Lawson were inseparable. What was so strange about it was that Westbrook was such a nice guy. He moderated Lawson somewhat. It was as if he acted as Lawson's conscience. Then when his brother was killed, Westbrook was inconsolable. He dropped off the face of the earth. Poor guy.

"After that, Lawson had no one to temper his behavior whatsoever. I'm convinced that I remained at the Pentagon as long as I did because Westbrook was there. Once he was out of the picture and Lawson was left to his own devices, my days were numbered. You couldn't have someone named 'Mohammed' working with sensitive classified data, could you? Never mind that I've earned about every medal this country has to offer."

The bitterness in his voice was palpable.

"Can I ask you why a New York local reporter and a federal agent have an interest in Colonel Jacob Lawson?"

The look of surprise on Allen's face was priceless. Hamedi smiled and looked at him.

"My guess was correct? I knew you weren't a newsperson; you gave off the aura of a federal agent. I figured law enforcement, but I was unsure what branch."

"You're very perceptive, Mr. Hamedi. I'm FBI Special Agent Will Allen."

"It's a pleasure to meet you. Now that's out of the way, let's return to Lawson. What is your interest in him?"

I spoke up.

"We believe that he and Alan Westbrook have teamed up again, but I don't think Westbrook is providing any sort of conscience this time."

"What do you mean?"

I looked at Allen, not knowing how much to reveal. He simply nodded.

"Mr. Hamedi, do you remember the big lottery a few weeks back?"

"Yes, some guy in New York won it, didn't he?"

"Yes, it was Alan Westbrook."

"Well, I'll be."

"And he's devoted his entire fortune to avenging the death of his brother, who as you know was killed on 9/11."

"Avenge? How?"

"He and his fortune have teamed up with Lawson to carry out a plan to blow up Mecca."

Hamedi was visibly shaken at the very image.

"Mecca? Blow up? You mean what that crazy preacher has been pushing is true? Is that Westbrook and Lawson he's been talking about?"

"Yes to all of it. Do you believe they could carry such a plan?"

"If Lawson's involved, yes they can. He's got his finger in so many pots around the world—including personally knowing practically every illicit arm dealer on the planet—it would be quite easy for him. How much money does Westbrook have?"

"Over $450 million."

"Lawson has enough dirt on many of these guys that he could get a device and deliver it for half that amount."

Hamedi paused for a second. Will and I gave him time as he was obviously reflecting.

"I made my pilgrimage to Mecca three years ago. It was the most exhilarating thing I've ever done. When I came back, I was a new and better man. I can't imagine a Muslim not having that opportunity."

"Can you offer any suggestions on how we can head this off?" Allen asked.

"I don't think the issue for Lawson will be getting his hands on one of these devices; the challenge will be how to deliver it to its target. Mecca is very heavily guarded. It's even more so now that a mad preacher is out there promoting its destruction. It's not like Topeka; you can't just mosey on up next to the Black Stone, leave a package and nonchalantly walk away."

"I don't think they're looking to do that." I observed. "My impression is that Westbrook is thinking of making the delivery himself, in a small aircraft on a one-way trip. He's planning on being a suicide bomber."

"That would, I suppose, make it a lot easier. Theoretically, a light plane could be flown in under the radar from the Sea to Mecca. It would be like the end of *Dr. Strangelove*."

"So you really think he's capable of pulling this off?"

"If Lawson is involved, yes I do."

"You knew Alan Westbrook. Did you also know his brother?"

"Yes, both very nice guys. Both very smart, but in different ways."

"How so?"

"Freddy was more of a dreamer, a policy wonk. Alan is a detail-oriented type. He's a very good lawyer but his first love has always been computers. He's a master. Believe me, Lawson will be making full use of that talent to execute such a plan."

"Did either brother have any love interests?"

Hamedi looked at me rather queerly, probably wondering whether there were any prurient motives behind my question. I was simply trying to gather any information I could on them, following any path to see where it might lead so he proceeded to answer my inquiry.

"They were both locked in on their careers so neither had a lot of time for romance. However, Freddy was frequently in the company of Captain Audra Fairchild. If there was anything romantic between the two of them, they did a good job of hiding it to the outside world. They were very discreet."

At that moment my phone buzzed. I looked down and saw it was Frank.

"Excuse me. I should take this'" I said as I walked away.

"Hi Frank, What's up?"

"Francine, I need you to get back here as soon as you can. There's something brewing in Paterson, New Jersey. A massive protest by the American Rights Organization is being planned for 4:00 this afternoon in the Arab section of town. They're the group that's loosely—or maybe not so loosely—affiliated with Reverend Warriner. I think they're going to be pushing the Destroy Mecca theme and I want you there to cover it."

"Sure thing, Frank. I'll take the first train back, or if there's too much of a delay, rent a car."

"Good. How's the interview going?"

"We're wrapping up now. I have a couple of leads to follow. I must say this Lawson guy generates a lot of hate wherever he goes. Nobody is reluctant to give me all the dirt they can about the good colonel."

"Well, be careful. As far as we know he's already tried to kill you once already. Speaking of which, I want Jonas with you in Paterson. I'll have him call you to make arrangements on where to meet."

"Sounds like a plan. Talk to you later, Frank."

I walked back and Will was thanking Hamedi for his time.

"Thank you, Mr. Hamedi," I chimed in, "You've been most helpful."

He looked me in the eye.

"Please, for the good of the world, stop Colonel Lawson."

"We'll do our best."

Will had previously indicated he'd probably stick around DC and have dinner with an old college chum he hadn't seen in ages but when I told him the reason I was rushing back he decided to accompany me.

"This sounds interesting; I'd like to tag along."

I sensed that he was not only viewing the upcoming protests from a law enforcement perspective but that he wanted to be protective of me as well. How could I not be safe having Jonas and an armed trained FBI agent by my side?

12

It's funny. I'll go anywhere in New York City without fear or trepidation. I'll venture to the sleaziest neighborhoods in any of the boroughs without batting an eye or feeling in the least bit intimidated. Looking back at some of the trips I made to cover a story, I was very lucky I didn't get my head bashed in once or twice.

On the other hand, on those occasions when I'd gone to cover stories in other cities I felt very uneasy and had a constant sensation of someone watching me. I had to do a piece in Newark a little while ago and I was on pins and needles the whole time. Frank and Jonas both said I appeared at ease on camera but inside my gut was churning.

The only time I'd ever been to Paterson was completely by mistake. Eddie and I were returning from a long weekend in the Poconos when all traffic on Route 80 came to a complete halt. Eddie decided to get off and try local roads. Well, among Eddie's many shortcomings was a complete lack of a sense of direction and it wasn't long before we found ourselves being extremely conspicuous driving our rented Mustang convertible down Main Street.

It wasn't long after 9/11 and I'm embarrassed to admit that I was more than slightly terrified seeing all the Arabic signs on the storefronts. I was surely relieved when we found our way back to a major highway.

I wasn't sure how I'd feel returning to this city all these years later.

Jonas met Will and me at the Newark Train Station and off we went to Paterson. I thought that Jonas appeared a little cold to Will, probably going back to having to rush to my defense way back when.

I didn't have any meetings or interviews lined up; I hoped opportunities for a story would present themselves. They did, in abundance.

When we arrived on Main Street around 3:00, people on both sides were starting to mass. Slogans were already being chanted; slurs were already being hurled back and forth. The police presence was not prominent at this point. I hoped they'd arrive in force soon before things got too ugly. Jonas had his camera rolling from the get-go, gathering great crowd footage. There was no shortage of individuals ready to plead their cases for the camera.

In amongst the anti-Arab protesters was Congressman Pete Connors, the one who appeared on stage at the end of Reverend McKenzie's performance. The Congressman appeared very out-of-place in this urban setting. As a representative from Georgia, nobody recognized him and he was content to be anonymous. He was lying very low, at least for the moment. Probably later on he'd be the firebrand he was noted for.

I grabbed Jonas and started to head over to the Congressman to see if I could get an interview before the crowd realized he was there. However, I acted too late. I was about thirty feet from him when from the left strode a hopping-mad Congressman Bill Parsons. He was heading straight towards Connors.

"Jonas, get your camera ready and make sure your microphone is on. This should be good."

Parsons was the liberal-leaning Congressman representing this part of Jersey. His views on nearly every single issue—gun control, abortion, immigration, welfare—were diametrically opposed to those espoused by Connors. Parsons did not look pleased that Connors was here in his district, probably to gather some headlines. Odds were that Connors had not even done the expected niceties of advising his Congressional colleague that he'd be attending an event here.

"Connors, what the hell are you doing here? Go on home to Georgia and spit your venom there! We want none of it here!" Parsons was seething.

In response, Connors remained calm and smiled.

"Why, Congressman Parsons, it's a pleasure to see you. Thank you for such a warm northern welcome to your southern colleague, Bill."

"Cut the bullshit. We all know why you're here; it's to spread your gospel of hate and intolerance."

"Bill, everyone knows that there are only four gospels I adhere to. They're named Matthew, Mark, Luke and John. Neither hate nor intolerance are listed there, I do believe."

The crowd was building around the two. I was glad Jonas was as big as he was. He wasn't going to get jostled out of the way and could shoot over the crowd. Will, for his part, was gallantly making sure I did not get crushed in the mob. Even with his help, I was struggling to stay close to hear the repartee when I noticed a Muslim cleric standing off to the side. I recognized him as a member of the Arab-American Friendship League. I'd seen him when I was with Farad but we'd never been introduced.

"Jonas, You keep shooting here. I'm going to go speak with that cleric over there."

Will started to come with me.

"No, you better stay here. This man knew Farad. I want to see what he knows. You guys still haven't released any details about his death, have you?"

"No, not yet."

"Okay, I won't let on that I know he's dead."

"I think I should go along with you."

The look of concern on Will's face was very endearing.

"Thanks for worrying about me, but I think I should go alone to talk with this gentleman. Remember how easily Hamedi made you? I'll be okay. Remember, I grew up in Spanish Harlem."

Will smiled and I started to walk away but to tell the truth I was sharing his concern. The Congressmen were going at it loudly and vehemently. Connors had dropped the 'aw shucks' country boy persona and was shouting back at Parsons. The crowd was swelling and taking sides. Things were starting to get ugly. It would have been smarter to stick around an armed agent and a six foot four behemoth, but I needed to talk to the cleric.

I fought my way through the crowd but the cleric and his assistants, also sensing the dangerous climate, had started to move away. I didn't know his name so I couldn't call out to him. I thought he was an imam, but I wasn't even sure of that. The crowd kept thickening and my progress had become minimal. Soon he was out of sight.

I turned to go back to the battling Congressmen when I felt a prick in my neck. Soon the world started spinning as a man grabbed my arm to steady me.

"You look a little faint, little lady." I heard as though from another room. I found myself leaning on this gentleman as he guided me away. I looked to see if I could find Will or Jonas, but my vision was entirely blurred by this point and the crowd was just too thick. Soon all went black.

13

I woke up in the middle of a field. Grasses and shrubs surrounded me. I slowly got up to my knees and then to my feet. I wobbled a bit and fell back to my knees. The pounding in my head was relentless. I tried focusing but my eyes had a life of their own, darting to and fro without any rhyme or reason.

I stayed on my knees for I don't know how long. During this time I took the opportunity to self-evaluate. I didn't seem wounded or injured in any way but from what I could see I was a complete mess. I was missing one shoe. My stockings were in tatters and my skirt was torn. I was absolutely filthy. I could only imagine NY Trend Magazine's reaction to me if they saw me now. I somehow doubt I'd be selected as New York's hottest reporter if the judging were done today.

I wondered whether I'd been raped but nothing felt tender or bruised. Still, I needed to get that checked out.

My head felt a little clearer so I made another attempt to get vertical. This time I was more successful as I got to my feet and stayed on them, swaying slightly. There were no buildings anywhere nearby, only overgrown vegetation. I could, however, hear a constant din of car and truck traffic not too far away. I could hear a train in the farther distance. I started to walk through the weeds in the direction of the traffic noise.

The ground was a little soggy but still relatively firm. It was difficult walking in one high heel so I took that shoe off and padded along in what was left of my stockings. After ten or so minutes I came upon a little creek. I was contemplating wading through it but I didn't know how deep it was or what sort of creatures inhabited it so I started walking alongside the bank of this stream. After another twenty minutes I reached a one-track railroad trestle that forded the stream. I climbed up onto the trestle to get a better look around to get my bearings.

Once on top I knew where I was immediately. Off in the distance I could make out the New York skyline. Between the skyline and me were miles of brown vegetation blowing gently in the breeze. I was in the Meadowlands.

I could see a major highway about a quarter mile away to the south. I began my journey toward this road. If I happened upon another creek or stream, I was going to plow ahead and wade across it. The water could only improve my condition.

I reached the highway. Cars and trucks were careening along at breakneck speed. I tried to flag one down to help me, but none would stop. Given the sight I gave them, I could hardly blame them for not wanting to stop. I plodded along the highway in the direction of the City.

After a short while I heard a car pull up behind me. I must say I'd never been so relieved to see a State Trooper in my life.

His voice soon emanated from his loud speaker.

"Miss, you can't walk along here."

I turned around and shot him a look. *Yeah, like this is the ideal place I'd pick for a stroll.* I tried to respond but nothing came out. I was tired of walking so I just sat down right there. He'd have to deal with me.

Slowly he got out of his car and headed over to me.

"Seriously miss, you shouldn't be out here."

Again, I tried to respond but could produce no words. I just looked up at him. A quizzical look came over his face as he looked down at what he probably thought was a homeless junkie who'd wandered out on the highway. Then a flash of recognition darted across his face.

"Are you Francine Vega?"

I nodded.

He leaned down to help me up and gently guided me over to his car. He placed me in the passenger seat and then went around to the other side.

"There's been a missing person's report out on you for the past two days. Have you been out here the entire time?"

Two days? I thought to myself.

The officer reached into a slot in his door and pulled out a water bottle that he handed to me.

"Thank you." I was finally able to mutter after greedily taking a couple of sips. "I don't know where I've been. I only just woke up in the middle of the marshes and wandered here. Everything is such a blur."

"I better get you to a hospital. You're in pretty bad shape."

"Thank you."

No more words were spoken the rest of the way to the hospital.

The next thing I knew, Frank and Jonas were hurrying through the door as I woke from a peaceful slumber. I looked down and found I was in a hospital gown, lying in a bed.

"Francine, thank God you're alright."

Tears were rolling down Frank's cheeks as he took my hand, careful not to jar the intravenous needle sticking in my forearm. Jonas came to my other side and took my other hand. He looked equality relieved and guilty.

"I never should have separated from you at the rally. I'm so sorry I didn't look after you, Frannie."

I squeezed both their hands tightly.

"Do you have any idea what happened to you?" Frank asked.

"I remember a prick in my neck and then everything started swirling around. Some man took my arm; he said he'd help me. That's all I remember until I woke up in the Meadowlands."

"Special Agent Allen's on his way over here. Usually there's a 24-hour waiting period to declare someone missing but once he lost you in the crowd he figured something was wrong and issued the alert immediately. He's been calling me nearly hourly since then to see if I'd heard anything."

I just smiled, too tired and emotionally drawn to say anything more. Then the doctor walked in and kindly asked the two men to leave so I could get some rest. We said our goodbyes and I settled back into sleep.

When I awakened, Will was standing over me with another man. I was a little more alert this time as I looked up at them. I took the other man to be an agency man as well.

"Francine," Will started, "I'm so glad you're okay."

I sensed that, like Frank and Jonas, he wanted to take my hand but right now he was in full professional mode.

"Thanks Will."

"Francine, this is Dr. Gary Allenworth. He's an expert in debriefing people who had been drugged to dredge out some memories that they don't realize they have about what happened to them. I spoke with the doctor and they've taken blood. I've asked that a vial be sent to the FBI lab for analysis. From what I can gather, the drug they gave you was very powerful. Something one of our more shadowy agencies would use to abduct a person to extract information from them."

"Sounds rather Bourne-like, but okay. I was telling Frank and Jonas that all I remember was feeling a prick in my neck and a man helping me. That's it until I woke up in the middle of the Meadowlands."

"The man, do you remember anything about him?"

"Not really."

"Was he tall?"

"Average, about your height and build."

"Was he dark-skinned?"

"You mean Arab? No, I don't believe he was."

"You said he spoke to you. Do you remember his voice?"

"It was a low, soothing, reassuring voice. I'd recognize it if I heard it again."

"I'm going to leave you with Dr. Allenworth for a bit to see what he can dredge from your subconscious. I'll come back in an hour or so."

"Thanks, Will."

I spoke with Allenworth for about forty-five minutes but I'm afraid he wasn't able to do much dredging. Perhaps there wasn't anything there to dredge. Perhaps I'd just been unconscious for the two days, although the doctor found that highly unlikely since he was aware of no drug that powerful. He thought it more likely that I had come to after a couple of hours and then they had drugged me again. He was searching to see if I could recall anything during those conscious moments. I kept apologizing when nothing came. He was very patient and persistent. At the end he said it was time to stop. Perhaps in a couple of days we'd pick up again and maybe by that time memories would come back to me.

Will showed up not long after that. I could tell he'd spoken with Allenworth and was disappointed there were no revelations. He sat with me for a few minutes when I announced I wanted to go home. I felt much better and saw no reason to remain further. Will tracked down the attending physician who came in to examine me.

"I think it would be better if you stayed overnight to make sure everything checks out but I don't think there'd be any harm if you went home to sleep in your own bed. Since we don't have any idea the type of drug that was administered, you have to be careful. Some types of hallucinogens can have recurring effects—sort of like waves—that will hit you hours later. Do you have anyone who can watch over you for the next day or so?"

I was about to respond that I lived alone but could probably get someone in the building to look in on me occasionally when Will spoke up.

"I'll look after her, doctor."

"Okay, I'll sign her release papers."

When I opened the door to my apartment it felt like I hadn't been there in months. Everything had a new, unfamiliar feel to it. Will suggested I go lie down but I told him I needed to get back into some sort of routine. I'd take it easy but I had to do something, not just lie in bed. He relented.

The first part of resuming my routine was to start going through my emails. I sat down at the desk and fired up the computer. I was soon greeted by 303 new emails, most of which would be garbage but I had to dutifully slog through the list to make sure I didn't miss anything.

I worked my way down and was about to delete one I didn't recognize when I stopped.

"Will, come over here will you? I think it's him."

Will sidled over next to me as I hit return.

```
Francine, I don't know if I'll be able
to save you next time. The person I am
working with was all for killing you
outright to keep you from snooping any
further. I told him I wouldn't work with
him anymore if he hurt you. In the end, I
prevailed upon him to let you live but I
doubt I can be as persuasive from here on
out. Please count this as a final
warning. Stop. Go back to reporting on
traffic accidents, corrupt politicians
and street festivals. Please don't dig
any further. Please.
    ASW
```

"So we now know who was behind kidnapping you."

I stared at the screen saying nothing. Will continued.

"Frankly, I agree with his suggestion. I never should have let you remain involved in this case. This is an FBI operation; your days as an amateur agent are over."

Now I was seething.

"Amateur agent! Just because you feel guilty about losing me doesn't give you the right to tell me I can't do my job! You feel guilty! Frank feels guilty! Jonas feels guilty! I'm not some fucking damsel in distress! I'm going to keep doing what I do, whether it's with you or not and I'm not going to be scared off by some wacko and his GI Joe friend! If I get killed in the process, then so be it, but it won't be your fault or Frank's or Jonas's; it'll be mine. There—

your conscience can be free and clear! Okay?"

As I finished my diatribe I was surprised to see Will smiling.

"Amateur or not, you'd make one hell of an FBI agent."

I could feel myself softening.

"I'd settle for being one hell of a reporter."

"Francine, it's only that I care—we all care—about you. I don't want anything to happen to you. In the matter of a few short weeks you've had two attempts on your life. And yes, I do feel incredibly guilty that I didn't do my job and protect you better. Sue me."

"Thank you for caring, Will. I'm trying to figure out why they have this interest in me. To tell you the truth, I don't know all that much more than anybody else. The whole world is aware of the destroy Mecca plan; Westbrook even thanked me for spreading the word."

"But the whole world—the whole world except for you that is —will stop keep digging after the warnings they've received. They'd move on. Lawson and Westbrook know you will not stop until you get answers. We have to figure out a way to get ahead of them and determine what answers they don't want you to dig up."

"Next steps?"

"Well, let's go interview Frederick Westbrook's old girlfriend and see if she has anything to offer."

"Thanks for not shutting me out, Will."

"Don't mention it."

"I'm all of a sudden feeling very tired."

"You go to bed. I'll be perfectly comfortable on the couch here."

"You're staying?"

"I promised the doctor, didn't I? I've already made arrangements for my kids to stay with Emma."

"Well, yeah, but I thought that was just talk to get me out of the hospital."

"Good night, Francine. I'll see you in the morning."

He settled down on the couch as I went into the bedroom. His gentlemanliness made me feel even more warmly towards him.

14

Frank told me to take as much time off as I needed but I had to get back into the saddle immediately. He understood.

Will and I took a train back to D.C. to speak with Captain Audra Fairchild. Before we left, Will handed me a new cellphone.

"I take it this is untraceable. Do you really think I need it?" I asked, knowing full well what the answer was going to be

"Who knew you were going to be in Paterson?"

"Frank, Jonas, you and me."

I paused for a second.

"And Westbrook. I was careful before and suspected as much, but old habits like answering my cellphone when Frank calls are hard to break."

"Well, break it. This is a clean, disposable phone that they won't be able to bug. Keep using your regular phone, but only for mundane things and for things we want them to know. For anything related to this case, use this one."

"I'll come to you to determine if something falls into the realm of mundane."

"Mundane is my specialty."

Using the disposable phone, I called Captain Fairchild to make our appointment. When I mentioned that I wanted to speak with her regarding Frederick Westbrook there was silence on the other end of the line.

"Captain Fairchild?"

"Yes, I'm here. Why do you need to talk to me about Freddy? He's been dead for over a decade now."

"I'd rather talk about this in person. It's important."

"Well, I don't know."

"Please captain, I won't take much of your time, but it's very important—important to our national security—that I speak with you. I'll be coming down with Special Agent William Allen of the

FBI."

Bringing in the FBI to stress how vital this was did the trick.

"Okay, can you come to my office at two tomorrow?"

"Yes, that would be fine."

"Come to the west entrance. I'll leave word and someone will come down to pick you up."

Will and I were escorted into Captain Fairchild's office precisely at two o'clock. The captain rose from her desk to greet us. She looked every part the well-groomed, perfectly fit army officer. She appeared to be in her early forties, and had dark brown medium length hair that was pulled back into a ponytail. She was what one would call a handsome but by no means mannish woman with prominent cheekbones and a somewhat square jaw.

"So," she started, "what interest does a New York reporter and an FBI agent want to know about a 9/11 casualty killed many years ago? Oh, in the interest of full disclosure, my mother lives in Queens and I've seen your reports on TV."

"Oh, you're the one," I joked. "We're here to talk to you about Frederick Westbrook because of an interest we have in his brother."

"Alan? Is he even still alive? Talk about the man who faded into oblivion. When Freddy was killed, Alan went all to pieces. I tried to reach out to him but by the time I did he was long gone, never —I thought—to be heard from again. How is he doing?"

"Well, that's a somewhat difficult question to answer."

Fairchild gave me a puzzled look. I decided to plunge in.

"Alan Westbrook was basically destitute but then he won $450 million dollars in the lottery that he has dedicated to destroying Mecca."

"You're kidding, right?"

"I wish I were."

"There's a preacher who's going around promoting destroying Mecca. He's even got some congressmen spouting that bile."

"The idea wasn't his, it originally came from Westbrook."

"Well, I'll be."

"Captain Fairchild," Will asked, "Are you familiar with Colonel Jacob Lawson?"

The expression on her face immediately transformed for one of mild curiosity to one of revulsion. I also detected a glimmer of fear in her eyes.

"What does he have to do with this? You didn't tell me you wanted to talk about him! I have nothing to say about him."

"Captain," Will explained, "Westbrook has hooked up with Lawson. The Colonel is helping him carry out his far-fetched plan. We know how resourceful and how ruthless the Colonel can be. We know that with Lawson's help, he could very well do it. Thousands if not millions of people could be killed. Ms. Vega and I are following any lead we can to try and stop them. One of the leads put us here in your office. Any help you can give us, even if you think it unimportant, can be vital."

"But you don't understand. You don't know what this man can do."

"Yes, Captain," I interjected, "I do. Colonel Lawson has attempted to kill me twice. I'm only alive because of the quick action of my cameraman and by pure dumb luck. The third time I won't be so lucky but I'm not going to back down from this bastard. I'm only a lowly beat reporter. I'd hoped that a captain in the U.S. Army would be made of stiffer stuff than me."

Fairchild mulled this over for a few seconds, then got up from her seat and went over to a credenza against the far wall. She opened the front left door to reveal a compact safe. She dialed the combination, opened the door and extracted a green folder that looked to contain about one hundred pages stapled into about twenty separate documents. She relocked the safe and sat back down at her desk.

She stared at the file before saying anything but then pushed it across the desk to Will.

"In this file you'll find various documents that implicate Colonel Jacob Lawson in the murder of Frederick Westbrook."

Will and I looked at each other, puzzled. I spoke up.

"But Frederick died on 9/11, didn't he?"

"Yes, he died on that date but I don't believe he died as a result of the terrorist attacks. 9/11 only provided cover; Lawson killed him and then planted the body amongst the ruins. As the first responders worked their way through the wreckage, they found Freddy. Nobody thought about it twice. He must have died after the plane hit, they naturally reasoned."

"What sort of evidence is in here?" Will asked.

"I didn't say there was evidence. There's nothing here that would stand up in a court of law as a smoking gun. What's here are numerous circumstantial evidence that together add up, at least in my mind, to an indictment of Lawson."

"Did you ever go to the authorities with your suspicions?" I asked.

"I thought about it, but Lawson's such a legend around here, I'd be tilting at windmills. But in case I had any thoughts, Lawson made sure I didn't do anything."

"How did he do that?"

"Go to the last page in the folder."

Will pulled out the sheet of paper. On it was typed the following:

```
Lenore Bettincourt
225 37th Avenue
Sunnyside, NY
```

"Who's Lenore Bettincourt?" Will asked.

"That's my mother. I found that under my windshield wiper about a month after Freddy died. It was a warning. He knew where my mother lived. I don't think he knew exactly what I had or if I had anything at all. If he did, I'd be dead now. This was just his way of covering his bases. Well, it worked."

My mind went immediately to the Frank Merrill, the reporter who killed himself. Lawson left him notes referring to his wife and daughter. Merrill ignored the warnings and a short while later his daughter was run down in the street.

"That's very smart of you, Captain. I know of someone who didn't heed his warnings and he suffered the consequences," I added. "Why tell us now? I'm sure the threat hasn't expired."

"Several reasons. First, my mother's got terminal cancer. Second, I'm tired. I got myself transferred to this office not because it's something I love doing. I'm here because it's the farthest I can possibly get in the Pentagon from Colonel Lawson. As a result, I haven't seen him or thought about him in years. But I do think about Freddy every day and it's been tough living with the guilt over this long time. It's a relief getting that file out of my office.

"Lastly, your story got to me. It made me ashamed that I've shrunk from him because of a threat. You've actually been attacked and yet you keep on going. We have to finally stop this prick."

I felt oddly proud for having survived.

"Is there anything more you can tell us?" Will asked.

"I think you'll find everything in that file is pretty self-explanatory and where it's not, I've inserted notes. I'm nothing if not meticulous. Like I said, there's no smoking gun here, but hopefully you being the FBI can put the pieces together and make something stick."

We thanked the captain and left.

"So, what's next?" I asked as we sat on the train heading back to New York. Will was already leafing through the file.

"We'll digest what in this file and, if there's enough here, I'm going to ask a judge for a court order to exhume Frederick Westbrook's body."

"Exhume his body?"

"Yes, our analysts should be able to determine if he was killed by any other way than dying in the attack. He wasn't cremated, was he?"

"I don't think so. The obit I read said he was buried with full honors at Arlington. It didn't say anything about cremation, but I don't know. If Lawson did kill him, you'd think he'd have pressured Alan to cremate his brother's remains to destroy any evidence."

"Let's just hope he didn't."

Will gave me half of the pages in the file to read through. The first document was a hand-written letter Frederick had sent to Captain Fairchild.

My dearest Audra,

I hope you are well. I dream of the time we can be in each other's arms once again.

As I've told you, I've long had my suspicions about Alan's friend Jake. Alan is in such awe of Colonel Lawson that you would think the guy walks on water. It has, I must be honest, created a fair amount of resentment in me as I've felt a wedge being driven between my twin brother and me. At first, I thought it was a case of pure and simple jealousy. Alan and I have been so close our entire lives that I could not fathom anyone (other than a woman for obvious romantic reasons of course) coming between us. I just chalked it up to Alan finding a new friend. I should be happy for him, I told myself.

However, the more I got to know Lawson, the less I trusted him. This feeling was only strengthened as time went on and I spoke to others about him. Believe me, his enemies are legion but his allies, hangers-on and associates (I never got the sense that he had any "friends") are an even greater number. In any case, many people have the same feeling about the guy, that he is involved in many shady and illegal activities.

He cloaks everything he does in uber-patriotism, but it's not an act. He fully believes that any crimes he commits—extortion, arms trafficking, even murder—are done to fulfill the larger goal of protecting the country and therefore must be condoned. As a fanatic, he's all the more dangerous.

I've dug up the attached files on Lawson. Most of these are innuendo and speculation, not admissible as evidence of wrongdoing. But there just seems to be too much of a pattern to be a string of coincidences. The man is in this shit up to his neck and must be stopped.

I think he may be on to my snooping and I really need to watch my back. I'm sending you this stuff for safe keeping in case anything happens to me. You must be extra careful yourself.

Love,
Freddy

While I was reading this, Will flipped through the pages, occasionally stopping on an item of interest. At one point, he looked up at me.

"What was the name of the reporter you told me about—the one who committed suicide after his daughter was killed in a hit and run?"

"Frank Merrill."

"Here are some notes about Frank Merrill. Like everything else in here, it's just rumor and conjecture. But there's a copy of a check attached to the notes. It's for $10,000 from an account titled 217 Management Corp., Inc. The check is made out to a Salvatore Roma. In the note section is written the initials "FM"."

"You think the FM refers to Frank Merrill?"

"I wouldn't be at all surprised. I'm theorizing that Mr. Roma did the dirty work in killing Frank Merrill's daughter and this is his payoff, or one installment of the payment anyway. We have to find Roma."

I liked the fact that he used the word "we".

"If it's true that Lawson killed Frederick, do you think we'll be able to drive a wedge between Westbrook and Lawson? Perhaps we can get Westbrook to divert his monies elsewhere to better uses." ●

"Perhaps, but let's not get too ahead of ourselves. We've got some work to do before we can think about that. First thing I have to do is convince my bosses that there's something here and I can continue this as my case. Right now my assignment is to investigate Farad Sahari's killing to see whether it's under FBI jurisdiction. We're moving a little far afield of that investigation and I want to make sure I'm not out on a branch sawing away behind me."

The mention of Farad's name filled me with sadness but I didn't want to bring our mood and excitement down.

"Ah yes, the bureaucracy must be fed," I quipped.

"And a voracious beast it is. I don't think I will get much resistance but I'm going to stay away from the "bomb Mecca" angle."

"Why? It's related and as far-fetched as the whole scenario is, the story's out there with Reverend McKenzie."

"That's exactly why, and in this case the reason is entirely bureaucratic. There's already a whole unit devoted to investigating McKenzie and his sermons. If I were to mention the Mecca tie-in, I'd be ordered to hand the investigation over to them. I don't want to do that."

"I don't want you to either."

Will looked me in the eyes.

"You know, technically I never should have gone to Paterson with you. There was no suspicion that the rally there was in any way related to Sahari's death. But I wanted to be there, to help take care of you. Not that I did a good job of that, did I?"

I took his hand.

"Will, I'm really touched that you wanted to protect me."

Then I smiled mischievously.

"I trust you'll do a better job next time"

He smiled back.

"I will."

15

On the one hand, I was anxious to tell Frank that we found a link to the death of his old friend, Frank Merrill. On the other hand, I worried about opening old wounds for him. He obviously was filled will sorrow just talking about it. I also sensed that he felt himself less a man because he fled DC for local news rather than sticking it out and continuing Frank Merrill's investigation. In the end, I decided the best thing was to be upfront and discuss it with him. Too much was at stake to skirt the issue because of a few hurt feelings.

This was my first time in the office since my abduction. As I walked in, all eyes were warily on me. After I'd returned from Paris the mood was much different, much more buoyant and relieved. Now that my life had been threatened a second time, my colleagues must have wondered what was up with me. Was there going to be a third attempt? And a fourth? And so on until they were successful? I wished I knew. I smiled and acknowledged everybody as I walked to Frank's office.

"Welcome back Francine," Frank said as he got up from his desk to give me a heartfelt hug and kiss. "How was DC? We're going to have to open up a satellite office for you down there, aren't we? Did you learn anything new?"

"Thanks Frank, it's nice to be back. I have a lot to tell you."

We sat down as he looked at me expectantly.

"I'm not quite sure where to begin. First, it appears that Frederick Westbrook may not have been killed in the attack on the Pentagon; we have reason to believe he was killed by Lawson."

"Wow, that's a biggie! Do you have proof?"

"Only circumstantial at this point but Will thinks it may be enough to exhume the body to look for clues that he was murdered."

"Will?"

"Special Agent Allen."

"I know very well about whom we are speaking. Will?"

"Oh, shut up."

I hoped I wasn't blushing as much as I felt I was.

"Anyway," I continued, regaining my composure, "we should know within a day or two whether he can get the court order."

"Why did he allegedly kill Westbrook? I thought he and the two brothers were the best of buds?"

"They were, that is until Frederick got suspicious of Lawson's dealings and started to do some digging and uncovered some of the dirt Lawson was involved in. Captain Fairchild provided us with a bunch of files Frederick had amassed. Special Agent Allen is reviewing them now."

I paused.

"And?"

"Frank, one of the documents in the folder had to do with the death of Frank Merrill."

As predicted, a pall settled over the room at the mention of Merrill's name as Frank turned his chair and stared out the window. I let him have his introspective moment. Finally, without moving his eyes away from the window he spoke up.

"What was in there?"

"Some notes, all of which appear to be circumstantial and conjecture. But there was also a canceled check for $10,000 made out to a Salvatore Roma. In the note section of the check were the initials F.M. Will's theory is that this may be a payment to Roma to run down Merrill's daughter. The check is from a dummy corporation and at present there's no way to directly link it to Lawson, but it's a lead."

"Thanks, Francine. Keep me posted."

I left him. Two minutes later my untraceable phone rang. It had to be Will; he was the only one who had this number.

"Hi, Francine. Well, I danced a bit but it's still my—or rather our—case. I'm preparing the paperwork to get Frederick

Westbrook's body exhumed. I've got to find a favorable federal judge to sign the order, especially without family consent. I've never attempted one before but I imagine it's not straightforward getting a body lifted out of Arlington National Cemetery. I'll let you know how that progresses."

"Anything on Salvatore Roma?"

"I asked one of our techs to do a search to see if he's anywhere in the system. If he is indeed a hit man, I can't imagine him not having a record. We'll see if we can find him. Did you tell Frank what we found?"

"I just told him. He's glad we're pursuing it but he's taking the news pretty hard."

"What are you going to do now?"

"I want to take a trip up to the Arab-American Friendship League and talk to them."

"Francine, you do realize the group is still on our watch list, don't you? Despite Westbrook's claim of responsibility for the Topeka bombing, we haven't officially ruled them out. They can be dangerous, we just don't know. Plus, I don't want you doing anything that inadvertently jeopardizes our investigation."

Two weeks ago if he had said the exact same thing I would have been irate, but I knew he was saying this mostly out of concern for me.

"I'll be careful. Will, we've gotten so focused on the big picture —you know, little things like trying to avert World War III—that we've back-burnered Farad Sahari's death. I have trouble believing Farad was involved in anything related to terrorism. He was also a pretty sharp guy; he'd know if a group he was so closely affiliated with was dirty. I need some answers."

"When you heading up there?"

"I've got an appointment at 2:00 with the director."

"Okay. I have to run. I'll talk to you later."

I was surprised he didn't make more of an effort to talk me out of it. If nothing else, I was a lowly journalist infringing on an FBI investigation. Legally, both he and I were treading on dangerous territory. He could be disciplined if his bosses found out he let me make this infringement. He did sound very distracted when he hung up so I passed it off as a lot on his mind.

Ever since the bombing in Topeka and the alleged claiming of responsibility by the Arab-American Friendship League, protesters have camped outside the modest 84th Street brownstone that the League called its headquarters. As time had gone on, both the number and vociferousness of the protesters had steadily deceased. As a result, the police presence—as well as the presence of submachine guns and bulletproof vests—had also diminished.

As I turned the corner onto 84th Street and saw the building, which was toward the other end of the block, I counted six protesters and one cop. They were all chatting very amicably together. As I got closer, however, I realized that only four of the six were protesters. One of the other people was the director, the man I was to interview. The fourth was Will. He saw me approach and waved.

"Francine," he called out, "come meet Mahmoud Fakhoury. We've all been having a most enjoyable conversation on our respective upbringings. And this is Esther, Willie, Billy and Oscar. And New York's Finest is represented by Officer Al Pescatore."

I shook all of their hands and then I took Will aside.

"Will, what are you doing here?"

"I got here about forty-five minutes ago, and after getting to know our protesters a bit, I went in and dragged Mr. Fakhoury down here. They were all reluctant at first but once we all got to know each other, everybody warmed up. It's always funny how attitudes can change once we get past the stereotypical images we have of each other."

Will paused for a second and then looked me directly in the eyes.

"Did you really think I'd let you do this interview alone? I tend to agree with you that this group is harmless, that they are what they say they are. However, until they are officially cleared of being suspects in Topeka or any other terrorist activity, you will not approach or contact them without me being present. Is that clear?"

I said nothing in response, defiantly meeting his stare.

"Let me put it another way. I will throw your beautiful ass in jail if I hear of it happening again."

Then he softened.

"Francine, I can't do my job effectively if I'm spending time worrying about you. I'm already breaking so many rules having you as a quasi-partner, but you're a vital asset to this investigation. Ask anyone how I was when I thought I lost you to the kidnappers; I can't afford to be that way again on this or any other case."

This was the first time since he first came to interview me that I saw him in full "official" mode. That time, however, he was just being a pompous ass. Now, he was absolutely correct; I was venturing into areas that were way out of my league. After almost getting myself killed twice, one would think it would make me more cautious. Instead, it made me more determined to plow ahead, ignoring the risks I was putting myself into.

I couldn't helped be moved by Will's touching expression of concern. He obviously cared for me.

Our stare-off was continuing. While I was ready to relent, it wasn't in me to play the helpless female, acquiescing to an authoritative male. I had too much of my mother in me. I had to figure out a graceful way to agree but still retain firm footing in his eyes.

"So, you think my ass is beautiful, do you?"

He smiled, knowing exactly what I was doing.

"Incredibly so."

"Always nice to hear."

"Shall we go inside and speak to Mr. Fakhoury, together?"

"I wouldn't have it any other way."

Mr. Fakhoury escorted us into the building and up to his office on the third floor. I just love these old brownstones. They have so much character. They were built to last forever. On the way up the stairs, Fakhoury said this particular building was built in the 1890s and belonged to a particular architectural style, whose name I didn't quite catch. He said he'd gotten some criticism from his countrymen because it was not decorated in an Arab style but was instead appointed with American antiques that gave the feel of the building when it was first built.

"To drag Arab artifacts into this beautiful quintessential New York structure would be like adding a minaret onto the White House. It just wouldn't fit. Plus, I tell my Arab friends that this is the Arab-American Friendship League. For most Americans, dealing with my staff and me is intimidating in itself, especially after 9/11. By furnishing the brownstone the way we have, at least they won't be intimidated by the surroundings as well. Hopefully, it creates a more conducive climate to meet our common objective of promoting peace and friendship. Can I offer you some coffee or tea?"

I hoped Will would not refuse. Farad had told me that refusing an Arabs offer of tea could often be interpreted as an insult.

"Some tea would be wonderful," Will responded, "I fondly remember the tea I enjoyed on a trip I made to Egypt some years back."

"I hope we do not disappoint," Fakhoury responded genially as he rang to his secretary to bring some tea in.

"Special Agent Allen, I would first like to thank you for forcing me to come out to talk with the protesters. I found it to be a most informative exchange of ideas, an opportunity that would have been lost as I would have been too afraid to venture out to deal with these fine people. My staff and I generally come in to the building through a back way so as to avoid confrontation. But I knew with you there, I'd be safe, and after talking with the protesters, I realize that I would have been safe in any case, but one cannot be too sure these days."

"You are most welcome, Mr. Fakhoury. I found it most enlightening myself."

The secretary brought in a tray with an elaborate tea set, which Fakhoury poured for all of us. He spoke while he poured.

"So what do I owe the pleasure of a visit by not only the FBI but by a member of New York's fine fourth estate? Ms. Vega, although we've never met, you come to me a known commodity as Farad Sahari had spoken very highly of you."

"That was very kind of him."

"Yes, I sensed he was very fond of you, or even beyond that. I once thought of warning him of entering into a relationship with someone from such a different world, but I quickly reconsidered. When love enters the picture, all practical considerations have a tendency to flee. Any protestations I may have offered would have fallen on deaf ears or created animosity between my dear friend and me."

"I miss Farad deeply."

"As do I, Miss Vega."

"Mr. Fakhoury, Farad Sahari is the reason we are here to see you today. I know you've already been interviewed by the Bureau regarding Mr. Sahari's death but I have a couple more questions."

"Most certainly."

"Did Mr. Sahari ever mention either Alan Westbrook or Jacob Lawson?"

"Yes indeed, he mentioned both of them. He said they are tied to the hate speech from that preacher."

"Yes, they're the ones actually trying to pull it off. We think they may also be somehow responsible for Mr. Sahari's death. I'm trying to figure out why they would target Mr. Sahari. Are you aware of anything he learned that Westbrook and Lawson feared would scuttle their plans?

"There is nothing I am aware of."

"You said that he mentioned the two of them, correct?"

"Yes, but only in a general way. He said that it was crucial they be stopped. But he did not share any specifics about them: where they were, the type of device they were looking for, who was to sell it to them. Nothing like that. I honestly don't think he knew anything. I'm sorry I can't provide you with anything more. I just don't know."

We chatted with Mr. Fakhoury for a few more minutes and then departed.

"Well," I observed, "that was a bust."

"On the contrary, I found that very useful."

"What did you learn?"

"First, it further strengthened my impression that this organization—at least not its leadership—has no involvement in terrorist activities. Fakhoury would have to be one hell of an actor to be someone other than what he says he is. Second, it also strengthens my belief that they had nothing to do with Sahari's death. They were genuinely close friends and Fakhoury keenly grieves his loss. Third, I had suspected that Sahari had gathered no information on Westbrook or Lawson. I think if he had gathered anything he would have passed it on to either you or Fakhoury."

"So why do you think Lawson had Farad killed?"

Will eyed me for a second.

"You only mentioned Lawson. You don't think Westbrook would have played a role in Sahari's death?"

"I honestly don't think he has it in him to be a murderer. He'd go along if Lawson was behind it but I don't believe he'd order such a thing to be carried out."

"Not for the cause anyway."

"What do you mean?"

"I think he'd do it for love."

"What are you talking about?"

"You and Farad Sahari had gotten very close in a very short time, didn't you?"

"I'm not sure that's any of your business."

"Don't get offended; I'm not prying into your private life. What I'm saying is that the two of you got close and most likely exchanged texts and emails that probably betrayed how close the two of you were getting. Since we know Westbrook somehow has access to all of your electronic communications, I think he became insanely jealous and killed Sahari because of it.

"Or, as you said, Westbrook doesn't fit the mold as the murdering type. A more likely scenario is that he became attracted to you but became distracted because your affections were directed elsewhere. Lawson needed him to focus on his work so he ordered the removal of the distraction."

"You're kidding, right?"

"Not in the least. Look at all the communications you've received from Westbrook. They're all very tender and warm. He intervened to save your life. The guy's in love with you. Furthermore, what about the story you told me about him helping out his old high school crush. The man is very impulsive and acts on those impulses."

"Well I'll be. Great, I have a conquest that is working to destroy the world."

"Don't worry, not all of us conquests are so inclined."

Will was not looking at me when he said this, so I wasn't quite sure what to make of his comment. He continued.

"If I'm correct about Westbrook, I think he's in the U.S., not in Europe with Lawson. Maybe they were together at the time you were in Paris, but he's back now. I can nearly guarantee it."

"Why do you say that?"

"Several reasons. First, Lawson wouldn't want him underfoot as he skulks around negotiating with arms dealers and go-betweens. Westbrook's not an agent. He'd be a clumsy liability in that world.

"Second, Westbrook's a computer whiz. I bet he's performing that service for Lawson as we speak, but it's something that could be done anywhere on earth. Setting up codes and software for a launch and detonation that can't be broken takes time and concentration. It would be something that Westbrook would accomplish more easily back here rather than constantly on the run.

"Third, if killing Sahari was indeed a crime of passion then

Westbrook has it bad. Having thousands of miles and an ocean between you and him would only be a further distraction. Being in the U.S. would at least give him the illusion that he has a chance with you. I haven't done a detailed profile on Alan Westbrook, but all indications are that he's a genius but highly unstable. Lawson needs the genius part but he knows that the unstable part must be considered as well and he's doing what he can to give him a little bit of stability so he can do his work."

"Wow, that's some analysis."

"This is all theoretical, of course, but it might be something we can use to our advantage."

"How?"

"I've been trying to figure out a way to drive a wedge between Westbrook and Lawson. Divide and conquer, you know? I thought getting the news to Westbrook that Lawson killed his brother might be the vehicle, but the more I thought about it, the less inclined I became."

"Why not? From all accounts, the Westbrook brothers were as close as any two human beings could get. Wouldn't he turn on Lawson in a heartbeat once he found out the truth?"

"I doubt he'd believe it to be the truth. He worships Lawson. He'd think we made this up to discredit his hero. I'd also be nervous about letting Lawson know too early that we're on to him. We don't know if he's tracking your calls and emails as well."

"So, what are you suggesting?"

"Let's smoke Westbrook out; make him come to us."

"How do we do that?"

"You're still occasionally using the cell phone he can access, right?"

"Yes, as we discussed I'm still using it enough for him to think that it's still my main phone."

"Good. From this point on we're romantically involved."

"We are?"

"Yes, and because I'm so besotted with you, I'll send you flowery, and not to mention suggestive, text messages over the course of a couple days. I predict that once he sees how madly in love we are with each other, his jealousy will take over.

"We should have pet names for each other. I can be Allie. That was a nickname I had when I was a kid but nobody calls me that anymore. Anything you want me to call you?"

"Everyone calls me Francine or Frannie. Not very imaginative, I suppose."

"It should be a name only I will call you. Francy? No. Vaigs as in short for Vega? No. How about Fava?"

My eyes watered instantaneously as if they had a life of their own.

"What's the matter, Francine?"

"That's the pet name my mother used to call me. When I was very young I couldn't quite get down the name Francine Vega and I called myself Fava. My mother adopted it as her endearment for me. There was a time when I'd roll my eyes whenever she used it but what I wouldn't give to hear her say it once again."

"I'm sorry. I didn't realize I stumbled into something so personal. Let's come up with a different name."

"No, that's quite alright. As a matter of fact, I'd like for you to call me Fava. It feels right."

He said nothing but looked on me fondly.

"What do you think is going to happen?" I asked trying to change the subject.

"We'll do some back and forth texts for a few days. In one of them I'll send you a picture of myself so he'll know what I look like. Then I'll suggest we meet at some out of the way place for dinner. There's a diner over on 11th Avenue that will fit the bill. I'll suggest we meet at seven. I'll show up at seven and you text me saying you'll be a half hour, forty-five minutes late. I'll tell you I'll get a table and wait for you. We'll see if he shows."

"And if he does?"

"He'll find out he's not dealing with an academic but a highly-trained special agent in the Federal Bureau of Investigation."

He laughed and I responded in kind.

Over the course of the next couple of days, every fifteen to twenty minutes my phone would buzz with another text from Will.

```
Fava, I can't wait to hold you again.
Fava, You were wonderful last night.
Fava, What are you wearing now?
Fava, I can't get the picture of your
beautiful face out of my mind, nor do I want
to. I don't want you to forget what I look
like so here's my picture.
Fava, I love you.
```

I'd respond to each of these messages in kind. At times, I'd find myself staring off into space like a schoolgirl, wondering what it'd be like if these fake messages were actually true, especially the last one. I was wondering if Westbrook was getting these as well. Only time would tell. Finally, the trap was set.

```
Fava, I can't stand it anymore. I have to
see you. Please tear yourself away from work
for an hour, just for dinner (and of course a
little hand-holding). Can we meet at the
Acropolis Diner on 11th Ave and 43rd Street?
It's a hole in the wall but the food's good
and it's out of the way. Shall we say 7?
```

```
Allie, Sounds great! I can't wait to be with
you.
```

At 6:50 I sent him a follow-up.

```
Sorry my love, got stuck at work (what
else?) be there around 7:45.
```

He responded.

```
That's all right. I'll get a table. I can't
wait to see you.
```

I sat back in my chair at my desk and waited. At 7:30 my phone rang.

"Francine," my heart dropped a bit, hoping he'd continue to call me Fava, "we have him. It all went as predicted. He's being taken to headquarters downtown to be questioned. I'd like you to be there. Can you hop a cab downtown?"

Will was downstairs at the guard station, waiting to escort me up to his office and the interrogation room where Westbrook was being held. On the way up, he described how it went down.

"I was sitting at a booth when he walked in and spotted me. He calmly walked over and sat across from me. He said, 'Allie, please come with me. I have a gun pointed at you under the table. Let's not make a scene. I don't want anyone else to get hurt.' I contemplated playing along to see if I could get any info from him but I thought against it. As unstable as he is, I was afraid he might just start shooting. So instead I just said 'Now' and immediately two red dots appeared on his chest. I told him if he so much as moved his hands in the direction of his lap, two bullets from high-powered firearms would enter his chest. He sagged, deflated, and we took him in."

"Not very dramatic, is it."

"No, I don't think he's really suited for this line of work. He didn't actually have a gun so I have no idea what he would have done."

"What now?"

"Well, we've tried interviewing him but he hasn't spoken a word since then. I'd like you to come in with me. Maybe he'll talk with you present."

Westbrook had cleaned himself up a lot since I saw him those short two months ago. Though the outside package had improved, when he looked up and saw me, his eyes had the same crazed look as when he stared into the camera and stated that at last he'd be able to avenge his brother's death.

"Hello, Alan."

"Hello, Ms. Vega."

From Will's account, these were the most words he'd spoken since he was captured. Perhaps I could get him to talk. I hoped that he'd overlook that I betrayed him and continue to talk to me.

"Alan, you know why you're here, don't you?"

"They haven't told me the specific charges or read me my rights yet, but I have a general idea."

"Where's Lawson?"

Will kicked me under the table, sensing that I was going too fast. Cutting to the chase immediately could make Westbrook clam up. He was right. Westbrook took to staring into space.

We got nothing more out of him. Nothing about Lawson, nothing about Farad, nothing about Mecca. We decided to get up and leave. Westbrook looked up at me as I rose.

"You betrayed me; you'll pay for this."

He displayed the same iciness as when he said he'd avenge his brother. Before this, even though he may have been responsible for the killing of Farad, a part of me had some level of sympathy for him. Now, nothing. Before I could respond, Will spoke up.

"Oh, by the way, Mr. Westbrook, we have evidence that your brother did not die in the 9/11 attack. Colonel Lawson killed him. Lawson used the plane crash into the Pentagon to cover his tracks. Just thought you had a right to know."

Not waiting for Westbrook to respond, we walked out. I headed back to the subway station.

I sincerely hoped Frank had a run-of-the mill assignment for me when I came in the next day. I wanted something banal and routine: a mugging, a sinkhole in the middle of Broadway, anything to divert me for a couple days. I was tired of Alan Westbrook, Jacob Lawson and the entire gang. I yearned for the mundane.

Frank did have an assignment. A five-alarm fire of suspicious origins had broken out in the Park Slope section of Brooklyn. A whole row of brownstones was up in flames.

Jonas and I hopped on the D train and made our way there. The conflagration was still in full force as innumerable firefighters did their utmost to contain it. I was able to get interviews with the Chief, who was on the scene, as well as several residents who were now homeless.

The Chief said the fire appeared to have been set, but they wouldn't know until the arson squad had completed its inspection. An emotional family lamented the loss of their home but said they were thankful to be alive. All in all, we got some good footage. It felt good to be working with Jonas on something like this once again.

Now that the FBI had Westbrook, I figured the saga to be over. Lawson was still out there but the loss of his bankroll neutered him somewhat. While I would have loved to be involved in bringing him to justice for his crimes, it really wasn't my area. Will was right. I was playing amateur agent and had almost gotten myself killed for it. It was just as well that I moved on to my boring and predictable life.

And Will, what was that? I had to knock myself out of yet another schoolgirl crush I'd had a tendency to develop lately. This man was a cop. He had two kids, for God's sake, that I'd never even met. I'd never dealt with kids before. If I was going to deal with them one day, they'd be mine that I would start from scratch, not inheriting somebody else's with all the baggage that entailed.

I don't know why I was getting so worked up over the fake texts he'd sent me when we were trying to ferret out Westbrook. Why was I pretending they were more than they were?

After Farad had died, Jonas sat down at my desk to ask me how I was holding up.

"Okay, I guess," I responded unenthusiastically.

"No you're not. Not now anyway," he shot back. "But you will. And you'll find someone new. Sahari seemed like a good man but I couldn't see it; the differences are too great. Frannie, you got to alter what you're looking for in a man. Flash ain't cuttin' it for you. Find someone with substance, someone who'll be there for you through thick and thin."

I made a joke about him moonlighting as a matchmaker but he just gave me a 'you know I'm right' look and walked away. His words played on my mind as I thought about Will but I probably misread the entire situation. Now that they have Westbrook, I'd probably never hear from Special Agent William Allen again.

Jonas and I finished our shooting and we headed back to the studio to finish the piece in time for the 6:00 news. We returned to Park Slope at 5:45 so we could do a live segment from the scene. By that time, the fire was under control. Because of the timing, we had a good report showing the fire at its worst, conversations with the heroes and victims and a wrap up at the smoldering wreckage. I was proud of the work Jonas and I did. I would have liked to celebrate, but I was beat. I was emotionally spent from dealing with Will and Westbrook over the past couple of days and physically exhausted from the day's shoot, editing and finishing. I just wanted to go home and sleep soundly in my bed.

I'd just gotten under the covers and turned off the lights when my phone buzzed. From the type of noise it made, I knew it was an incoming text. I considered ignoring it but my journalistic instincts kicked in and I grudgingly pulled myself out of bed and headed over to the dresser. I located the phone in the dark and pressed the button to activate it.

The message shone brightly in the darkness:

```
Fava, I love you.
```

16

"I'm sorry, Francine. I got home last night. The kids were already asleep. I went in, gave them each a kiss and then settled down in front of the TV to unwind before going to bed myself. I just couldn't get you out of my mind. I screwed up enough courage to send you an impersonal text message but not enough to tell you to your face. It was highly inappropriate of me. I never should have sent it."

Will looked so distraught sitting across from me at the coffee shop near my office as he made his confession. I found it extremely endearing. All my life I'd been drawn to the self-confident charmers. In many cases, such as Farad, the self-confidence was well placed. In others—Eddie being the prime example—the self-confidence was a facade, a mask to the world hiding the fact that there wasn't much substance to back up the boasting. Still, I fell for the charm and was blind to the truth until it was too late.

Don't get me wrong; Will had plenty of confidence in himself and what he did. But it was a matter-of-fact confidence rooted in his abilities, not in his desire to impress or fool others. Underneath he had a genuinely shy, gentle nature. I was finding it quite nice to have such a man interested in me.

But on the other hand, what would I be getting myself into. I'd known other wives of law enforcement officials. Many couldn't take it, having the constant worry of not knowing whether their husbands would come home on a given night. In my job, I've also interviewed more than a few grieving widows whose husbands didn't come home.

And there were the substantial differences between us. He was at least a decade, if not more, older than me. He had two kids I'd never met. Did I want to get involved with two little monsters?

Is this the type of life I'd choose for myself? I could easily nip this in the bud. The FBI had Westbrook. They could hold him for all sorts of violations of the Patriot Act as well as implicating him in the death of Farad. Will would move on to another case; there'd be no obvious reason for us to stay in touch. We could go about living our own separate lives. His feelings for me would dim over time. Now was definitely the time to make a clean cut before it went any further or got serious.

I reached across the table and took his hand.

"Will, I'd like to address various points of what you just said. First, as I told you, only one other person in the world ever called me Fava. The only way I'd accept another person using that name for me would be if that person loved me deeply and I loved them in return. So, from now on you will call me Fava, understand?"

Will looked at me, wiping a tear from his eye as he nodded.

"Second, when am I going to meet these kids of yours? I've seen the pictures you have in your wallet but that's hardly what I would call a relationship. I want to get to know them."

"I'd like that very much. They'll fall in love with you, too. I just know it."

"We'll see. Third, I couldn't think of doing it any better than the way you did it. If you had blurted out your love to me in person, God knows how I'd have reacted. This way you sent the text and I had a little time to mull it over and come to the realization that I loved you, too.

"So, all in all what you just said was not a great statement by an FBI agent, one who's dedicated to the truth. I'm sorely disappointed."

Will smiled.

"I'll try and do better next time."

"See to it."

We both laughed.

The next day I arrived at his house in Queens for dinner.

Will opened the door for me. Peering out from behind his legs was his four-year old daughter, Stella. Once she got a good view of me she tugged on her father's pant leg. He squatted down so that she could whisper in his ear.

"Yes, she's the woman on TV, just like I told you."

She whispered something more.

"Yes, I think she's very pretty, too."

Will stood back up.

"Fava, welcome to our home. This distinguished lady, who is quite pretty herself, is Stella. Stella, this is Francine."

"But Daddy," corrected Stella, "you called her Fava, not Francine."

"Yes, he did," I responded. "That's a name only special people get to call me and so I want you to call me Fava, too. Is that okay?"

After I spoke to her, Stella shyly shrank back further behind her father. I still hadn't gotten a full view of her but from what I could see she was a beautiful girl with blond hair pulled back into a pony tail and eyes that were as dark as mine.

I looked around.

"And where is Albert? I'd hoped to meet him as well."

"Well," Will responded, "we had a bit of a scene before you arrived. I'm hoping he'll come down to join us for dinner, but I'm not overly optimistic."

"I understand," I responded. And I did.

We sat down to eat. I was about to compliment Will on the delicious beef stew he prepared but before I could, he made sure to point out that his nanny/housekeeper, Emma, made it that afternoon. I thereupon tried to win over Stella, but did not seem to have much effect.

"Stella, do you know what you want to be when you grow up?"

Stella nuzzled into her father's side, embarrassed by the attention.

"Well, you have plenty of time to figure that out. Enjoy being a little girl for now. Before you know it, it's all over."

As we ate our dinner, I could sense Stella looking over at me but as soon as I looked back, she would hide away. I was sorry when the evening ended and I hadn't made much headway with her and Albert never did come down to join us. I had an early morning assignment the next day and needed my sleep so I had to leave. I gave Will a peck on the cheek. I didn't want to embarrass him or Stella with a full kiss on the lips.

"Thank you, Will. I had a lovely evening."

Will, obviously embarrassed by his son's behavior and his daughter's reticence, appeared ill at ease and uncomfortable as he said his good-byes.

"I'm so glad you came."

As I was heading to the front door, I detected movement out of the corner of my eye at the top of the stairs. It was Albert, looking down on us. I didn't let on that I saw him there.

"Will, tell Albert I'm sorry I missed meeting him," I said in a voice loud enough for Albert to hear. "Also tell him I'm not looking to replace his mother. It's just that I think his father's a special guy I love and want to spend time with."

"I'll be sure to let him know."

I leaned over and gave Stella one last little wave and then turned to head out the door. I hadn't taken one step when I heard little footsteps running my way. I turned and looked down. Stella was holding her arms up to me. I picked her up and gave her a big hug.

"Fava, you come back?"

"Yes, Stella my little darling, I'll come back very soon. You can count on it."

17

I couldn't believe how deliriously happy I felt the next day. I had some work to do a puff piece on the upcoming Fashion Week, but other than that it was a blessedly slow day at work. Frank was at a company retreat in Phoenix. Jonas would be shooting a piece with another reporter. I took my time getting ready before heading to the station.

I contemplated calling Will just to hear his voice, but I didn't want to make a pest of myself. I'd content myself dreaming about him.

I was mulling this over when my phone rang. I was surprised; it was the untraceable one Will gave me when we didn't want Westbrook listening in on my conversations. With Westbrook out of the picture, I'd stopped using it. In fact, I'd forgotten I still had it on me. Will had probably just lost track of which phone he was calling.

"Why hi there," I purred, "let me tell you once again how much I loved meeting your kids, at least one of them."

Will didn't even pause a second to respond in kind.

"They cut him loose!" he blurted out.

"Who? What are you talking about? Who cut whom loose?"

"Westbrook!"

"The FBI let him go? That's impossible. You have an ironclad case against him."

"The evidence collected at Sahari's crime scene, it's gone."

"Gone?"

"It's not in the evidence room. It's nowhere to be found. They have record of me signing it in but no record of anyone signing it out. It's just vanished. As a result, my bosses cut him loose. And they did it without consulting me.

"And it gets better. I understand that in the next couple of days they're going to arrest Mahmoud Fakhoury and charge him with

Sahari's death and maybe even Topeka."

"What?! We know he didn't commit either of those crimes!"

"Fava, I've been given direct orders to move on. I'm not to touch the Farad Sahari case or Westbrook anymore."

"Will, is there anybody you can talk to who will tell you what really happened? Not just the public sanitized version?"

"I've tried. I have a couple calls in but nobody's talking. Some people I've known for years aren't returning my calls. It's like Westbrook was never here; like he was a complete figment of our imaginations."

"Do you think it was Lawson?"

"Lawson has tentacles everywhere, probably even here."

"What are you going to do?"

"Do? There's nothing I can do. I've been given a direct order to back off."

"But a man was killed. You had the man who did it or is at the very minimum is a material witness. He subsequently threatened me. Will, you've got to keep going. I know your inner sense of justice won't allow you to stop."

"Fava, you know I want to but I risk arrest if I disobey a direct order. I can't risk it, for my kids."

At that moment in time, I wished he hadn't called me Fava. On the other hand, I understood. He couldn't risk leaving the kids fatherless. When I didn't respond, he continued as if he was reading my mind.

"I'm sorry, Francine."

He hung up. My doorbell rang. I looked through the peephole but could not make out who was there. I called out.

"Who's there?"

Without identifying himself, he answered.

"He's wrong, you know. You're both wrong. Jake wouldn't do that. He was Freddy's friend, the same way he's mine."

There was no way I was going to open the door. Farad was dead because of him. He said I betrayed him and there was no predicting how he would react to that. We were going to have our conversation through the thick door to my apartment.

"Alan, I saw the evidence. I spoke with your brother's former lover, Audra Fairchild. Do you remember her?"

There was no answer.

"We exhumed your brother's body. A forensic pathologist took a fresh look at it. He found things that were overlooked the first time because no one thought to look for them. There were injuries that could not be explained by the crash; he was stabbed by a knife. Your brother was on to Colonel Lawson's past activities and he became a liability."

"Lies! All fabricated to bring Jake down. He has many enemies who are always looking to trip him up."

"Why would Captain Fairchild wait ten years to reveal all this? She did not want to talk about Lawson. She only talked after we'd pressured her. She decided to do it for your brother. He'd been denied justice for too long. If she was so intent on bringing down Lawson, she would have gone public with all she had a long, long time ago."

There was silence. After a few minutes I wondered if Westbrook had left.

"Alan? You still there?"

"Yes...Yes I am."

I could tell by the tone of his voice that he was gradually accepting that I was telling the truth. He sounded totally defeated. I went to open the door. Still, to be safe I first grabbed the canister of pepper spray from my purse. I unbolted the door and he walked in. I motioned for him to sit down in a chair opposite me as I sat on the couch.

We sat there, me looking at him, he at the floor.

"Alan, did you kill Farad Sahari?"

"I didn't mean to. I just wanted to scare him, to make him never see you again. You'd think all the time I spent around Jake I'd know something about guns, but I don't. I didn't realize the safety wasn't on and when I shook the gun in his direction it went off. I'd never killed anyone before. I can't get the look on his face out of my mind. Jake came up with the idea of dumping his body in an old abandoned warehouse in Queens. I'm sorry."

I was shocked that he actually did do the killing, not some hit man as we theorized. I also really believed he was sorry.

"Alan, do you know why they let you go?"

"I'm not sure but I think it may be because they want us to succeed."

"Who wants you to succeed?"

"Why, the government, of course."

"The government?"

"Yes, they want us to destroy Mecca, but we have to do it on our own. They need to keep their hands clean."

"How do you know this?"

"I've listened in on some of Jake's conversations: CIA, military brass, even an elected official. At first they were skeptical that we could pull it off but as time went on and public opinion headed in our direction, they said to themselves: *What if they really could pull it off? That would destabilize the entire region and we could sit back and then come in at the right time.*"

"What about now? Do you believe in Jake? Do you really want to partner with him any more?"

"It doesn't really matter. He has the bomb. It was surprising how easy it was to obtain one. It's a vintage Soviet model. Weighs about half a ton. It was tricky trying to get a modern computer to properly interface with the bomb, but I finally got it to work.

"Jake purchased a state-of-the-art drone to get it to Mecca. This thing has all the bells and whistles. It will fly under and around any radar or detection system. He has the rest of my money. It doesn't matter."

He said this in such a deadpan manner and lack of emotion that he could have been reading a shopping list. There was nothing left inside this man.

I excused myself. He responded as I left the room.

"Yes, you go call your FBI friend. You're going to need to talk this over."

I looked at him as he sat there silently. I left the room and dialed.

"Hi Francine," he offered.

"It's Fava to you. Will, Westbrook is here. He's in my living room."

"He's what? You let that wacko into your apartment?"

"He's quite harmless, actually. He claimed killing Farad was an accident and I believe him. I've convinced him that Lawson killed his brother. I'm by no means a shrink but I think we took the last remaining bit of humanity from him. His brother and Lawson were his world. After his brother died, he only had his hero. There's now only a shell sitting there."

"You be careful. This guy is extremely unstable; he could change in a heartbeat. I'm coming right over."

"I appreciate your chivalry, Will, but I'll be alright. You're going to have plenty to do. I haven't told you the big news."

"What?"

"Westbrook said that Lawson has a bomb. Not only that, he has an unmanned drone that can get it to Mecca. And, he has the remainder of the money. Lastly, he confirmed that people high up in our government are supportive of their plan. That's why he was freed. Somebody very high up knows he is a key to helping Lawson successfully launch the drone."

"Oh my God."

"My thoughts exactly. He made it sound like the launch could be any day now."

"Meaning it will go off without warning, possibly killings hundreds of thousands if not millions."

"What do we do?"

"Fava, before I make a commitment to go full steam ahead on this can I ask a favor of you I have no right asking? I'll fully understand if you say no."

"Yes, Will, I'll do it."

"You don't even know what I'm going to ask."

"You're going to ask me to look after your kids if you get

arrested. Of course, that is provided that I don't get arrested, too."

I couldn't bring myself to add "or killed".

"How did you know?"

"I've come to know the kind of man you are. I know you'd never be able to look Albert and Stella in the eye again if you sat back and did nothing. But you want to make sure they are taken care of if anything happens to you. How'm I doing?"

"Nail on the head. I'm going to start making some calls. I have a few CIA contacts that I can make discreet calls to. See if I can get some intel. I'll be in touch."

I walked back out to the living room. Westbrook was still sitting there, motionless and detached.

"Alan, do you know where Lawson is?"

"No, ever since I returned from Paris he's never let on where he was. I'd get calls or emails from him but he'd never tell me where he was or exactly what he was doing. It was for my protection, he said. And I trusted him."

"And now?"

"I don't know."

"Alan, you were able to follow me, to track my whereabouts by monitoring all my electronic devices. Can you do the same with Lawson?"

"He's military, you're not. I'm pretty good, but it's going to take a lot more to break through the barriers and firewalls the military puts up."

"Alan, do you still believe in this cause? Knowing that you aren't avenging your brother's death; knowing that all you'd be doing is killing thousands of people who never did anything to you; is that what you want to do? I've only known you a short while but I don't believe that's you. It's not who you are."

Westbrook catatonically stared off into space. I thought I lost him into whatever world he escapes to. Then he snapped out of it and looked at me.

"No, it's not who I am. He should be stopped. I'll do whatever I can."

18

Will wasn't having any luck getting information or even having anyone hear him out. Everyone he talked with either feigned ignorance or obviously was not in the loop on what was really happening. Given the sensitivity of this issue, most likely the latter was the case. The people who actively supported an effort to destroy Mecca must be a very small—but also a very powerful—cadre of officials. I hoped he wasn't exposing himself too much. I didn't want to see him get arrested, or worse.

Alan stuck around my apartment for a couple more hours, mostly sitting there in a stupor, like he's been drugged. Then at one point he suddenly sat up and announced he was leaving. I had no power to stop him, nor did I really want to. He creeped me out. His behavior was extremely unpredictable and mercurial. I had no idea if or when he could resort to violence.

Before leaving he told me he'd stay in touch. He also said he was going to keep up his contact with Lawson, not letting on that anything had changed. He was going to try was to lead Lawson on, perhaps getting him to delay when the attack would take place. This would give us more time to figure out what we wanted to do.

Personally, I was without a clue as to what my next step could be. I'd talked to all my contacts that could be of help. I'd followed every lead I could and now was dry. I wracked my brain but could not come up with anybody. I called Frank and talked it over with him, but he couldn't think of anything either. I couldn't just sit around while the fate of the world teetered towards destruction.

I headed to the station. I needed the distraction of work for a bit. Perhaps something would come to me there. Ever since my kidnapping, Frank had been very lax about my schedule and my work assignments. I had to admit I took advantage of his leniency, picking and choosing when I went to the office and the stories I worked on. Perhaps it was unfair of me. Frank still felt guilty about putting me in danger's way and I knew he wouldn't say anything to me in the way of a reprimand for my slack attitude, at least not for a while yet.

Anyway, I decided to grace the office with my presence. I went into my purse to get my lipstick to touch up some when I found Inspector Paul Murat's card. I'd completely forgotten I had his card. That ill-fated trip to Paris was a blur to me, like someone else had taken it.

I wondered.

I looked at the clock and did a quick calculation. It would only be 3:30 in the morning in Paris right now. I had to wait at least six or seven hours before calling. I pulled myself together and headed to work.

"Francine, come on in," Frank called out as soon as he saw me. I walked into his office. He closed the door behind me.

"Francine," he began, "you have to move on. I know you feel sorry about Sahari. I know you think the fate of the world rests on your shoulders. But you're not the police. You're not the FBI. You're a damn good reporter and I need you back here full time. With the recent budget cutbacks and our consistent low ratings, it's all hands on deck, everyone needs to give their all."

"I'm sorry, Frank. I know I've been slacking off lately, leaving you in the lurch. I've taken advantage of your good nature, and not to mention your guilt, and I'll get better."

Frank held up his hand, cutting me off.

"Okay, I got that off my chest and you responded appropriately. Now, you can tell me what you're really going to do. Before you respond let me tell you that, despite the little speech I just gave officially for the record, whatever you choose to do I'm behind you one hundred percent."

"You are? Because I was just going to tell you that despite my response, I have a new lead I want to follow up to help stop Lawson."

"Good," his tone was decisive, "you can tell me or not. Don't stop going after that motherfucker. You and Allen make a good team, in more ways than one if you get my drift."

I did. I left his office energized.

A few hours later I dialed the international access number, the country code for France and the prefecture of police for the First Arrondisement of Paris.

"Bonjour," a sprightly female voice intoned over the line.

"Hello, Inspector Murat, please. This is Francine Vega from New York."

The voice, which switched immediately to English and seemed a trifle colder, responded.

"One minute, please."

A few seconds later a male voice came on.

"Allô, Ms. Vega."

"Hello, Inspector Murat. I wasn't sure you'd remember me."

"Yes, Miss Vega, I remember you very well. To what do I owe the honor of this call?"

"Have you discovered who murdered Captain L'Eglise?"

"No, unfortunately we have not made any arrests yet."

"I believe I may have some additional information about his murder."

There was silence. I didn't want to let on that I knew this information back when the inspector interviewed me in Paris. I didn't want an obstruction of justice, or whatever they called this type of charge in France, leveled against me.

"What is this information?"

"I know who murdered him, or at least who made the arrangements for the killing."

"And how did you come to obtain this information?"

"It arose out of a story I've been working on."

"I see. And who is the murderer?"

"His name is Colonel Jacob Lawson."

"A colonel?"

"Yes, in the United States Army."

"I see."

I could tell he didn't believe me, although why I would make an intercontinental call a month later to lie to him was beyond me.

"Ms. Vega, why do you believe that this American colonel is wandering about killing French policemen?"

This was going to be harder than I thought. I was beginning to wish I hadn't called.

"Inspector, I know because his accomplice confessed it to me. He knew details that could only be known by someone who knew or who was responsible. He knew that Captain L'Eglise's death had nothing to do with a mob hit. Rather, it was related to the fact that the captain was a boyhood friend of an Arab named Farad Sahari and was helping Sahari."

"I see."

This time the way he said 'I see' gave me hope that maybe he thought I wasn't leading him along.

"What was he helping this Mr. Sahari do?"

"Foil a plot to destroy Mecca, in Saudi Arabia."

There was silence again as he absorbed what I'd just said.

"Why don't you start from the beginning?"

I laid it all out for the Inspector: the lottery, the Westbrook brothers, Lawson, the five pillars of Islam, Farad, L'Eglise, my kidnapping, all of it. I didn't bother with the latest revelation that Lawson had in fact killed Frederick Westbrook; it didn't seem relevant to L'Eglise. I even confessed that the reason I gave for being in Paris was not what I had told the police. The Inspector politely let me tell the entire story, only occasionally interrupting for a clarification on something that I did not explain clearly.

"Miss Vega, you do realize how preposterous this story sounds?"

"Yes, I do. I realize that I must sound like a raving lunatic, but it's true. Feel free to contact Special Agent William Allen of the FBI to confirm my account. He can be reached at 212-555-1236."

"Let us assume everything you tell me is true. Why are you calling me? What do you hope I can do for you?"

"I called for two reasons. First, Captain L'Eglise should have justice. His murderer should be hunted down. Perhaps this information can point your men in a different direction."

"And the second?"

"Lawson has the bomb and a drone to get it to Mecca. He has to be stopped."

"How can I do that?"

"I think he may still be in France. Maybe even in Paris. I believe someone very high up in the U.S. government is helping him; they actually want him to succeed. We're being stymied here and I was hoping you could help."

"Miss Vega, this is a lot for me to comprehend. I will have to talk with my superiors here before we can do anything."

"I understand. But you must hurry. He may be planning to detonate the bomb any day now."

"I will get back to you soon. Good bye."

Fifteen minutes later my untraceable phone buzzed. Knowing it was Will, I answered without a greeting.

"I guess he didn't believe me, did he?"

"No, Fava, he really thought you were crazy. Good move on your part, getting the French authorities involved. The Inspector was good; he asked all the right questions. He was a little annoyed that you didn't divulge information earlier but I talked him out of pursuing any charges."

"Thanks, Will."

"Although it would have been kind of eerie if I had gotten a call to pick you up on an international warrant for obstruction of justice. In any case, he said he was going to do some digging and was going to talk with the French version of the CIA to see if there's been any chatter about a high-level arms deal going down.

"In the meantime, I've finally found someone who will at least talk to me, off-the-record of course."

"Who?"

"Well, talk about full circle, it's Edward McKenzie."

"The State Department guy?"

"The same. It was one of those friend of a friend of a friend things. When I identified myself and told him about what I was looking for, his response was: 'Oh my God'. He told me about talking with you and Sahari and that he didn't take you seriously and blabbed the whole thing to his brother, who in turn made himself a national figure. After I explained that there actually was a plot to destroy Mecca, I could literally hear him kicking himself, calling himself and his brother 'world-class assholes'."

"That pretty much sums it up."

"Well, he's seeing the light now. At least we have one ally in another Federal agency. I told him to be careful, that there were very high-level people actually backing this plot. Some of them could even be in the State Department. He appreciated the heads-up and said he would be discreet in his inquiries."

"Will, I still can't get my head around the fact that anybody in an official capacity could support this."

"Why not? Given the reaction to Reverend McKenzie's sermons, there's obviously some level of public support, even if it's only the more ignorant segments of our society. And there are plenty of supposed patriots like Lawson who firmly believe we never extracted enough revenge for 9/11 but they know that the US can never officially take the appropriate action. This set-up provides them with the perfect scenario: a wacko uses his newfound fortune to finance a private ultimate attack while the government can stand back and say: shame, shame. They can further deflect blame by pointing at the reverend. After the fact, they may make a big show of going after Lawson, of course killing him before he can say anything."

"Lawson's a pretty smart guy, isn't he? Don't you think he's thought this all through to the end, including an escape?"

"Oh, I'm sure he has but I'm certain he'd be perfectly comfortable if he were captured and killed. In his own eyes, he'll die a hero and a patriot. But like you said, I wouldn't be surprised if he has an escape scenario all worked out. Remember, he has the rest of Westbrook's money."

"This is all very depressing. If that's the way we are, maybe we should just let it happen. We'll have World War III that will obliterate all of us and the remnants can start over again, just like one of those old apocalyptic movies."

"I still have some residual faith in humanity."

"So what's next?"

"We should perhaps give Mr. Fakhoury another visit."

"I thought you said you'd cleared him of any wrong-doing."

"I did, but perhaps he can help us save the world, Fava."

19

"So, to what do I owe the pleasure of a return visit?" Mahmoud Fakhoury asked as we sat once again in his office. "May I offer you some tea?"

We declined the tea, preferring to launch into our foreboding litany of possible events that could be devastating to his people. For the most part, it was a reiteration of what I'd told Inspector Murat. Will did most of the talking, with me filling in a few details here and there. When we were done, Fakhoury was ashen.

"When we talked before, it all sounded so theoretical, so preposterous. Now, you are telling me this may actually happen."

He paused and gazed out the window.

"No wonder Farad seemed preoccupied with something momentous in his last days. I must assume it was this news that was such a burden on my dear friend. Is anyone looking for this man Lawson? Shouldn't there be world-wide alerts or something?"

"There should be, yes, but we're having problems getting anyone to take us seriously."

I didn't want to mention that there were actually people in the government who supported this plan.

"We'd heard about that preacher who promoted such evil, but nobody took him seriously. There were those in my country who said we should be more forceful in our protest of the hateful things he was saying, but I thought he would get a few headlines and then disappear into obscurity. I said the worst thing we could do was to voice our objections, especially after my organization was blamed for the bombing in Topeka. Our protests would have prolonged his place in the news even longer. Little did I know he was a seer of the future. What can we do now?"

"We don't know when the bomb will be launched or from where," Will explained. "Initially, we were assured by Mr.

Westbrook that it would be a time when the fewest number of pilgrims were in Mecca. He also made it sound like warning would be given so that people had a chance to flee. I don't think Westbrook was ever pulling any of the strings. He was just the purse. What I'm saying is we don't know. It could happen in five years or it could be happening right now as we speak. Lawson could very well want to do it in the middle of the Hajj, which I understand begins in a week."

Mahmoud Fakhoury was too dumbfounded to respond. Will continued.

"We came to you to appeal to your Muslim friends to stop the Hajj, to keep the pilgrims out. You also should see if you can evacuate the town."

"You just don't understand. Attempting to stop the Hajj is like trying to stop the ocean waves from lapping up on the shore. The people come from the four corners of the earth. Even if you told the world of the dangers, the people will come."

"Can you plead with your governments to step up their patrols and monitoring? We don't know where this drone will be coming from and it will be flying very, very low to avoid radar detection but a vigilant air force would be able to spot it crossing your border and shoot it down."

Fakhoury smiled.

"Mr. Allen, you must be mistaking our military capabilities for that of America or Israel. Our military forces are designed to keep people in check and to repulse a traditional attack. Something as small as this would undoubtedly evade detection. But, I will see what I can do. I fear I may receive the same reaction from my people as you got from yours, but I will try."

When we left Mr. Fakhoury, we were even more depressed than we already had been. Will and I kissed and each of us headed back to our respective offices to do some actual work.

An hour later my phone, my official phone that is, beeped. I recognized from the sound that a text had just come in. I looked at it.

Thursday, was all it said.

Westbrook had contacted Lawson and gotten the date. He was aiming for six days from now, which was also the second day of the Hajj, a day when there could be a million or more people in or around Mecca. He truly was looking to murder as many Muslims as he could. We didn't have much time to get people to believe us. We had to act. But what could we do?

Every bit of information we had was laced with innuendo and suppositions. Everyone we spoke with who knew Lawson fully believed he was not only capable of pulling this off but would also be fully willing, all cloaked in super-patriotism.

The Parisian Inspector was at least willing to pursue further inquiry, but what could he do? If Lawson was still in fact in Paris, that could be a positive. But we didn't know how good Inspector Murat was at his job, what resources he had at his disposal, how full his workload already was, how successful he could be at convincing his bureaucracy that he needed to invest time on this case, etc.

We'd run dry on this side of the Atlantic, however. I didn't like us having to take matters into our own hands, but it was heading in that direction.

20

My cell phone rang. It was the untraceable one so I assumed it was Will.

"Hi Will, what's up?"

I was taken aback when a different male voice responded.

"Miss Vega, this is Agent Willoughby."

Willoughby? What was he doing on the line? My mind raced back to the encounters I had with him, none of which were good. My first thought was that he was Lawson's man inside the Bureau, but Will swore for him.

"Hello Agent Willoughby, where's Will?"

"Special Agent Allen asked me to call you. There's been a development."

I hated this bureaucratic speak. I wished he just got to the point already.

"Somebody's taken Stella, Allen's daughter."

"What? No!"

"He arrived home last night to find his son and their nanny tied up and gagged. There was a note: Back off or she dies. He wanted me to tell you all this."

"Where is he?"

"He's off the grid, gone underground. We won't hear from him until he's found her."

I could sense Willoughby choking up a little before continuing.

"Will's the best. If anyone can track her down, it'll be him. I've seen it. He tracked me after I was abducted and saved my life.

"He didn't share what he knew or who exactly he suspected, but I believe he had a pretty good idea. He'll get Stella back. You mark my words."

"Thank you for letting me know, Agent Willoughby."

"You're welcome, ma'am. There's one more thing. Will told me to tell you to keep on, don't let this deter you from doing what you need to do. Full speed ahead. Those were his exact words, full speed ahead. He said you'd know what that meant."

"I do."

I hung up and then marched into Frank's office, closing the door behind me. Frank looked up from his paperwork, but he didn't look entirely surprised to see me. I sat down and launched into what I wanted to do.

"Frank, I want to do a piece that will undoubtedly get us both fired, or worse."

"I do have to say, Francine, that in all my career that is absolutely the worst pitch for a story I've ever heard. But then again, you do have my attention."

"Then it can't be the worst, can it? Frank, Lawson's plot to destroy Mecca, it's real. He's planning to send a drone carrying a nuclear device into Mecca next Thursday. It's the second day of the Hajj. There could be over a million people around Mecca at the time.

"We've tried everything, but nobody seems to be taking this seriously. We think high government officials may be involved. I believe we may be getting close, however. Special Agent Allen's four year-old daughter has been kidnapped. Will's trying to find her right now but he's told me to keep on course, doing everything I can to thwart this lunacy."

Frank sat there thunderstruck.

"You're sure about all this?"

"Do you mean I have a smoking gun? No, most everything I have is circumstantial and speculative but there's so much of it that, yes, I'm absolutely positive about this."

"And you want to do a story on the air."

"Yes, I want to expose Lawson. Perhaps this would flush him out."

"You do remember Reverend McKenzie, don't you? He became popular overnight supporting the exact thing you're saying the public will rise up against."

"I'm still an optimist. I hope the people clapping the loudest for McKenzie were the lunatic fringes. The rest of us just looked at him as a diverting freak show."

"You are starry-eyed, aren't you? Well, I'm going to hope your optimism is well placed and tell you to go for it. You're going to name names, right?"

I nodded.

"Since we're obviously not going to go through legal, this piece is going to have to be the tightest you've ever done. You have to get everything you want across in the first 45 seconds, max. I can't guarantee that the plug won't be pulled anytime after that. Got it?"

"Yes, Frank."

"We're going to have to disguise it on the schedule. It has to sound like an innocuous puff piece. Perhaps the suits won't even be listening until it's too late. Then we'll see how the chips fall. I'm proud of you Francine, following through like this."

"Thank you, Frank, for everything. I better get to work."

As was getting up to leave, Frank happened to glance at his computer screen.

"Hold on, Francine."

I sat back down.

"We may not have to disguise this at all. I just got an alert. The FBI and NYPD are at this very moment raiding the Arab-American Friendship League headquarters. Mahmoud Fakhoury has been taken into custody. The charges haven't been officially announced but it's speculated they'll be related to the bombing in Topeka and then the subsequent murder of Farad Sahari, who was going to snitch on the group."

"What? This can't be. Will had cleared them. They didn't do anything. They're being framed!"

"You and Jonas get over there right away. See what you can dig up."

Twenty minutes later Jonas and I walked up to the brownstone. Numerous agents and police officers were walking down the front steps carrying boxes of files, computers and whatever they could get their hands on. Everyone doing the carrying was in some sort of uniform, either the police blues or the windbreakers with FBI emblazoned on the back. Standing off to the side was a stocky man with brown wavy hair and a gray suit. Will had once pointed him out as one of the agency's press spokesmen. He was very green, having just started with the bureau a month or so ago.

"Come on Jonas, start shooting. And keep shooting regardless of what I say."

We walked over to him.

"Excuse me, I'm Francine Vega with Action 6 News. You're with the FBI, aren't you?"

"Yes, I'm Richard Cowen, public relations specialist for the New York office."

His glance darted back and forth between the camera and me.

"Can I ask you a few questions about what's going on here?"

"I really don't know how much I can tell or if I should really be talking on camera. I'm just waiting for my boss."

"We can just talk, if you like. It will be totally off-the-record."

I signaled for Jonas to lower his camera, which he did. But, as he rested the camera on his hip by his side, he kept the lens on the FBI rep and the trigger depressed. Normally, my journalistic ethics would not have allowed him to tape this interview after I said we wouldn't record it. However, this was not about the story; it was about possibly saving the world.

"Thank you. What do you want to know?"

"Can you tell me what charges have been made against Mr. Fakhoury and the Arab-American Friendship League?"

"I'm not at liberty to discuss that right now. It will come out in due time."

"I happen to know that Mr. Fakhoury and the League were cleared by the FBI of any involvement in either the Topeka bombing or in the murder of Farad Sahari. Have there been new developments?"

"I'm not sure where you got your information that the Arab-American Friendship League and its officials have been cleared."

"I was told this by Special Agent William Allen."

"Special Agent Allen is himself under investigation. A warrant has been issued for his arrest."

"What?"

"Yes, we have an all-out alert for his arrest. He suddenly disappeared from his office and we haven't yet apprehended him."

"He disappeared because his daughter was kidnapped!"

"I know nothing about that, ma'am. If it's a kidnapping, I'm sure other units of the bureau are actively hunting for his daughter, if in fact she has been kidnapped as Special Agent Allen alleges."

I was furious with this bureaucrat and his smug answers but I had to keep my cool, for Will's and my sakes. I decided to ask a few more inane questions to make Mr. Cowan continue to believe he had the upper hand.

"Can you tell me what was being removed from the League offices?"

"Mostly financial records, primarily to ascertain if there is any involvement with terrorist activities."

"I see. Can you tell me what will happen next?"

"I'm really not sure. Most likely Mr. Fakhoury and the others will be charged and indicted."

"Well, thank you for your time."

I shook his hand and turned to walk away. I took one step and then turned back.

"Oh, one last question: Do you know Colonel Jacob Lawson?"

The question definitely caught Cowan off guard. I could see a flash of recognition in his eyes before he composed himself.

"What was the name again?" he stalled.

"Colonel Jacob Lawson, he's Army in the Pentagon."

"No, I'm not familiar with the name. Why?"

"Oh, nothing, I'd heard his name in conjunction with the League and wanted to see if there was any truth. Thanks again for your time."

Jonas and I headed back to the subway.

"Did you get it all?" I asked him as we walked along.

"Yup, and not bad either, considering how I had to hold it. Gives new meaning to shooting from the hip, huh?"

"Very funny, let's get back."

We decided I would do a live spot from the studio, weaving in footage from the FBI raid. My mind kept racing, worrying about Stella. Lawson was absolutely ruthless and amoral. He'd show absolutely no remorse about ordering a four-year old girl murdered. I wondered if Will had any leads to finding her. Now that he was wanted himself, I wasn't sure how seriously the FBI was taking the kidnapping threat.

I'd never heard anyone speak about another human being the way Willoughby spoke about Will, however. It was beyond hero admiration; this was absolute reverence. Willoughby fully believed that Will would find Stella, unharmed and no worse for wear.

In the meantime, I had this piece to do. It had to be absolutely perfect and the tightest thing I ever did. I could just imagine the network's attorneys' blood pressure shooting through the roof the first time I mentioned that the government was involved or at least tacitly condoned a terrorist plot. I agreed somewhat with Frank that, once I did get into the meat of the story, I had to be right to the point. There would be a short window before Frank got the call to pull the plug. However, I did think I had to take a minute or so to set the stage. The raid gave me the perfect opportunity to do just that.

Frank was allocating me three minutes, an eternity in broadcast news. In the first minute I'd be able to describe the raid and offer some speculation about why it happened. Although the FBI still had not officially stated the charges that were to be filed against Fakhoury and the League, enough sources were unofficially talking that it was pretty obvious what the charges would eventually be. Network executives would not be threatened and may even be lulled into a false sense of security, if they were watching me at all.

The Arab-American story was to be third on the schedule, right after we came back from commercial break. Gil Patrick, our 6:00 anchorman, was a little surprised when the first segment ended and Frank escorted me out to sit in a chair beside him. Frank explained that the piece was to be done live and was allocated a full three minutes. Gil, who was very organized and could get easily flustered if things did not go precisely as scheduled, seemed rather disjointed. He asked a lot of questions about what his role would be. Frank repeatedly told him to introduce me and then just sit back. I'd be handling the entire segment. Gil was skeptical and none too happy, but there was nothing he could do.

We were about to come back from the break when Frank rushed into the studio. Jonas was with him.

"Francine, quick, come with me. You have to get out of here."

He turned to Gil.

"Gil, we're going to skip the Arab-American story. Go on to wounded veterans. We'll figure out what to fill in later."

To emphasize that he wasn't kidding, he grabbed me by the arm and started pulling me toward the back exit.

"The FBI, they're on their way up. They have a warrant for your arrest. We have to get you out of here."

We raced through the door to the back stairs.

"Arrest? What do they want to arrest me for?"

"I didn't get any details. I just know you have to get out of here. I'll deal with them. I anticipated you'd need to make a hasty getaway after your story so I already have a car waiting for you. Jonas will go with you."

Jonas and I ran down the thirty floors to the parking garage. We exited the building through the loading dock.

As promised, a sedan was waiting for us. There was a driver I didn't recognize but that didn't bother me. We were always hiring somebody's cousin or nephew for these types of jobs.

Because of his size, I told Jonas to sit in the front as I slid into the back seat. It wasn't until I was already in that I noticed another man back there. I tried to exit but he grabbed my arm as he instructed the driver to start driving. When Jonas began to protest, the driver pulled out a handgun that he laid across his lap, thus ending any further discussion.

My mind immediately went back to Paterson. I was being kidnapped again, and there was nothing I could do about it. This time, however, Westbrook wouldn't be able to intervene. I was going to die. My main regret was that I'd dragged poor Jonas into this. If I didn't deserve this fate, Jonas certainly didn't either.

We drove on in silence for a few minutes when a loud thud came from the trunk area. My backseat companion didn't seem to notice. When it happened again he turned to me.

"That's the person who was supposed to drive you. He's quite all right. He'll be released, along with his car, when we get to our destination."

"Which is?" I asked.

The man said nothing in response but looked forward, resuming his silence.

When we entered the Mid-Town Tunnel, my heart began to race. All I could think of was that Farad had been killed in Queens and that was to be my fate as well. I needed to figure out a way to get Jonas and me out, but these men were armed. And while they lacked Jonas's size and bulk, they both looked exceedingly fit. We'd be no match.

We merged onto the Long Island Expressway and worked our way across Queens. Soon we were out of the city. Twenty minutes later we turned off the highway and were on the local streets of Hicksville. I was totally out of my element now. I was going to be rubbed out in the suburbs. We pulled up to an abandoned warehouse. As we started to slow, Jonas made his move.

He dove on the driver, reaching for the gun and shouting to me at the same time.

"Run, Frannie, run."

I opened the door and before the guy in back could have a chance to reach for me, I bolted. I saw the driver pick up his gun and bring it down hard on the back of Jonas's head. His body slumped; he was unconscious. I was torn. Part of me wanted to help him but I knew I'd be more help if I were free.

I ran as fast as I could around the corner of the warehouse. As I turned the corner, a door opened. I could not change course and ran directly into the person emerging through the door. I assumed it was the man designated to kill me.

After our bodies crashed, we both went flying, me much further than him. I got up to continue my flight when he called out to me.

"Fava! Wait!"

Hearing those words made me the most relieved I'd ever been in my life. I ran into his arms. Almost immediately, my thoughts of joy vanished.

"Stella! Do you have any news?"

"Better than that."

As if on cue, the door opened once again and Stella flew into my arms.

"My little girl, are you okay?"

"Fava, Daddy came and got me," she replied matter-of-factly.

"I'm sure you were very brave."

"I was," she responded seriously.

I gave her one more hug as Will told her to go back inside.

"It was rather easy finding her, actually. A couple amateurs had her. They were more scared than she was. Even if Lawson gave the order, I doubt they'd have killed her. Still, they're lucky to be alive; Willoughby talked me out of putting bullets in their heads. But I couldn't let them off scot-free. Let's just say they're going to walk with limps the rest of their lives."

Will escorted me into the warehouse. A generation ago it was a pickle and vinegar factory. The not overly unpleasant smell of vinegar still pervaded the interior all these years later.

Will's men extricated the driver from the trunk and helped Jonas, who was just coming to, out of the car. A few minutes later we were all sitting in an old office in the warehouse.

When we walked in, Willoughby was already there.

"Francine, you know Agent Willoughby and this is Agent Fallon and Agent Broderick. I'm sorry about the cloak and dagger stuff. A miscommunication fuck-up, I'm afraid. I had to get you away from the station after your broadcast so I arranged for your escape with Frank. Unfortunately, we didn't have a lot of time to firm up the details. So when my men showed up and there was a driver there, they had to act. Likewise when you showed up early with Jonas, they didn't feel they could let on who they were or that they were with me until it was safe.

"I apologize, Jonas, for the lump on your head. Likewise, Mr. Langford, I apologize for you being manhandled and your subsequent ride in the trunk."

Langford looked like a deer in the headlights as he accepted Will's apology. Jonas was rather sullen as he nursed the bump with a bag of ice.

"You gentlemen are free to go."

Broderick handed Langford the keys to the car we'd just arrived in.

"Francine and I would sincerely appreciate it if you didn't go to the authorities, at least not for 48 hours or so, but the choice is yours. We did break the law in abducting you."

As I mentioned earlier, often times the workers who shuttle us around a relatives of station executives. Langford I knew to be Frank's nephew so there was a good chance he wasn't going to say anything. He took the keys and started for the door. He looked back to see if Jonas was following him. Jonas looked up.

"I ain't going nowhere. I'm staying with you, Frannie."

Langford headed out the door and a few seconds later we could hear the car drive away. Will turned to Broderick.

"Rick, you know where you're going, correct?"

"Sure thing, Will. Don't worry, she'll be safe. I'll call you when I get there and then I'll stay there until you tell me otherwise."

Will put his hand on Broderick's shoulder.

"You're a good man. Thanks."

Will went in to another room and emerged with Stella. He knelt down beside her.

"Honey, you're going to go with Uncle Rick now, okay?"

"Can't you come along, Daddy? And Fava too?"

"Not right now, but we'll be with you soon. Daddy and Fava have some things we need to do. But soon you'll be with Albie and Emma. You'll be at Emma's mommy's house out in the country. You remember we went there last year for a visit?"

"Yes, Daddy."

"We'll come and get you as soon as we can. I need you to be very brave, okay?"

"Okay."

She didn't look overly convinced, but she would soldier on. She looked over at me.

"Don't I get a hug goodbye?" I asked.

She ran into my arms once again. I held her tight and then let her go. She took Agent Broderick's hand as they walked away. I returned back to Will.

"Where's he taking her?"

"You remember Emma, our housekeeper slash nanny? Her mother's got a place upstate. Emma and Albert are there already; Stella will join them. They'll be safe, especially with Rick there, too.

"I still don't understand how you found Stella so quickly."

"I have to admit that I did have some help."

We walked into a separate room and hunched over a laptop computer on a wooden table was Alan Westbrook. He was so intent on clicking away that he didn't hear us enter.

"He came to me after he got news that Lawson had ordered Stella kidnapped. He'd already soured on Lawson once you convinced him that Lawson had killed his brother. He offered his help in tracking down Stella. He sat down at the computer and a few clicks later he had a bead on her captors. He was able to get the morons' cellphone numbers and then home in on their GPSs. We raided the house and got her back. Then he came here with us, offering his help to stop this insane plot."

"You trust him?"

"I don't have a lot of choice."

"What's he doing now?"

"Trying to get into Lawson's computer."

Despite the fact that we were standing right next to him, we'd been talking about him as if he weren't in the room. He was so intent on his computer screen, we might have well not have been there. Then, without greeting or acknowledgment, he looked up and spoke to us. In the vernacular of a teenager: he was so over me.

"I designed his computer system; you'd think I'd be able to hack in but he's had somebody else insert a new code. This is going to take me awhile. I have a couple things in there that should help me get around whatever they installed."

He paused as he unleashed a furiously paced series of clicks on the keyboard. As he continued typing, I asked him a question.

"What do you hope to accomplish by hacking into his computer?"

"I'm hoping to stop him from launching the drone. He must suspect I've turned on him, since the computer isn't responding. He must have had someone reprogram it to get rid of my access. Little does he know that I buried secret codes deep within the algorithms of the computer, just in case. I have to remember how to get to them and how to access them remotely without his catching on. So, if you'll excuse me I have a lot of work to do."

Will and I let him be, leaving the room and closing the door behind us.

"What's going to happen to him?" I wondered out loud.

"Well, he's going to stand trial for Sahari's death. He's admitted he did it and is very sorry. He said that it was a mistake. At the time, threatening him seemed like the right thing to do but now he knows it was very wrong. He said he's not going to accept any deals and is willing to serve the maximum sentence. However, I suppose if he's instrumental in helping us to save the world, that would have to say something."

Will turned to me and took my hands in his.

"What do you think should happen to him, Fava? I know you were very close to Sahari."

"I honestly don't know. He's obviously a very troubled person, brilliant but troubled. Farad deserves justice, but there are all sorts of issues at play here. The one thing that I'm thankful for is that Westbrook's infatuation with me has waned substantially."

"I guess I'm safe then."

"We'll see. I do have legions of men irrationally devoted to me. You can never tell what they'll do."

We laughed and then settled in. There was nothing for us to do, not until Westbrook made a breakthrough. Of the five of us—Will, me, Jonas and Agents Willoughby and Fallon—only Willoughby was doing anything worthwhile as he listened through headphones to police frequencies to ensure that no one was on Will's or my trail as of yet.

Fallon got up, proclaiming he needed a cigarette and was going to step out for a few minutes to smoke. Will said he needed some air and offered to join him. Jonas's head was feeling better and he asked if could tag along.

As they left, Willoughby took his headphones off for a little break himself.

"Anything of note on those things?" I asked him.

"Cops are responding to a burglary about four blocks from here."

"Maybe I should head over to cover it. I'd probably beat all other reporters there."

"Yes, I'd imagine you would," he responded.

"So, are you here in any official capacity?"

"Hell no. I doubt I have a job anymore, but I wasn't going to let Will fight this alone."

"That's very loyal of you. You did say he saved your life?"

"I was a green rookie and stupidly got myself captured by a couple of meth-heads. Boy, were they out of their gourds. I was sure I was going to be shot any moment. Just when I thought they were going to do it, Will dropped out of the ductwork in the ceiling and took them out with one shot each. He said it took him nearly forty-five minutes to crawl through the ducts to get to me. He was all scraped up by the ordeal but he kept on. Our bosses were planning on a frontal assault, but he was sure I'd get killed in the process and so he volunteered to make the crawl. So, yes, after that you can say I'm loyal and will do anything for that man."

"I totally understand. He said you talked him out of killing the men who took Stella."

"I doubt he would have gone through with it, regardless of how blind he was with fury. He's just not that type of guy. Didn't stop him from putting a bullet in their kneecaps, though. But then he ordered them dropped off in front of the hospital."

The thought of a man I was involved with coolly shooting someone in the kneecap gave me a shudder. But then again, I've come to love Stella in a very short time, and she wasn't mine. I'm not sure I wouldn't have done the same thing if I were in his shoes. A part of me, however, didn't think it took too much convincing by Willoughby—if any at all—for Will to only maim rather than kill the men who'd kidnapped his daughter. Despite his love for Stella, Will was not a murderer.

Not long after, Will, Jonas and Fallon came back and we assumed our previous positions in silence. We occupied ourselves as best we could, either with old magazines or by surfing on our smart phones. I'm not sure what we were waiting for. I guess we were each hoping Westbrook would suddenly barge in with news that he'd disabled Lawson's computer, stopping the launch, and had contacted authorities who in turn had taken Lawson into custody.

We'd been waiting a couple of hours when Will's cellphone rang. He answered it, said thank you and hung up.

"Rick's at the place. Stella's safe," was all he said.

An hour later, Westbrook burst into our room with news.

"Well, good news and bad news. I've located Jake. He's in

Israel. But I was unable to disarm the bomb or stop the launch. Someone has completely altered the codes and put in a new firewall that I can't get through. The codes I've buried still allow me to get the computer's location but not much more than that."

"Israel?" Will asked.

"Yes, the coordinates indicate he's somewhere in the Negev Desert. My guess is that the drone and bomb are also located somewhere in the Negev, but not super close to him."

I suspected that Westbrook knew more—perhaps the exact location of Lawson or even how to disarm the bomb—but he was playing his cards close to his vest. He was aware that if he divulged too much, his usefulness would be greatly diminished. He wanted to stay involved.

I looked at Will and the look on his face indicated that he suspected as much too. A set of GPS coordinates provides an exact location, not just "somewhere in the Negev." Will and I both knew that you could push a person in as tenuous mental state as Westbrook only so far. Cross over that line and Westbrook would shut down completely. We needed him. It was better to play along and coax information out of him gradually.

"So you're saying that someone needs to get to Israel, track down Lawson, neutralize him and then figure out how to disarm or at least divert the bomb?"

Westbrook nodded but said nothing more. Will stood there, thinking. I pulled him aside so that Westbrook could not hear us.

"Shouldn't we contact the Defense Department, the CIA, somebody who can take the steps to stop him?"

"That would probably be the most logical thing to do, but we have less than two days. Remember, we've both become persona non grata. By the time we convince anybody that they should actually listen to us, the drone will be on its way."

We hadn't noticed Westbrook sidle his way over to us like a cat and was listening in.

"Plus," he interjected, surprising us out of our skins, "destroying or shutting down the computer won't work. The computer on the drone is specially designed to take over if it stops receiving signals from the base program. There would be no way to stop it from taking off or the detonation sequence from initiating. Jake picked a drone to deliver the bomb because it is so small. By the time the authorities figured out that they weren't tracking a bird, Mecca would be obliterated. Furthermore, the drone is state-of-the-art. It has anti-radar technology on it so once it's on its way, it'll probably take visual sighting to bring it down.

"I can probably figure out how to disarm it, but it'll take me a few days, by which time the launch will happen. I need to be there."

Now he was basically bragging about his work. I wanted to slug the guy, but he was correct: we needed him.

"Well, there's no way I can trust you, so you can't go alone but I have no way of getting us out of the country," Will replied in exasperation.

"Hold on a second," I told them both. I grabbed my cellphone and walked out of the room. A half hour later, I walked back in.

"Okay, we have three tickets on El Al for Tel Aviv. The plane leaves in four hours out of JFK. Alan, do you have a passport?"

"I have it on me."

"Good," I then called out to Agent Fallon, who came in.

"Agent Fallon, we need you to go to our places and pick up our passports. Here's my address and keys. As you enter my apartment, my office is the first room on the right as you walk in. My passport's in the top left-hand drawer of my desk. Tell the doorman you're there to pick up something for me. I'll call him and tell him to expect you. Will, give him your keys and any special instructions."

Will was rather bewildered but complied without objection. Fallon left.

"Fava, what's going on here? How can we leave the country? I'm sure we're on watch lists and will be stopped in the terminal."

"We're going to be traveling under emergency diplomatic visas. We're going to be escorted through customs by the

Department of State. And, we'll be picked up in Israel by the Israeli Army."

"How'd did you do this?" Will asked.

"I'll explain later."

An hour later, Agent Fallon returned with our passports and then drove us to the airport. As I predicted, a member of the State Department was there. He gave us each our special papers to ease our travel. I felt like we were in *Casablanca* and Rick was handing us our letters of transit that would ensure we could go anywhere without question.

The State Department man, who never did identify himself by name but said he was a close friend of McKenzie, also handed over a small plastic computer attachment to Westbrook. It was a device that would enable his computer to access the Internet via satellite anywhere in the world. Where we were going, it was doubtful he'd be able to tap into a reliable wi-fi source.

The agent, or whatever he called himself, escorted us through security to a waiting room, where we waited for about an hour at which point we were escorted onto the plane. We were provided first class accommodations. I worked it so Will and I would sit together and Westbrook would be a couple of rows ahead of us. That way, we could talk in confidence and Westbrook could be alone with his thoughts, which I think is where he preferred to be anyway.

"Okay," Will asked once we were settled, "how'd you arrange all this?"

I was more than a little proud of myself for pulling this all together.

"I made two phone calls. The first was to McKenzie. You said you spoke to him and he was full of remorse at blabbing to his brother. I called him and explained the situation and he felt even more guilt. He at first said that this should be handed over to other agencies, probably the CIA. I explained about Westbrook and his computer skills and how he probably would not work with anybody but you and me. After that, he put me on hold and started the wheels turning on this end."

"And the second call?"

"While I was on hold, I called Inspector Murat in Paris and went through the same deal with him. After he'd called you to verify my credibility, he'd done an awful lot of work and was able to verify that Lawson had been in Paris and had worked with a well-known high-level arms dealer who was based in Switzerland. He worked with the DGSE, France's equivalent of our CIA to kidnap the dealer, bring him back to Paris and extract information from him."

"I'm guessing 'extracting information' is a euphemism for torture."

"I didn't ask nor did I especially care. Anyway, they confirmed that he'd secured a small nuclear device for Lawson for about $200 million."

"A real bargain."

"The dealer also knew that the bomb was delivered to Israel though a certain faction in the Israeli secret service."

"I'll bet there are certain Israelis who'd think obliterating Mecca a lovely idea."

"Lawson subsequently left for Israel to unite with his bomb and obtain a drone. In the meantime, our good friend Alan—who was still in the thrall of his friend Jake—worked on the computer program to guide the drone and arm the bomb."

"I guess our newfound companion here is a bone fide genius?"

"It was hard to guess when I first met him. But the guy was a top-notch lawyer as well as a computer geek. His apartment was a hovel, but there was computer equipment all around. When I talked to the super, he said Westbrook told him to take it all."

"Sooner rather than later he's gonna have to let on where Lawson is."

"He will, but he'll dribble the info we need out bit by bit so he can maintain control and stay involved. He needs us. I think we're the only "friends" he has. That's pretty sad. Losing his brother was such a blow to him."

"It's amazing what a person will do or how he reacts or changes when a loved one is lost or threatened."

Will let the thought dangle in the air.

"So, you put bullets in their knees."

"Not my proudest moment."

"I have no problem with it. Willoughby said that he didn't think you have it in you to kill them in cold blood, that he didn't have to talk you out of it."

"I don't know; I really don't. All I saw when we busted in was my little Stella cowering in the corner. These two clowns were playing cards, awaiting instructions. I knew they were just hired flunkies, but still, abducting a four-year old girl? How low can you get? Given my status, I could hardly turn them in but I couldn't let them go either. So after I disarmed them, I took one of their guns and calmly kneecapped them to give them something to remember the rest of their lives. I guess it's to my credit that I had them driven to the closest hospital."

"Like I said, I have no problems whatsoever. You're right, you never know how any of us would react if someone we love is lost or threatened. I don't know what I'd do if anything happened to you."

He reached over and took my hand.

"We have a long couple of days ahead of us. We probably should try to catch as much sleep as we can."

21

During the flight, Westbrook worked on his computer, never getting up, not even to go to the restroom. I wasn't sure what he was working on, but he was very intent.

Will and I were able to catch a few moments sleep here and there but before long we were starting our descent into Tel Aviv. As promised, an Israeli official, Colonel Aram Light, was there to greet us and shepherd us to our next flight. Knowing the upcoming danger, Light handed Will a loaded semiautomatic pistol, which he gladly accepted.

Before going anywhere, we had to get more precise information regarding Lawson's location out of Westbrook. It wasn't until we were walking on the tarmac to the second plane that he said anything. And then he said only two words.

"Mitzpe Ramon"

I looked at Will. Neither of us had any idea what Westbrook was talking about or even what language he was speaking. The Israeli officer did, though.

"Town of about 5,000 people in the north Negev. There's a landing strip there. Let's go."

We climbed on board a small but fast prop plane, a Hawker Beechcraft, that sat eight to ten passengers plus a pilot and copilot. Colonel Light was the pilot. Because the pilot seat was rather cramped, Light had to take off the belt on which his sidearm was holstered. He placed it in an open bin behind his seat. Will had a small knapsack that he also placed in the bin. We all strapped ourselves in and we were off. The trip to Mitzpe Ramon would take about an hour.

About fifteen minutes into our flight, Will got up, announcing he needed something out of his bag.

"What do you need?"

"My notepad, there are a few things I want to write down while they're still fresh in my mind."

"I have a pad," I announced trying to be helpful.

"Nah, I like my own, plus there some other related notes in there I want to look over."

Will wasn't much of a note taker so I thought it a bit strange but I simply responded, "suit yourself."

He went over and started rummaging through stuff.

"Of course, why is it whatever you need is always hidden on the bottom?"

As he was rummaging, he struck up a conversation with Colonel Light.

"So Colonel, where do you fit into the scheme of things?"

The colonel, while keeping his eye out the window and paying attention to his flying, responded in perfect English with a slight British accent.

"I'm in military intelligence. And yes, there's the same joke in Israel as in the States: military intelligence, that's an oxymoron."

"Ever been to the States?"

"Yes, a number of times. I'm a real sucker for New York City. I love it."

"Me too. Ah, there it is. I better leave you to your flying now."

Will returned to his seat with his pad. I looked over and he was just scribbling nonsense. I figured he was up to something so I wasn't going to say anything.

I then looked over at Westbrook who was still working feverishly on his laptop. At one point he looked up. Seeing me eying him, he called me over.

"This is where Lawson is."

He showed me an aerial photograph of a very small building.

"It's about five miles south of Mitzpe Ramon. Very secluded. Mitzpe Ramon is in the middle of nowhere; this shack is nowhere itself."

We landed on an airstrip east of the town. When we got off, Light's uniform was the only credentials he needed to impress the few people manning the landing strip. We marched unmolested over to an SUV he'd ordered be available upon our arrival.

We could see the white buildings of the compact town but other than that, in every direction we looked was sand and rock. Mitzpe Ramon was located on the edge of what was known as the Ramon Crater.

I'd vacationed in the Arizona desert once. While Arizona's searing dry heat was comparable to what I was now experiencing, the striking difference was that in Arizona, there were at least the huge cacti; here there was nothing.

We set out heading south down one of the few roads leading out of town into the heart of the desert. Eight minutes later we pulled up in front of the building Westbrook had highlighted on the aerial shot. There were no signs of life. I could see tire treads from a truck that had recently been there. Similarly, there were footprints out of what appeared to be the only door in and out of the building.

The building itself looked relatively new. It was a fabricated corrugated metal structure that measured about twenty feet square. In addition to the door, there were two small windows. Off to the side there was a propane tank and a small generator, which was whirring away.

Both Will and Light drew their firearms and each moved very slowly to the two windows to peer inside. Not seeing anyone, Will carefully opened the front door and crept in. Satisfied the place was abandoned, he called for the rest of us.

I went in first followed by Westbrook. Light came in last. Will had holstered his gun but Light kept his out. Will turned to Westbrook.

"Are you playing games with us? We travel halfway round the world to this God forsaken place based on your fuckin' GPS coordinates and there's nothing here. Either you're not the genius we thought you were or this is all part of your insane plan."

"No, this can't be," Westbrook responded. "Look, my readout says the computer's still here. On this very spot. We need to look around."

There wasn't much to search. There was a table and chair and an old wooden file cabinet. I started opening the drawers in the cabinet, starting from the top. The first two were empty but the third had some sort of electrical box that looked somewhat like a computer hard drive.

"Look," I told everybody. Westbrook came over.

"It's a type of transponder that relays signals to and from the primary CPU. That's what I'm reading. Jake would have the actual computer. It should take me just a few minutes to reprogram this to give us new coordinates."

"Back away."

It was Light giving this order. The pistol was still in his hand. At the moment it was aimed at Westbrook but as soon as he started to back off as ordered Light re-aimed it at Will, knowing he was the most dangerous of the three of us.

"Jake said you were very clever, Mr. Westbrook. He said that despite having one of my men reprogram the computer, you'd track him down and he was right. Jake wanted to booby trap this cabin so that it blew up as soon as the three of you entered but I talked him out of it. Kids from town come down here to play and I didn't want them hurt."

"That was very noble of you," Will noted with a large dose of sarcasm in his voice.

"I'm a softy, what can I say. But we can't have you three continuing on, threatening Colonel Lawson's holy endeavor."

With that, he raised the gun and aimed it at Will's head and pulled the trigger. Will didn't flinch as the gun harmlessly clicked. Light pulled the trigger again and again, all with the same result. After the fourth click, Will wheeled around and delivered a kick directly to Light's sternum. As Light went down, he involuntarily dropped his gun. Will quickly stooped to pick it up.

"Thing about firearms, they're not much good without these."

He opened his left hand to show all the bullets he had extracted from Light's gun when he went to get the notepad out of his bag. He quickly slipped one of the bullets into the chamber and aimed the gun at Light. He walked closer to him.

"Did you really think I wouldn't notice that the firing pin on the gun you gave me had been sawed off?"

With that he brought the gun down on the side of Light's temple, knocking him out cold. He turned to me.

"Don't worry, his knees are safe."

Then he turned to Westbrook.

"Okay, Alan, do your stuff."

Westbrook pulled out a wire and plugged it into his computer and then into a port on the transponder. Then he started typing.

"Okay, I've established an interface," he announced.

"I don't need progress reports," Will gruffly responded, "just let me know where Lawson is."

Westbrook went back to typing. I've never seen anyone's fingers fly so quickly. In another life he would have made a great concert pianist. The expressions on his face ranged from concentration to concern to aha and back again.

"Okay, I have a location. It's about fifty miles from here."

"Let's go. We have to track Lawson down."

Westbrook kept typing.

"C'mon Alan, let's move!"

"Oh my God! Oh no!"

22

"But you said Lawson wasn't going to launch until Thursday!" Will was screaming at Westbrook.

"He accelerated the schedule. He knows we're onto him and moved it up."

"You can't override the command and order it down?"

"No, I'm afraid not."

"Can you tell when the drone took off?"

"Ten minutes ago."

"Quick, take off Light's uniform. Alan, you're about his size. Put in on in the car. Fava, grab my gun off the floor."

"But it's worthless."

"The bullets aren't and it's the same make as this gun. We'll need as many bullets as we can get."

Westbrook took off the colonel's uniform, leaving him lying there unconscious in his underwear. We ran and piled in the car.

"The locals didn't seem to know Light," Will explained as he started the car and headed back towards Mitzpe Ramon as Westbrook changed in the back, "but they were intimidated by his uniform. I'm hoping they'll be just as intimidated and won't look too closely to see that it's a different person."

"What are we planning to do?"

"We're going to get back in the plane and try and hunt down that drone, hopefully without dying in the process."

"Can you fly this thing?"

"Remember, I was a fighter pilot for five years before I hooked up with the FBI. The Hawker Beechcraft is pretty basic. And it moves pretty quickly for a prop plane."

I'd forgotten Will had told me that about himself.

"Alan," Will asked, "How fast will the drone go with this payload?"

"It's a MQ-9 Reaper. Jake set it to go relatively slow figuring it would be even less detectable. The payload of a 70's era bomb will make it go even slower. It'll go around 120 miles an hour."

"The Hawker can get over 300 so we should be able to overtake it. We just need to find it."

We arrived at the airstrip and as expected, the locals shied away from the uniform and let us proceed hurriedly to the plane. Will sat in the pilot's seat and started flicking all sorts of switches. The engines suddenly started to warm up and the props turned, slowly at first but soon they were whirring away. I went to close the door when Will stopped me.

"No, we'll need it open. Strap yourself in the seat beside it."

I did as he commanded.

"Alan, I want you up here with me. I also need you to make a best guess as to where the drone took off from."

"I already have; I triangulated."

"I don't need details how you did it!"

"Here are the coordinates."

"Now get me the line directly from where it took off to Mecca. That's where we're going to look for it."

"Okay, Fava, take my gun."

He gave the gun to Westbrook who in turn handed it to me.

"You ever fire a gun before?" Will asked.

"No," I nervously responded.

"Crash course time. Hopefully, I'm speaking figuratively here."

He held up the other pistol, the one Light had given him, to illustrate while at the same time maneuvering the plane out to the runway.

"This switch is the safety. When the time comes, you need to press that switch; otherwise the gun won't fire. Then put your right hand in place with your finger on the trigger and brace the handle with your left hand. Hold it out in front of you with a slight bend at the elbows. The pistol is going to have quite a kick so you need hold it tight but not so tight your hands go numb. You're going to fire in quick succession so you can't allow for much recoil.

I want you to practice a shot so it doesn't come as a surprise."

By this time the plane was in full flight. Will banked the plane so we were heading east. When he leveled off I aimed the gun out the open door, released the safety and fired. The sound of the explosion filled the cabin. Despite Will's advice, the gun nearly flew out of my hands. I knew I had to grip harder and keep my arms more rigid.

"Get it?"

I nodded, hoping I'd convince myself as well as him.

"What are your coordinates, Alan?" Will asked.

Westbrook gave them and Will adjusted his flight accordingly. We were flying at no more than a quarter mile off the ground. When we were over the spot Westbrook gave him Will aimed the plan in a south by southeast direction and slowed the plane to as slow as he could without us falling out of the sky. I'd say we were going around 200 at that point. Will opened up the throttle somewhat to increase our speed, but not so much that everything would be a blur and we'd miss the drone entirely.

"Now I believe I'm heading straight towards Mecca as the bird —or drone—flies. If we guessed right about where it started from, hopefully we can establish visual contact with it within a few minutes. We have to bring it down within the next half hour or so. Otherwise it will be over more populated areas. We have to knock it down in the Negev."

"Are you saying I'm going to shoot it down? You can't be serious."

"That's our first option. If our friend here can win a $700 million lottery, I figure anything's possible. I'm working on Plan B right now."

We flew for five more minutes, seeing nothing but the arid and barren desert countryside. Will looked forward to the left and Westbrook forward to the right. Because I was sitting at the open door on the left side of the airplane—which I've since been informed is the port side—I had the narrowest field of vision off to the side. Yet it was me who spotted the drone.

"Will, off to the left. A couple miles away, I'd estimate. I saw the sun reflect off something."

Will banked to the left and headed in that direction. Neither man saw anything at first but finally it came into view. What I thought was a couple miles turned out to be closer to ten!

"That's it, Fava, you found it."

Will aligned our plane behind the drone. He'd align us slightly to the right of the drone so I would have a good view of it as we passed by. My job was to squeeze off successive shots starting well before the drone and ending after it, hoping that at least one bullet would find its mark. We'd repeat this process until I either downed the drone or ran out of bullets. If it were to be the latter, Will would then commence Plan B, not that he'd yet revealed to us what Plan B was.

I got myself into position and had the gun ready when I saw Will look up towards the heavens.

"We've got company," he announced, "change of plans. Quick, Alan, you take the controls. Just keep it straight. Fava, I need you here to transmit any commands I have for Alan; I doubt he'll be able to hear me."

We did as we were told. Will jumped out of the pilot's seat and Westbrook moved in. I moved forward to the seat directly behind the copilot's seat, although there wasn't much for me to do as Westbrook seemed to have it under control. As Will headed back he took the guns from me. He then took the seat belt, tied it around his right arm and leaned out the door.

"It's not military, it's another freaking prop plane, practically a crop-duster," he shouted, more to himself than to us. I could see the plane now. While the plane was smaller and much less powerful than ours, their weapons were not. A man was hanging out the window and began attempting to spray us with machine gun fire. I could hear one bullet hit our fuselage. Will appeared unfazed as he steadied himself.

"Alan, pull back on the throttle, just a bit, to slow us down, but don't lose sight of that drone!"

I was concerned about us slowing down given the firepower our opponent had, but I dutifully transmitted the command.

"Where's the throttle?" Westbrook responded. I tapped Will on the arm and asked him. Will in turn pointed at the middle between the pilot and copilot and made the motion of pulling back. Westbrook got it and pulled, at first too far as the engine sputtered somewhat. Will motioned for him to push it back some, which he did and the engine revved some, but not to the level it was before. Will gave the okay sign and leaned back out the open door.

Meanwhile, the gunman was spraying our area with bullets, for the most part ineffectively but I'd hear an occasional ping as he struck the plane. Will aimed and then released a burst of bullets until he emptied the magazine. He ejected the magazine and inserted the one from the other gun. Steadying himself again, he let fly another stream. A few seconds later, smoke started to emanate from the engine of the other plane. He'd struck something vital. Soon, the aircraft started losing altitude. The gunman had paused as he tried to assist the pilot in keeping them alive. It was to no avail.

Soon the small plane started to spiral towards the earth. We lost sight of it as Will climbed back in.

"Nice shooting," I complimented him.

"Thanks," he responded as he shooed Westbrook from the pilot's seat. Soon we were back to full speed, catching up to the drone. It was only then that we noticed a hole in the windshield and that Westbrook had been hit. Blood soaked his shirt around his shoulder.

"Fava, help Alan. There's a first aid kit over there." Will pointed at the starboard wall behind him.

I opened the kit and took out some gauze. Westbrook took off his shirt and I proceeded to press the gauze on it to stem the bleeding. He didn't react one way or another. I happened to glance up at his face and saw that he was staring at me. But it wasn't a stare that conveyed love or infatuation. It was one of deep sorrow.

"I'm truly sorry for all this, Francine. This is all my fault."

I couldn't disagree with him, so I said nothing and continued to dress the wound. Soon the blood had slowed down sufficiently for me to put a final dressing on it that I would tape down. He sat there silently as I climbed into the copilot seat.

"We're out of ammunition, aren't we?" I asked Will.

"Two bullets left, Time for Plan B."

"Which is?"

Will didn't respond but instead started to lower the landing gear. It then occurred to me that he was going to try and clip the drone's propeller with a wheel, sending the drone to the desert below.

"Will, no disrespect, but are you a good enough pilot to do this?"

"We'll see, won't we?" he smiled.

He opened up the throttle and started to descend. The drone was getting progressively larger as we approached it. We were literally yards behind it when he took it down further. Soon we were passing over it.

"Missed it that time."

Will ascended some and then banked to the right, making a large loop to come around behind it once more. Another pass, another miss.

He tried twice more with the same result.

"How much more time do we have?"

"About ten minutes. After that it will be close to populated areas. Next pass I have to do it."

Will was obviously afraid of our propeller clipping the drone or of the drone being thrown up into our plane. In either case, we'd undoubtedly die. But there was no time for such caution. He made his loop and, as he started his last approach, he took my hand.

"I love you, Fava. I love you very much."

He let go of my hand and made his approach. The drone disappeared under our plane. The next thing I knew, there was a loud crash. It was the drone's propeller hitting something. Will lost control of the plane but it was only momentary. Soon we were leveling off again.

He made a loop to see what had happened to the drone. We came around just in time to see the drone's nose bury itself in the sand.

"Damn, I'm good," was his summary of the situation. I couldn't disagree. Will knew he couldn't rest on his laurels, however.

"Let's get the hell out of here," he stated, "Alan, that bomb's still going to go off, isn't it?"

"The crash could have dislodged the timing device and maybe it won't go off."

"But there's as much chance that the clock is still ticking, right?"

"Yes."

"How much time do we have before that blows?"

Alan looked rather ashen from the loss of blood, but he was holding his own.

"About two hours," he responded.

"Okay, I want you to get on your computer and send out whatever messages you can to the world to stay the hell away from the coordinates where that bomb is. Fava, I want you to get on the emergency radio frequencies and give them the same message. See if they can patch you through to a radio or television station out of some population center. We need to get word out. I don't want any air traffic passing through here. Me, I'm going to fly this thing as fast as it will go without busting apart."

We each did our respective jobs as efficiently as we could. On my first call, I got a young woman who could only speak Hebrew and I wasn't able to communicate with her. On the second, I got an older man who spoke English but admonished me for playing such a prank on an emergency channel. It wasn't until my fifth call that someone actually took me seriously.

"Mayday, mayday," I said hoping it had the same meaning over here as it did back home.

"Hello, can I help you?" responded a middle-aged male voice with a distinct Israeli accent.

"Yes, my name is Francine Vega. I'm a news reporter out of New York. I'm currently in a small plane flying across the Negev Desert. I need to get word out that a large bomb is set to go off in the desert in approximately an hour and a half. We need to warn people to stay out of the area. I need your help to connect me to a radio or television station in Israel and Jordan or anywhere to spread the word. We especially don't want any air traffic in the region. Please help me."

There was silence on the other end of the line.

"You're in earnest, aren't you?"

"I've never been more serious about anything in my life. Please, lives may be lost if we delay."

"Hold on one second."

"Thirty seconds later, the line came to life again. This time it was the station manager for the Israeli state television station out of Jerusalem.

"My name is Yitzak Levy. Would you please repeat what you told the gentleman who called the station?"

I repeated everything, pretty much verbatim. Again, there was a period of silence after I finished.

"Do you have any corroboration of this wild story?"

"I wish I did. All I can say is that I saw the drone with the bomb go down in the middle of the desert 150 miles north of Eilat. I wish it weren't true, but it is."

"And what if this is a prank?"

"If it is, then all it will cost you is some embarrassment. If it isn't and you wait around for the corroboration you naturally seek as a journalist, the bomb will go off and people who could have been saved will die. You fill in the blanks."

A few more seconds of contemplation and then he came back on.

"I will get this on the air immediately. If indeed you are who you say you are, thank you."

I breathed somewhat in relief as I hung up. Will looked me.

"Any luck?" he asked.

"An announcement will be going out on the Israeli state television station in a few minutes."

"I knew you'd do it."

I took his hand.

"Are we safe yet?"

"Yes, I believe so, and we have an hour further to go before the blast. How's Alan?"

"He's doing okay. A pretty good field dressing, if I do say so myself. Where are you flying to?"

"Back to Tel Aviv. We'll see what's waiting for us there."

"Any speculation as to what's next?"

"We'll have to see if the thing blows or not. If it does, Israel isn't going to be too thrilled about a nuke going off on its soil. All sorts of inquiries and all that. Hopefully, they'll track Lawson down and hold him accountable."

We sailed along. Will had slowed the aircraft down somewhat to conserve fuel, which was getting scarce. He was pretty sure we had enough to get all the way to Tel Aviv, but he wanted to be careful.

As the time of the scheduled blast got closer, Will called back to Westbrook asking him to monitor various websites to see if there were any reports of a nuclear explosion in the south of Israel. I looked back and saw that he was asleep. I went back to check on his dressing, but it seemed secure so I didn't wake him.

I went to the radio and put on the headphones to monitor the Israel Broadcasting Authority. Much of what they were saying was in Hebrew, so it didn't mean a lot to me. I scanned the dial to see if I could come up with an English station and finally stumbled on one.

At the moment, some analyst was droning on about American protective pricing and tariff policies on agricultural products. He sounded like he knew what he was talking about and I'm sure it was truly important, but I wished he'd shut up. I stared out the window, hoping his monotone wouldn't put me asleep too when a woman's voice cut in. I flicked the button putting the broadcast on the speaker so Will could hear as well.

"Excuse me for interrupting, Moshe, but we've just received an unconfirmed report of a nuclear blast somewhere in the Negev. The Israeli military is on high alert. The Prime Minister and his Cabinet have been rushed to an undisclosed secure location. That is all we know at this moment."

I turned the radio off as Will spoke.

"Well, we may have saved millions of lives but who knows if we averted World War III."

"You think once the truth comes out, there'd still be war?"

"I don't know, Fava; I just don't know. I don't have a good feeling about this. We'll be in Tel Aviv in about ten minutes. You better strap yourself in tightly and make sure Alan is as well. Make sure his computer is secure. I don't think this is going to be a smooth landing. I have a feeling the drone's propeller did a job on our landing gear. I tried pulling it in earlier and it didn't respond."

Will called the control tower at Tel Aviv, requesting permission to land and advising them that our plane had been damaged and that we would most likely need emergency vehicles on stand-by. Because of the heightened security, however, we were advised that we were being diverted to a smaller airstrip twenty miles west of the city.

"I don't like it," Will stated.

"Why? It makes sense, doesn't it?"

"It almost sounded like they were expecting us and they're diverting us away from a large airport to a smaller one where they can handle us better."

"I'm sure that during a nationwide alert, the military has first priority landing and taking off at the major airports. Probably lots of planes have been diverted for this reason."

"You're most likely right. I'm being overly paranoid, but indulge me. I just don't think Lawson is done yet. We know he has at least one high ranking officer in his pocket; what's to say there aren't others and they're shifting us to a different airport where we can be taken into custody without commotion or anyone noticing. Let's find somewhere else to land, and it has to be soon or we'll be completely out of fuel. Alan, you back with us?"

"Yes, I'm awake now."

"Can you find me a nearby field to safely land this plane?"

"That shouldn't be too difficult."

I gave Westbrook back his computer and he tapped away on his keyboard and within one minute handed Will a set of coordinates.

"Aerial photos indicate this is a vacant field. Looks pretty remote, just an adjacent farmhouse. I don't know how old these shots are. For all I know, there could be an apartment building there right now."

"We'll have to take that chance. Running on fumes. I calculate we'll be there in four minutes. Strap in and put your heads down."

Westbrook and I did as we were told. He held his computer close to his chest. I worried about Will, who had to remain upright to pilot the plan through this landing.

I could feel the plane's slow descent. Finally, there was a jolt as a wheel bounced on the field. We bounced a few more times as Will quickly adjusted the wing flaps to slow us down. As we slowed, the right side of the plane dipped until the right wing hit the ground and we did a cartwheel. I lost number of the times we somersaulted until we finally came to a grinding halt. But the plane was all in one piece. We survived.

23

"Fava, you okay?"

"Yeah, a bit shook up but okay."

"How about Alan?"

I looked over and I wasn't sure whether Westbrook was alive or dead. His wound had opened again as the dressing was filled with blood. He was definitely unconscious, but beyond that I couldn't tell. I worked my way over to him and felt for a pulse. There was one.

"He's out cold, but alive. I don't know how badly injured he is. His wound has opened."

"Let's get out of here. I don't know if this thing's going to blow."

I unhooked Westbrook's belt and he flopped over onto the floor.

"Will, I need help with him."

We each took him under an arm and lifted him up as we awkwardly started to walk toward the door. Along the way, Will grabbed anything he thought we might need: cellphones, the working gun, the computer, etc. Eventually we were out of the plane. I smelled fuel and Will said to hurry. I didn't need to be told a second time.

A stocky gray-haired man of about seventy came running out of the house towards us. He seemed very agitated. His stout wife trailed along behind. The man shouted at us in what I assumed was Hebrew as he pointed at the crops we'd ruined and the large furrows we'd made in the soil. Will's body assumed an 'I don't understand a word you're saying attitude' as we kept walking with an unconscious Westbrook between us.

The man was still shouting at us at the top of his lungs when the plane blew up in a great ball of fire. We all hit the dirt, but we were far enough away that no debris came our way. When we got up, the man and his wife looked at the conflagration in wonderment as we continued to walk on. Eventually, he realized we were leaving and started up his Hebrew diatribe once again, but his heart was no longer in it. We left the field and started walking down a narrow road.

We walked for ten minutes when a van came barreling along. Will flagged it down and headed toward the driver. He was a thin man in his mid-thirties. The lines on his face indicated he was a man who spent a good chunk of his life outdoors.

"Do you speak English?"

"Yes, little."

"Can you give us a lift? We were in that plane crash over there."

The man followed Will's outstretched arm and could make out the fiery wreck through the bushes and the smoke billowing up into the air. He looked back at Will with and expression indicating he was impressed we'd survived such a crash.

"We need to get our friend to a hospital. We don't know how badly he's hurt. Is there one close by?"

"Ten kilometers. Come, get in."

The man climbed down and helped us lift Westbrook into the back of the van, laying him on the floor. We climbed into the seat beside the driver.

"My name's Will Allen. This is Francine Vega. Thanks again for helping us."

"Yehuda Mendl," he said as he tapped himself on the chest.

"You American?"

"Yes, we are."

Yehuda's face lit up.

"I have uncle in Lakewood, New Jersey. You know New Jersey?"

"Yes, very well. We're both from New York City, right next door to New Jersey."

"Some day I go New Jersey. See America."

"We'll be very happy to show you around when you come."

Then Yehuda got serious.

"I in army. Probably get call soon, after bomb."

We couldn't really say too much after that. We arrived at hospital about five minutes later.

Will shook Yehuda's hand and thanked him again for the ride.

"I wait," he responded.

Will told him he didn't have to, but he seemed determined to continue to help us so we didn't argue any further. We walked Westbrook into the emergency room. A nurse spotted us and called for a doctor who came immediately. The doctor's grasp of English was a lot firmer than Yehuda's so it was easier explaining the situation to him.

We helped the doctor and nurse lift Westbrook onto a gurney. He regained consciousness for a moment, grabbed Will's arm and put something in his hand. Then he was out once again.

Soon they disappeared behind a screen as the doctor began his examination.

We expected the nurse to ask us for information, insurance cards, and the like but when she didn't return to the front desk we decided to head out.

"He's in good hands. We can't wait around," Will declared as we walked back out. As promised, Yehuda and his van was where we'd left them.

"Your friend, he okay?" he asked.

"He'll be fine. The doctors will take good care of him. Yehuda, how far is it to Tel Aviv?"

"One hour and one half."

"We need to rent a car to get there as quickly as possible. You know where we can rent a car?"

"No rent. Get in."

"Yehuda, we can't ask that of you. It's way out of your way."

"Get in. We go," he gleefully pronounced.

We got back in.

"Yehuda, we need to get to the American Embassy in Tel Aviv. Do you know where that is?

"We find."

After that, we drove in relative silence. I looked out the

window, thinking about nothing in particular but realizing I was exhausted. We hadn't slept in over two days and my adrenaline was running out. It was all catching up to me. Still, I couldn't fall asleep, not yet anyway.

"I've always wanted to take a trip to Israel," I pronounced, "but I thought I'd actually get to see the sights. Maybe someday I'll come back...if there is a someday."

Will kept his eyes straight ahead but reached over and took my hand.

"Why don't we come back, on our honeymoon?"

The word didn't sink in for a few seconds but then it did.

"Did you say 'honeymoon'? Are you asking me to marry you?"

"That's exactly what I'm doing. After Kati died, I swore I'd never remarry. I didn't want to go through the pain again. But I didn't count on running into you. We've only known each other for a very short time, but sometimes it just feels right. I know I'd be asking you to take on a lot—what with two kids and all—but I can't imagine myself without you. Fava, will you marry me?"

I also looked out the window.

"I too promised never to remarry, but for a different reason. Mainly, the men I'd been attracted to were flashy and exciting. I thought I'd never be able to take someone on as a husband because I didn't trust my judgment. Eddie made such a great first impression; I was swept off my feet. But you know how that worked out. Farad was debonair and sophisticated and I was certainly falling for him but our worlds were so different it never could have lasted. You are the exact opposite of anything I'd ever have looked for in a man."

"I'm boring, I admit it."

"Let's just say you're steady and solid."

"I'll accept that."

"I'm glad I got beyond a rather unimpressive first impression and got to experience the truly wonderful man you are. In addition, there's no way anyone can say that you've shown me a boring time the last couple of days, can they?"

"No, no they can't. So?"

"My answer? I thought in a roundabout way I had answered. Yes, Will Allen, I will most definitely marry you. But I do have one condition about our honeymoon."

"That is?"

"Albert and Stella have to come along."

"Deal."

We hugged and kissed. During our whole conversation, Yehuda had been trying to listen in on our conversation but because of his tentative grasp of English, he was only perplexed. Will reached over and patted him on the back.

"Yehuda, this wonderful woman has just agreed to be my wife. Now, if we can avert war and we all survive, you are the first person to be invited to our wedding. When the time comes, we'll pay for your trip to the states!"

Yehuda flashed a broad smile.

"Mazel Tov! I accept!"

We drove on for a bit in silence after that when something occurred to me.

"By the way, what did Westbrook hand you when we left him at the hospital?"

"It was a computer flash drive. I have no idea what's on it. I've noticed that, even after all we went through together, you still refer to him by his last name."

"I can't get it out of my head that he's the one who killed Farad. I appreciate all that he did, but he still murdered someone I knew and cared about."

"Which he admits and he told me he wants to come back and take responsibility for what he did."

"I know that, too, which is why I can't hate the guy. Life is so complicated these days."

"You just said a mouthful, Fava."

We entered Tel Aviv. It was a modern, bustling city. Soldiers were all over. They looked us over a couple of times but decided we were okay.

As a seaside town, I'm sure Tel Aviv had a lot of nightspots and great beaches, which of course we were not going to see. Yehuda made several stops to get directions to the American Embassy. Finally, a man went through multiple hand gestures and gyrations while Yehuda continually nodded. He shook the man's hand in thanks and climbed back in. I was dubious he could remember all the turns the man told him to take but fifteen minutes later, we had pulled up as close as we could.

The building was an unimpressive concrete five-story building that took up about one third of a city block. There were barricades encircling the building, blocking all access. I wasn't sure whether these barricades were permanent fixtures or had been hastily installed after the latest incident.

There was one entrance through the barricades that led into a parking lot for the ambassador and the embassy staff. Yehuda stopped the car and we got out.

"You can go on back home now, Yehuda. We're okay from here on. We have your information. You'll be hearing from us again. Thanks for all your help. You've been a good friend."

We all shook hands and then Will and I headed over to the opening. Two armed marines, a sergeant and a corporal, were stationed there. They'd been eyeing us ever since we stopped.

"Sergeant," Will addressed the senior of the two, "it's urgent that we speak with the Ambassador."

The sergeant looked us over. We hadn't cleaned up or changed since our crash and, in our disheveled state, it was no wonder the marines summarily dismissed us.

"No one is allowed in or out today, sir."

Will had not yet shown his badge, but he had it ready. He did not want to appear that he might be going for a weapon. He showed it to the sergeant.

"My name is Will Allen, I'm a Special Agent with the Federal Bureau of Investigation on assignment here in Israel. I have some information that is vital the Ambassador hear."

The sergeant appeared to be wavering somewhat but still his

orders were to let no one pass.

"Listen sergeant, in the past 36 hours I've been shot at and in a plane crash and I haven't had a minute's sleep. Plus I have information he'll want to know about today's nuclear blast. If I don't get to speak to the Ambassador, we may very well find ourselves in World War III. I suggest you run inside and advise your superiors. Otherwise, the death of millions of people will be squarely on your shoulders. That's not what you signed up for, son."

Will's softened conclusion did the trick as the sergeant headed inside. A few minutes later he appeared accompanied by a young man in a grey suit. He appeared to be around thirty years old, wore horned rimmed glasses and spoke with a hint of a lisp.

"Listen, whoever you are,"

"FBI Special Agent William Allen,"

"Yes, Special Agent Allen, please turn right around. In case you haven't heard, we are in the middle of a crisis and the Ambassador cannot be disturbed."

"I know. We're the ones who forced the bomb to explode in Israel."

The aide looked especially taken aback.

"You what?"

"We intercepted the drone carrying the nuclear bomb and forced it to crash in the Negev Desert. To confirm what we are saying, I can give you the exact time it detonated, the type of nuclear device it was, its origin, the exact coordinates of the detonation, and any other information you may need on it. If you look it up, I'm sure you'll find that most of the information we can give you will be highly classified and will only be known by the President, the Ambassador and maybe five other people. And us. That's why it's vital we speak with the Ambassador. Otherwise, there's a strong chance this may spiral out of control into a world war."

The aide looked us over one more time.

"Come with me."

We accompanied the aide. On the way in he introduced himself as Heinrich Muller. He laughed at our reaction of such a German name working in Israel. He said he was Jewish and was named after his grandfather who had escaped from the Nazis at the last minute in 1940.

Soon we were on the fifth floor as Muller knocked on the door to the Ambassador's office. The Ambassador, Peter Shapiro, opened the door, clearly agitated.

"Muller, I thought I made it clear I was not to be disturbed!"

"Sir, you're going to want to hear what these people have to say. It's regarding this morning's blast."

The Ambassador glowered but then relented.

"You have two minutes."

We walked into the office as Shapiro closed the door behind us. He was obviously a man of great wealth, evidenced by the various pieces of original artwork and statuary—including an original Miro—that adorned the space. He sat behind a lavishly ornate mahogany desk and we sat in two luxurious leather upholstered chairs facing him. The chairs were so comfortable it took all my willpower not to instantly fall asleep.

"Mr. Ambassador, I'm Special Agent William Allen of the FBI. This is Francine Vega; she's a reporter out of New York. As you know, this morning at 7:41 local time a nuclear explosion occurred in the Negev Desert, approximately 130 miles north of Eilat. The device was a relatively old but obviously still functional nuclear fission gun-type design. It was manufactured in the Soviet Union in the late 70s."

The Ambassador's eyes opened widely.

"How do you know such detail?"

"You mean how do we know such information that is obviously classified? It's simple. We're the ones who forced the drone that was carrying it down. The drone was intended for Mecca."

"You mean it was meant to destroy Mecca, just like the drivel that that crackpot preacher talked about a few weeks ago?"

I spoke up.

"Exactly. We knew that what he was spouting was not just a diatribe but was an actual plot that I exposed to his brother in the State Department when I first learned about it."

Ambassador Shapiro took all this in. I continued.

"There are a number of powerful people in government—both in the US and here and Israel—who aided and abetted this plot. We were nearly killed by one such Israeli officer who called it a 'holy endeavor.' We're taking a chance talking to you; for all we know you could be supportive as well."

"I certainly am not, and neither is the President! I can assure you of that."

Will re-injected himself.

"Sir, I know it's none of our business but have you received any communication from Israel as to what its next steps are?"

The Ambassador eyed us, deciding whether he could divulge the contents of such top-secret communiqués to people who obviously did not have sufficient clearance to hear such things.

"The main reason I ask," Will continued, "is that the person behind this, a Colonel Jacob Lawson, is very resourceful and will stop at nothing. We foiled his plan to destroy Mecca but I'm sure he's calculating how to use the present situation to his advantage. He'd like nothing better than for there to be a full-scale confrontation between the East and the West, between the democracies and the Muslim states, believing we'd come out on top in a new world order."

The Ambassador gave a resigned sigh.

"Yes, but what kind of world will be left for us to rule over?"

24

After meeting with us, the Ambassador said he was going to reach out to the Israeli government and relate our side of the story. He was also going to make some inquiries about Colonel Jacob Lawson.

Noting the state we were both in, he graciously offered us accommodations in the embassy. We graciously accepted. He even had staff hunt down a change in clothes for both of us. After a shower and change, I felt like a new girl. I could have gone to sleep that very minute, but the Ambassador also offered for us to dine with him, which we accepted.

For a variety of reasons, he had not been back to the States in nearly two years and he was anxious to talk about New York. Before this posting, he'd lived in New York for over twenty years and found it to be the most exciting place on earth, although he did admit that Israel could be exciting on a number of levels. He sheepishly admitted that, although he professed to be a news junkie, he could not recall seeing me on TV when he was there. One of the downsides of working for the fourth rated station in New York, I explained.

After dinner, we retired to our rooms. I was so looking forward to actually sleeping in a bed for the night. I'd only just gotten to sleep when there was a rather quiet knock on my door. I put on the robe they'd provided and went to the door. I opened it and it was Will. I invited him in.

I can't say that Will was the best lover I've ever experienced, but I can't ever remember being more satisfied when we were done. We went to sleep in each other's arms.

Next thing we knew there was another knock on the door. Sunlight was seeping in through the curtains, so I knew it was morning. I went to the door and Muller was there. He looked in and saw Will was also there.

"Good, that saves me from having to wake you as well," he said as he entered uninvited. "The Ambassador needs to see you in his office immediately. Please get dressed and come down right away."

We did as we were told and walked into his office. There were three televisions on the wall; each one was paused.

"Please, have a seat," the Ambassador coolly commanded, "As I mentioned last night, I'm a news junkie and when I get up in the morning I have all three televisions going at once, often in different languages, to catch up on what had happened the night before. Well, the piece on the center screen especially caught my attention and I thought you would find it of interest as well."

He clicked the remote and the picture came to life. On the screen young dark-haired woman, obviously a reporter, spoke into a microphone.

"This is Esther Rabin reporting live from in front of the Knesset in Jerusalem. We have just received word that two Americans have been closely linked with yesterday's detonation of a nuclear bomb in the Negev Desert in southern Israel.

"The Americans have been identified as William Allen, an agent with the United States Federal Bureau of Investigation and Francine Vega, a reporter for a New York television station."

As she stated this, our photos replaced her face on the screen as she continued to talk. I couldn't even remember when that photo had been taken.

"Sources have told us that Mr. Allen and Ms. Vega were allegedly paid millions of dollars by the Republic of Iran to carry out this plot to attack Israel."

The reporter re-appeared on the screen. The scene then shifted to the mangled airplane in the field.

"The Americans escaped from this plane after making an emergency landing outside of Tel Aviv. It has been reported that a third American, who is at this time unidentified, may have also been involved in the attack, but that is unconfirmed."

Back once again to the reporter.

"Mr. Allen and Mr. Vega are believed to still be in Israel. Both also have outstanding warrants for their arrest in the United States.

"Anyone who sees either of these persons or has any information about their whereabouts should contact their local police authorities. They should not approach these individuals as they are considered to be armed and dangerous."

The Ambassador clicked the remote, re-freezing the reporter.

"So, you two are financed by Iran. I'd never have guessed it. Should I be worried?"

"In your line of work, I'd be surprised if you weren't worried all the time," Will responded.

"So right you are. After you went up to your rooms—or should I say room—I made some calls. In fact, I made a bunch of calls: about you two, about Colonel Lawson, etc., etc. The conclusion I came up with is that I believe your version of the story, not what's being put out into the public."

A wave of relief rushed through my body.

"That's good to know," I responded.

"This morning I was awakened by a call from the Israeli Prime Minister. He'd gotten a report you were here in the embassy and he demanded that you be turned over to Israel so they can question you. I asked him to have his staff fax over pictures of you so I could check to see if you were in the building. I assured him full cooperation in this matter."

The man was definitely enjoying this as evidenced by the glint in his eye.

"But I also begged him not to rush to action based on news reports and speculation. I told him that I believed there might be an alternative explanation to an Iranian connection. He said he was open, but he said the Iranian evidence was very compelling. So after I spoke with him, I made some additional calls and discovered that deposits of $10 million were made into each of your checking accounts and that the deposits came from an account tied to an Iranian terrorist organization."

"$10 million? We're rich!" Will sarcastically remarked.

"Any idea how those deposits found their way into your accounts?"

"Lawson. The man is extremely resourceful. He couldn't kill us or scare us off so now he's using us and discrediting us at the same time. Rather clever of him, I'd say."

"Yes, my sources tell me Lawson is quite the fellow. The type who gets what he wants, considers himself the ultimate patriot, doesn't take no for an answer, has his fingers in everything and connections everywhere. He'd be fully capable of doing this, and more."

"What's next?"

"Let me make one more call. Give me a half hour or so."

We left the Ambassador and sat in an anteroom off of his office.

"Will, has it seemed to you that Lawson is all over the map."

"What do you mean?"

"What I'm referring to it the level of competence of people he has assisting him. The guys who kidnapped me, for example, seemed highly professional. Likewise, the men who killed L'Eglise. On the other hand, the plane that tried to shoot us down in the Negev was, as you put it, practically a crop-duster and the felons who abducted Stella were a couple of lowlife flunkies who were very easy for you to track down. I just find it interesting. People are usually consistent in how they act. Someone with the talent, smarts, connections and money that Lawson has should be able to put together a little more professional operation. That's all I'm saying."

"That usually happens when someone is put off their game and they have to improvise on the fly. And I know exactly what's put him off his game."

"What?"

"You."

"Me?"

"Think about it. Lawson has a pattern of handling people who get in his way. He intimidates them. Often that's enough to get them to back off. Look at how Captain Fairchild backed off with just a simple note with her mother's name. Then, if they don't back off, he goes for more drastic measures. I bet if we dug, we'd find a message was sent to L'Eglise that he either ignored or didn't understand. Lawson ordered him taken out. You'd have been a twofer."

"I still don't understand what I've done that's so special or different."

"Well, you've had all sorts of things done to you and you persevered. He's not used to that. I'd think that most reporters, after being shot at, kidnapped, chased around the world and survived a plane crash would have requested a gig doing traffic reports for the rest of their careers. But not you. That's what put him off his game. I'm hoping we can use that and hit him when he's vulnerable and a little confused."

I considered what he said, but I still didn't believe I was all that extraordinary or different.

We sat for a bit more when the door opened and Shapiro walked in.

"Well, you're going to turn yourself in," he grandiosely announced.

"What!" I exclaimed.

"I exaggerate a little. I called the Prime Minister back. I admitted that you were here but I told him I believed you to be innocent of what they are accusing you of. In fact, I told him you probably averted a great war. He wasn't convinced, but agreed to hear you out in person. As you can imagine, he can't exactly leave Jerusalem right now to come to the embassy so I said we'd go to him."

"Don't we become open targets out there?"

"I have an armored vehicle with tinted windows, so no one will know you are being transported. Plus, the Prime Minister has given me his word that after we speak, you can return with me back to the embassy, which is U.S. soil. It's our best and only chance. I suggest we take it."

We were both uneasy but had little choice in the matter, so we agreed. We headed down to the parking garage located in the basement of the embassy. Muller was already standing by the car, waiting for us; he'd be our driver. The car was a black Chrysler sedan. The Ambassador climbed in the front, Will and I in the back.

The distance between Tel Aviv and Jerusalem is a little over thirty miles. Even with checkpoints that had sprouted up since the blast, given the way people drive in this country and a modern highway that connects the two cities, we expected to be at the Prime Minister's residence in a half hour.

At one point Muller took an exit off the highway. The Ambassador was looking at some papers and didn't seem to notice. Will, however, did notice not only the detour but also the fact that Muller had kept his gloves on as he drove. Will grabbed my arm, indicating I should be alert. Eventually Shapiro looked up and noticed we were not on the highway.

"Heinrich, why did you get off?"

Muller said nothing but kept driving.

"Heinrich, I asked you a question. Why aren't we on the highway? We need to get to Jerusalem as fast as we can."

Again nothing. The road we were on was practically deserted. Up ahead I saw a van. We were anticipating the worst. I pulled out my untraceable cellphone. Keeping it very low so Muller couldn't see, I texted Jonas: NEED HELP! I sent the message and stuffed the phone in my sock. I'm not sure why I thought of stuffing it in my sock, but that seemed to be the one place where they may not think to look if I were to be searched.

I had no idea what I thought Jonas could do or what help he could provide. But I knew that he was never without his phone, constantly texting or checking emails. Frank, on the other hand, would often leave his phone on his desk and wouldn't check messages until the end of the day. I don't think he even knew how to text. If anyone would get it, it would be Jonas.

Of course, Jonas was an ocean and thousands of miles away. What he could do—and how soon he could do it—was highly questionable. By the time something happened, I'd probably be dead.

The Ambassador raised his voice once more as we pulled in behind the van.

"Heinrich, I demand that you drive back to the highway and on to Jerusalem! Now."

Muller stopped the car, put it into park and at the same time pulled out two guns. One he aimed at Shapiro, the other he whipped around and aimed at me. He fully realized that Will was the most dangerous of the three of us but that he would not risk me getting shot so he kept the gun on me.

"I'm sorry to have to do this. I like you sir, I really do. You're a good man."

Before the Ambassador could reply or offer any protest, Muller squeezed the trigger, shooting him between the eyes. The Ambassador slumped over dead. Then he turned back to us.

"In case you hadn't noticed, Special Agent Allen, this is the gun we took off you when you came to the embassy. Your fingerprints are all over it. The murder of an Ambassador, who also was a close friend of the President, should seal your fate for good. Now, we're all going to take a little trip. Personally, I'd just as soon kill the both of you but I have orders to keep you alive. You're in for a special treat."

Two other men, both armed with submachine guns, got out of the van and opened our doors, ordering us to get out. Muller took my bag and looked inside. He took out my official cellphone and checked it.

"What kind of an American woman are you? There are no messages or calls within the last couple of days."

He pulled out both of our passports, which I'd been carrying.

"I'll let you keep these, although I doubt you'll have much use for them anymore. They'll serve as positive identification when they find your bodies."

He looked through the rest of the bag and, after deciding everything else in there was harmless, handed it back to me. He then patted down Will and determined he was clean. He handcuffed us to each other and led us to the back of the van.

"I apologize for the poor accommodations, but it won't be very long, I assure you."

We climbed in the back and then the door slammed behind us, leaving us in the dark. Our only light were the slivers that seeped in around the doorframe. As promised, we were not in luxury as we bounced around on the metal floor. After about ten minutes, the van stopped. The back was opened and we both had to adjust to the bright sunlight as we were led out and into a small wooden house in a small town.

Muller shut us in a windowless room, telling us to behave ourselves and that he'd be right back. Again, he was a man true to his word as he reentered a few minutes later with his two friends as they led us up a set of narrow stairs to a room in the third floor of the three-story building. This time they all stayed with us as we waited.

Ten minutes later the door opened and a single man walked in. He appeared to be in his upper fifties or low sixties but would be mistaken for a much younger man. He was about six one, had ruggedly handsome looks and a mane of light brown hair. He perfectly filled out an Israeli-style khaki uniform. We eyed him as he approached.

"Colonel Lawson, I presume," Will said, beating me to the punch.

"Special Agent Allen, Miss Vega," he said as he bowed to each of us in turn, "I can't tell you how much of a pleasure it is to finally meet you. It truly is. Miss Vega, I can totally understand why Alan fell for you the way he did."

"It was just one of those things," I replied.

"Yes, amour. How fickle the heart can be, however. I doubt Alan even thinks of you anymore."

I was going to answer, but thought better of it.

"Well, the two of you have been a thorn in my side for quite a while now but that is ending. I went back and forth whether to keep you alive or kill you. There are pros and cons to both choices, and until I decide or until it's obvious that you've outlived your usefulness, you will be my very-much-alive guests.

"Now, I have something I need to take care of in Jerusalem but I'll be back in a couple of hours. Until then, you will have to count on Mr. Muller and his associates for hospitality. I leave you in their very capable hands. Good bye."

He made mock bows to us and then turned on his heels and went back out the door. We could then hear a car engine starting and the car drive off.

"You might as well make yourself comfortable," Muller told us.

There were two chairs in the room, which I got the impression the henchmen wanted, but we sat in them as we awaited our fate. Our three captors leaned against the wall or semi-sat on the table that was against the far wall.

We remained like this for about fifteen minutes when suddenly the door was kicked in with a crash. Our captors tried raising their guns to fire at the intruders, but they were too late as shots burst from the semiautomatics of the two men entering the room. Will grabbed me, pulled me to the floor and rolled on top of me.

The gunfire was over almost as quickly as it started. Will raised his head and looked around. As he did, I was also able to get a glimpse of the carnage. Muller's torso was torn to shreds and his associates were no better off. Will rolled off of me.

"Willoughby? Fallon?"

"Hey boss," Agent Willoughby answered in return, "good morning, Miss Vega."

I nodded dumbly back at them.

"What are you doing here?"

"We've been in Israel for a couple of days now, in case you needed us. We were in Tel Aviv since we've been tracking Ms. Vega's phone's GPS. When she texted her coworker, he told his boss, Frank. Before coming over, I'd told Frank to call me if he heard from you. He called and we followed you out of Tel Aviv to here."

"Very resourceful of you, Willoughby."

"I learned from the best. You've been pretty busy of late, haven't you, Will, starting a war and all?"

"Don't forget assassinating an Ambassador."

"Well, about that."

Willoughby showed Will the Glock that had been used to kill the Ambassador.

"I believe this was yours. It's been wiped clean."

He knelt down and, wearing gloves, he took Muller's lifeless hand and put it around the handle of the gun as well as making sure his fingerprints were elsewhere on the barrel and chamber. He even took the bullets and made sure Muller's fingerprints were on them. Then he put the gun in Muller's holster, taking the pistol he'd been using.

While he was there, Willoughby searched his pockets until he found the keys to the handcuffs. He proceeded to uncuff Will and me.

"There, when they match the ballistics to the bullets that killed the Ambassador, they'll have a match. Now we should get out of here. We weren't as quiet as we should have been. Finding firearms in Israel was not difficult but it was impossible getting our hands on any silencers."

We headed down to the jeep Willoughby had rented and got out of town as quickly as we could. He'd already chartered a boat out of Haifa that would take us to Istanbul and from there we could work our way back home. Will told him no.

"We need to get to Jerusalem. I figure we have 24 to 48 hours before Israel retaliates, probably with a nuclear strike on Iran. We have to stop it."

"How do plan on doing that?" Willoughby asked. "You can't exactly walk up to the Prime Minister's house and ring the bell. Your pictures are plastered all over Israel. You'd probably be shot on sight. Even going back to the States is risky, but you'll have a better chance there of getting the truth out."

"That's true, but we have to try. There's got to be something we can do to stop this from happening."

"I have an idea," I interjected. I pulled out my phone and dialed. A familiar voice answered.

"Hi Frank."

"Francine, thank God you're okay! Where are you?"

"Agent Willoughby got to us just in time. You're aware of what's going on here, aren't you?"

"Of course, you're international news."

"Exactly, and I want to use my newfound celebrity status to hopefully stop World War III."

"What do you need me to do?"

"I need to get on the air here. We need to somehow get to the Prime Minister to convince him of the true story. The American Ambassador has been murdered; we probably will be blamed for that, too."

"My God."

"Keep him out of it. I need you to use whatever sources you have to make contact with a major news outlet here in Israel and broker a deal for us to be interviewed, and it all has to be done in the next couple of hours."

"I'll be back to you soon."

We dug our belongings that Muller confiscated out of the van and went back to the place Willoughby had rented in a little town halfway between Jerusalem and Tel Aviv. He had a computer with a satellite hookup there. Will dug the flash drive Westbrook had given him out of my bag. I'd sewn it into the lining hoping that no one would find it if they looked. They hadn't.

Westbrook, as I suspected, had been extremely organized. There were fifteen folders into which were organized a hundred or so files. The first folder that caught our eye was labeled "Vega-Allen deposits". The files contained therein described the process and provided links explaining how Lawson went about depositing the $10 million into our accounts.

All the other folders were equally detailed and organized. They ranged from providing the where and how Lawson obtained the bomb to a file detailing the arrangements Lawson had made to kidnap Stella.

"Damn it if it isn't all here," Will exclaimed. "Everything we need to prove our innocence and implicate Lawson is here. Along the way, this may provide us with enough to stop a war from happening. Remind me not to get on Alan's bad side. God only knows what he can dig up on me."

We were so focused on the screen that when my phone rang, about an hour after I spoke with Frank, we all jumped.

"Hi Frank."

"It's all set up. You anywhere near Tel Aviv?"

"Half hour, forty five minute drive."

"Good, you have to be there in an hour. The address is 145 Menachim Begin Road. The reporter's name is Rachel Stern. I understand she's a pretty well-known investigative reporter."

"Can we trust her?"

"I have no clue. The person I spoke with knows someone who's dealt with her in the past on a story. This friend-of-a-friend-of-a-friend vouches for her, but that's the closest I could get on such short notice."

"It'll have to do. Thanks, Frank."

"She said she'll give you about a half-hour for the interview after which she's obliged to call the cops. Frankly, I think she's pushing it not turning you in immediately but a reporter is a reporter and the ability to get an exclusive with a suspected terrorist is way too tempting."

"Thanks again, Frank. If I survive this, I owe you a drink."

"Hiram Fennessey gets a bottle for some DMV info and all I get is a lousy drink for helping you save the world?"

I laughed. I didn't even know he was aware of that.

"You got me Frank. A bottle it is."

"Good luck, Francine. You stay alive, you hear me?"

"Yes sir."

I turned to Will and Willoughby.

"Okay, it's all set. We need to go back to Tel Aviv."

Will looked up from the computer screen at Willoughby.

"How long would it take to download these files and then send them on to the FBI and a couple of other places?"

"The files don't look that complicated. A couple minutes. Tops."

"Okay, do it, but don't remove the files from the flash drive. Do you have any more of these drives?"

Willoughby nodded.

"Copy the files onto those as well. Give me two of them and you keep the other."

Willoughby sat down and typed in a handful of keystrokes. Five minutes later he looked up.

"Done."

"Okay, send them to the FBI, somebody you trust, and also to Frank and to Captain Audra Fairchild. Here's her email address. She'll know what to do when she gets them."

Willoughby did what he was told and a few minutes later we were heading out the door. We were nervous the entire ride back to Tel Aviv. All around us a country was gearing up for war; soldiers and military equipment were everywhere, mobilizing at a frenetic pace. We stayed off the main highway hoping to avoid checkpoints. I was sure we were going to be taken into custody somewhere along the way but we arrived back in Tel Aviv unmolested.

We could be driving into a trap, but we didn't have any choice. I had to trust my instincts and Frank's assertion that a "reporter is a reporter." At the moment, we were big news and this scoop was too big to pass up. This was a golden career move for her: either she got an exclusive interview with the people responsible for starting a nuclear war, or she was instrumental in averting such a war.

When we arrived at the address, Willoughby and Fallon got out of the car to survey the situation.

The area was primarily light industrial. The particular address we were going to was a drab modular two-story house and fit in well. I had a feeling that this was an out-of-the-way spot that Rachel Stern used on occasion to conduct sensitive interviews that required a great deal of discretion.

Willoughby and Fallon got out a few block away and then we approached the front door. I noticed the drapes on a window on the second floor being drawn back and then let fall. A few seconds later, the door opened.

"Ms. Stern," I said in introduction, "I'm Francine Vega and this is FBI Special Agent William Allen. I'd go into more detail about ourselves but you probably know all about us."

"Yes indeed I do. You'll go through all that for the camera anyway and we don't have a lot of time. Please come in."

We walked into what would loosely be called a living room as it had a couch, two chairs, a coffee table and a couple lamps. But that was about it. Opposite the couch, Stern had set up a camera on a tripod. I was impressed with the camera; it was a very modern and sophisticated HD camera. Jonas would have a field day with this equipment, I thought.

The camera was aimed at the couch, where Will and I sat. Rachel was to be off-camera the entire time. She pressed a button and the red light appeared, indicating the camera was running.

"Please, identify yourselves for the camera."

We did so. Stern proceeded to ask us questions.

"Please, tell me why you came to me."

Will spoke first.

"We came to you with the hope that through this broadcast, we will be able to avert war."

"And how do you think that can be accomplished?"

"By telling the truth about the nuclear explosion that occurred in the Negev two days ago."

"The two of you are wanted in Israel for setting off that bomb. There is evidence that you were responsible for the blast because you were paid millions of dollars by the government of Iran. Can you address these charges?"

"The charges were fabricated. I have documentation on this flash drive that proves we are innocent."

"Why would anyone fabricate these charges against you?"

"To discredit us so that the government of Israel will believe that it was Iran that ordered the detonation of this bomb and will initiate the process to begin an all-out nuclear war with that nation. Other nations will soon choose sides and the end result will be a world war pitting the west against the Islamic nations."

"Please tell me how you came to be aware of such a plot."

I fielded this one.

"It all started innocuously enough with a winning lottery ticket sold in New York. The winner was a distraught and unstable man who had lost his twin brother in the attack on the Pentagon on 9/11. This man swore to use his newfound fortune to avenge the death of his brother by attacking Islam itself."

"How did he propose to do this?"

"He was aware that one of the pillars of Islam is the requirement to make the hajj, the pilgrimage to Mecca. Destroy Mecca, he reasoned, and one of the pillars on which the religion resides crumbles, bringing down the religion with it. As you may know, a preacher in the U.S. publicly promoted such a scheme and the result was rioting. Once that died down, the preacher was dismissed as a crackpot but we came upon evidence that the plan was in fact real and a schedule had been set. He had an able accomplice, Army Colonel Jacob Lawson. An old Russian atom bomb was purchased from arms dealers and an unmanned drone was also secured. It was programmed to fly from a remote spot in the Negev to Mecca.

"Special Agent Allen and I were able to obtain an aircraft, locate the drone and then force it down in the Negev. We apologize to Israel that the bomb was detonated on its soil, but we had no way to stop the detonation and our only choice was to force it down in the desert where loss of life would be minimal. Otherwise, hundreds of thousands if not millions of people would have been killed."

"Why did you come to me and not go to the Prime Minister or others in the government?"

"We actually were on our way to see the Prime Minister yesterday. We met with Peter Shapiro, the American Ambassador to Israel, who believed us. He was taking us to see the Prime Minister when our car was attacked. The Ambassador was murdered by assailants and we were taken captive but we were able to free ourselves."

I was surprised by the lack of reaction Stern exhibited. She had a list of questions she was going down, checking them off one at a time. Then I saw her furtively check out the window. I'd been in enough of these interviews to recognize it wasn't going well. But there was something more. Then it dawned on me. I got up.

"C'mon Will, we need to get out of here. She's called the cops already. It'll only be a matter of time before they get here."

We made to leave. Stern tried to protest but it was obviously half-hearted. Just before we left, I turned to her and looked her in the eyes.

"I do hope you'll be able to live with yourself after war comes and millions are dead. You had a chance to stop it, but you took the easy way out."

We climbed back into the car and sped out of Tel Aviv, picking up Willoughby and Fallon along the way.

24

"So, what do we do now?" I asked to no one in particular. No response was forthcoming.

I felt particularly inept. I'd always believed in the power of the press to influence public policy but we were stymied every time we tried to go that route. The world was cascading out of control toward war. I had the means to stop it but I wasn't good enough to make it happen.

Similarly, Will experienced intense powerlessness. Neither of us knew what our next step would be. We returned to Willoughby's flat in silence. Fallon went out to get us some food while we waited. After about fifteen minutes there was a knock on the door. Figuring that Fallon wouldn't knock and that anybody else we could think of who'd find us probably wasn't a good thing; both Will and Willoughby drew their guns. Willoughby opened the door quickly.

"Hi."

Westbrook walked in. He was wearing the clothes he'd worn when we checked him into the hospital.

"How'd you get here?" I quickly asked.

"They took out the bullet and patched me up. While I was convalescing, a terrific row took place outside my door between one of the doctors and an Israeli officer. While my grasp of Hebrew is non-existent, I deduced the officer wanted to take me away into custody but the doctor said I wasn't ready to travel. My money being on the officer, I gathered up my clothes and computer, which they very nicely kept in a drawer for me, and climbed out the window. Luckily I was on the first floor. Finding you after that wasn't that difficult as you insist on keeping that phone on and the GPS led me here."

"Alan," Will asked, "Do they know who you are?"

"I don't think so, not unless you told them when you dropped me off. I didn't have any identification on me. I was totally out of it and don't remember talking with anybody. My computer is password protected so they couldn't find out there."

"Good. You may be our key to stopping a war."

We would have liked to immediately pile back in the car and make the drive back to Jerusalem, but we all realized how exhausted we were. We needed at least a couple hours sleep.

The plan we designed after waking up was very simple. We'd drive to Jerusalem, again by back roads to avoid checkpoints. Then we'd go straight to a local police station. Since our pictures were plastered all over Israel, neither Will nor I could very well go up to anybody in authority and tell them we needed to talk to the Prime Minister. But Alan Westbrook could. Nobody knew him, yet.

To ensure he'd be taken seriously, he was to go into the station, tell whoever was there not only that he had information on the bomb but that he had information about another bomb that was set to go off, and relatively soon. He needed to speak with the Prime Minister immediately. Then he would calmly sit down and wait for the wheels to turn. We hoped this lie, combined with his crazy manner, would be enough to have him taken seriously.

Calls would go up the chain, ultimately reaching the Prime Minister himself. We would have to battle the old mantra that Israel doesn't negotiate with terrorists, but we hoped that the fact that, if there was a suspected bomb ready to go off, they'd at least pass the word along that Alan needed to be taken seriously and that he wasn't asking all that much, just a chance to speak.

We explained the risks to Alan. He could be thrown into prison and tortured to get information. He was fully aware of all this.

"I'm the one responsible for this this whole mess. Whatever they do to me, I deserve."

I took Will aside.

"I don't know about this. I really doubt he can pull this off. In case you hadn't noticed, Alan's not overly adept at dealing with people. He's much more comfortable losing himself in his computer. Wouldn't Willoughby or Fallon be better suited for this?"

"Fallon's too green; his nervousness would shine through. Willoughby is just as inept at dealing with people as Alan but I'm afraid he would try too hard to think on his feet. Alan will impart his natural desperation but at the same time will project an innocence that will make his message stronger. He'll do fine."

"I hope you're right."

We rehearsed in the car as we drove to Jerusalem. The more Alan rehearsed, however, the worse he did. After a bit, Will just ended to process, giving me a look like maybe I was right. But at this point we didn't have any other options.

Alan had searched the web and gotten an address for the Jerusalem district of the Israeli Police. We stopped two blocks away from the station.

"Good luck, Alan." It was the first time since he came to my apartment that I had used his name to his face. He appreciated the gesture and reached for his computer. Will questioned whether he needed it. Alan responded that it was like a security blanket. Plus, he had an idea. He opened the computer and typed about twenty keystrokes.

"Good, I'm ready."

And he was on his way.

A half hour later he arrived back at the car. He was still gripping the computer, which was open as he walked.

"Well?" Will asked.

"Like clockwork. The Prime Minister will meet with us at his office in forty minutes."

"What's with the computer?" I asked.

Alan opened up the computer and turned the screen toward me. There was a digital clock counting down by the hundredths of a second. The clock read 1 hour, 25 minutes and whatever tenths and hundreds of a second your eye could latch onto at a given moment.

Under the time display was a box marked 'Deactivation Code'.

"I walked into the station and told the desk clerk I needed to talk to someone in charge immediately. After being initially brushed off, I showed her the screen and told her this was the time before a second atomic bomb will be detonated somewhere in Israel. I told them this one was much newer and more powerful than the one that blew in the Negev. It was also in a populated area. The only way it could be averted, I told her, is if I enter the appropriate code into the box and that it was a code only I knew. I also told her that I could bypass the code and immediately set off the explosion by pressing the tab and delete keys at the same time. If any harm came to me, I'd press the buttons.

"Soon I was talking with her higher ups at the station and ultimately I was patched in via teleconference with various national security officials. It was then I told them my demands: for us—the three of us—to speak face-to-face with the Prime Minister. I gave them ten minutes to respond. I sat down, waited ten minutes and then got up to leave, gripping my computer tightly. They then agreed to my demands. We're to drive to the Prime Minister's residence and we'll be admitted."

"Alan," Will noted, "that was brilliantly done. You thought of a way that made it impossible for them to take you out without exposing themselves and the country to a very great risk. Plus, the demands you were making were not all that unreasonable. Brilliantly played."

Alan looked very proud of himself.

We drove to the Prime Minister's residence, also known as Beit Aghion in an upscale neighborhood of Jerusalem. Will had Willoughby and Fallon get out of the car about five blocks from the residence so that they could trail along behind, keeping an eye out for us in case we were jumped or any other trouble occurred.

We pulled up in front of the residence and five agents immediately surrounded the car. Will and I got out of the car with our hands raised. Alan also got out but both his hands were clasped on the computer. His eyes were crazily darting back and forth, giving the impression he'd press the buttons at any moment.

The agents patted us all down and, after confiscating Will's firearm, led us into the residence. None of them had guns drawn but they ensured we had the impression they could extract them at any second. We were led into a windowless conference room and the door was closed behind us. Five minutes later Prime Minister Moshe Rosen stormed in.

"We do not negotiate with terrorists!" he scolded us.

"Nor should you," Will responded, "in any case, we're not terrorists."

"You're the Americans who took money to bomb my country, aren't you?"

"We're the American's who have been accused of such, but not one word of it is true. And we can prove it."

"If you're not terrorists, why are you threatening us with a second bomb?"

"There's no bomb," I offered, "it was the only way we could get in to see you without ourselves being killed."

"I don't understand."

"You made an appointment to see Ambassador Shapiro. Was that only yesterday? It seems like months ago."

"Yes, but he was killed on the way here."

"We were with him. We were coming to talk you out of war, to tell you that none of what you heard was true. There is no Iran connection. There is no country at all involved. It was all an elaborate scheme concocted by a well-financed rogue American Army officer, abetted by officers within your own military and probably officials in your government as well as our government."

There was a pause before the Prime Minister responded.

"Yes, I know all that, although I wouldn't refer to Colonel Lawson as a rogue. He's a fine officer and a hero, although he assured me that the launch would not come from inside Israel. That will remain our little secret, one that you will take to your grave, I'm sorry to say."

Will visibly deflated.

Prime Minister Rosen had a long Israeli military heritage. His grandfather had been a general during the 1948 war. His father was a general in 1967. He himself had risen to the rank of colonel before he entered politics. It would only make sense that he was an acquaintance of Lawson.

"I should have known as much," Will noted. "It was way too easy getting to see you. We walked right into your trap."

"Yes, you did, but I do commend your motives. Trying to stop war is a very pure objective, but in this case you are wrong. War is sometimes very necessary. I was supportive of bombing Mecca, but perhaps you did us all a favor. The people will be one hundred percent behind me and, since Iran drew first blood—and a nuclear one at that—we should have strong support throughout much of the civilized world once we respond in kind.

"Unfortunately, in the eyes of the world the three of you are to remain terrorist outlaws who will be hunted down and killed. I will leave it to my security team to decide where your bodies will be found."

With that, he pressed a button and the door opened and four burly men walked in with guns drawn.

"Goodbye, my friends. I will be sure to give Colonel Lawson your regards."

Our hands were bound behind us. We were led outside and put into a black van. Sitting in the back, behind us, were two of the soon-to-be assassins; the other two sat in the front seat. I was about to say something when I heard Will mutter something very softly. He was speaking down into his chest.

"Black Audi A55 Cargo Van, license 2952165. Leaving now. Four men."

Then he said nothing as we began what I thought would be our final journey. Alan sat very placidly off to the side. He looked odd, not being bent over his computer, which had been taken from him at the Prime Minister's residence.

The van pulled into a clearing outside of the city. The four men ordered us out. Their orders were clear: we were to be executed.

"So, who's in charge here?" Will asked.

The burliest of the four, who also happened to be our driver, responded.

"I am. I do hope you're not about to plea for you lives. It won't do any good."

"I fully understand that. I'm just curious what's going to happen to us after we're dead."

"We'll probably leave you here for a couple of hours and then you'll be found. At that point we'll put out a broadcast that the bodies of the terrorists who were working closely with Iran were found."

"I see. You think maybe you could get a message to my kids, telling them I wasn't actually a terrorist? It's going to be tough enough on them as it is."

"I don't think so."

"Well, it was worth a try. Where do you think you'll be fighting next year at this time?"

"Fighting?"

"Of course. Everyone in Israel is in the reserves, aren't they? Once the Prime Minister declares war and launches a bunch of missiles, you'll be attacked from all sides. My guess is you'll be right here, defending the homeland. At least your kids will have the privilege of knowing their father's a hero, that he died to protect Israel."

"Let's get this over with."

"Whatever you say. You're the one who's going to have to live with your actions. Hope you can sleep, killing innocent people like this."

"I'll sleep like a baby."

As he finished the word 'baby' blood began to spurt from a large hole that appeared in his neck. He dropped his gun and fell to his knees, clutching his throat. A few seconds later, he toppled over completely.

Within seconds of the first shot, the second man went down. He was holding a wound in his chest. The other two spun around with their guns extended, trying to locate where the shots came from. It was all to no avail as they each fell in a similar fashion.

The three of us stood there, towering over our would-be assassins as Willoughby and Fallon emerged from behind trees on opposite edges of the clearing.

"Nice shooting," Will observed, "I see you were finally able to track down some silencers."

"Yeah," Willoughby responded, "pretty damn good ones at that. We probably should just use this van to get out of here. The piece of shit car we lifted to follow you isn't very big and is about ready to fall to pieces. You're lucky we didn't stall getting here."

"Well, thanks, you guys. Let's get out of here."

26

We hadn't averted war but we were still alive. I supposed that was a step in the right direction, although how long we'd stay alive was entirely problematic.

"What now?" I asked.

Willoughby drove out of Jerusalem. At one point he took a Smith & Wesson pistol out of his jacket pocket and handed it to Will.

"Don't lose this one, okay?" Willoughby told Will.

"Very funny," was the response.

"What happens how?" I asked.

"That depends on how good a recording we got," Will replied.

"Oh, it's clear as a bell," Willoughby observed. "You can hear every word and it's obvious who's speaking."

I was totally in the dark.

"Recording of what?"

"I was wearing a wire, Fava."

Will pointed to his chest and I noted that one of his buttons on his shirt was a slightly different color than the rest.

Will continued. "Willoughby always travels with the latest gadgets in his bag and he wired me before we went to see the PM. You remember me mumbling in the car? I was giving directions to my friends here to follow us and save our lives, which probably wasn't necessary since this button also has GPS capability.

"Given how easily we got in to see the Prime Minister, I suspected something must be up and I put a wire on. I wore the gun when we arrived so I could turn it over, hoping that at best they'd do a cursory frisk to look for any other weapons but not expect a wire. We lucked out and they were satisfied with the gun. Then when we went in, everything that was said was being recorded by Willoughby and Fallon."

"What do you plan on doing with this recording?"

"We're going to re-visit Rachel Stern."

"Why?"

"You said it yourself: This is too good a story for a reporter to pass up. Before, all she had was our word on things. Alan had put together some files and such, but those could have been doctored. Now we have something concrete; we have the Prime Minister on tape admitting to knowing all about the blast but still willing to use it as an excuse to drag his country into a nuclear war. No journalist worth her salt will pass that one up. Plus, we'll have the element of surprise on our side. Before, she had time to make arrangements with authorities; this time, she won't. We'll force her to listen and to come up with her own conclusions."

Will and I jumped out of the van a few blocks from the TV Station while Alan, Willoughby and Fallon stayed in the vehicle. Will didn't have any need for Alan to come along with us. If truth be told, Will probably didn't need me either but we'd been through so much together, he wasn't going to separate us now.

As we approached the television station, we went around to the back where the loading dock and vehicle parking were. We hid behind an adjoining building and surveyed the situation. The loading dock was empty at the moment. There was one door to the rear and no windows. We tested the door, which was locked. We waited.

After five minutes, the door opened and a maintenance worker stepped out for a smoke. His ID card, which would also open the door, hung from his belt. Will sauntered over to the man.

"Got a smoke?" he asked.

As the worker looked down to pull out a cigarette, Will took out his gun and rapped him solidly on the back of the head. He went out instantly. We dragged his body around the corner and took his card.

"He'll be okay," Will assured me, "a pounding headache but that's about it."

The station was a drab looking three-story structure with about six rooms on each floor.

"My guess," I speculated, "is that Rachel's office is on the second floor. She's important enough to the station that she'd have a corner office but not on the top floor; that would be for management."

We went up the steps to the second floor and started walking through the floor.

"Just look like you belong in the place," Will advised, "People may not know you but if you look confident, they'll believe you should be here."

We walked along the hallway, looking for Rachel's office. As I predicted, it was one of the corner offices. She wasn't there, but there was evidence she was around. We entered and closed the door behind us.

Ten minutes later, the door opened and Rachel walked in. A shocked as well as frightened expression filled her face when she saw us. She tried to go back out but Will had already slipped behind her and re-closed the door.

"Hi Rachel, surprised to see us?" I asked.

Rachel headed over to her desk.

"I'm going to call security."

"Good luck with that," Will noted as he held the disconnected phone jack up in the air.

"All we're asking is that you hear us out," he continued.

She sat down and eyed us intently.

"Okay, I'm listening."

Will sat down and pulled out Willoughby's recorder. He hit play. Rachel seemed confused when she heard the Prime Minister's distinctive nasally voice.

"Where did you get this?" she asked.

"In his office, this morning, just before he ordered that we be killed."

Rachel listened to the recording. Her eyes nearly bugged out of her head when she heard him admit he was trying to start a war on bogus charges. When he was ordering our murder, she gasped a quick 'Oh my God.'

At the end of it all, she said nothing.

"Everything we've been trying to tell you is true," I interjected. "As far-fetched as it all sounds, it's all true. And now, even the Prime Minister is involved. The question is: Are you going to do your job as a journalist and report this or are you going to take the easy way out and bow to the state, and in the process allow a thermo-nuclear war to start?"

She looked me in the eye.

"If I have my way, this is going on the air."

She started to get up. Will rose to stop her.

"Don't worry, I promise I'm not going to report you. I have to run this by my boss."

A few minutes later, Rachel returned with a gray-haired spare man, introduced as Chaim Goldberg. We replayed the recording for him. Rachel then pleaded our case for us.

"I believe them, Chaim. The recording is backed up by numerous documents and other materials. I've seen them. This is big and I think we should run it. As a matter of fact, I think it's vital that we run it, for the good of the nation."

"That bastard," was all he could say.

Goldberg asked a few more questions, all of which Rachel handled with ease. Their interaction reminded me of Frank and me and how we worked together. Chaim pondered, looked at his watch and then shook his head yes. They were going to run the piece.

"I need to review a script in a half-hour."

He walked out of the room. Rachel turned to us.

"Let's get working."

We sat down and started to frame out the piece. Rachel called up our earlier interview on her computer. She would have liked to have redone some of the footage—mainly because she didn't believe us then and she thought that might come across—but we didn't have time. Instead, she would cut and paste various portions into the whole.

Unlike American TV, news segments in Israel and in many

other countries tended to go into a great deal of depth. Instead of one or two minutes, a piece could be five to ten minutes long. We didn't have that luxury here. She'd have to get across her point across in two to three minutes.

She decided she'd introduce us first. By now, our faces were known all over Israel. Having us front and center would grab people's attention. She'd use the introductory Q & A from our previous interview. Then she'd cut to us live, introduce the recording of the Prime Minister and play it as we listened on. We'd then be asked about how we came to record this conversation and to describe our subsequent near-murder.

At the end of the piece, she'd appear solo on camera and talk to the Israel people one-to-one. She'd talk about abuse of power, how the leader of the country was playing on the people's fears and blood lust to start a war that could easily escalate into a world war, and how a nation of laws was being subverted for fanatical purposes.

She quickly drafted the script and let me look it over. I had a couple technical comments, but other than those, I thought it perfect.

Rachel had a reputation for being a fearless but fair journalist. We did not see that in her before, but now it was in full view. She and Chaim were taking great risks. They could be arrested, accused of treason and face a host of other charges but they were doing what they believed to be the right thing. I don't think I've ever had more admiration for anyone, other than my mother and Will, in my life.

She rushed out with the draft and came back a short fifteen minutes later. Chaim approved the piece but had one addition.

It was obvious that neither Rachel nor Chaim were fans of the Prime Minister, who was noted before his hawkishness even before this. However, Chaim thought it fair to at least give the Prime Minister's office a chance to respond. He did not want to expose his hand too early, though, and have the government shut down the broadcast beforehand, in the interest of "national security". What he proposed was for Rachel to play the recording for the world to hear and then on the air call the Prime Minister's office to get their reactions. It was a gutsy plan that could either work brilliantly or result in all of us spending the rest of our lives in prison.

"C'mon, let's get mikes on."

At the last moment, she shifted gears and decided to do the entire interview live. She'd just ask the same questions as she did of us earlier.

The camera began to roll.

"Good evening, this is Rachel Stern reporting live from our studio here in Tel Aviv. With me today are Special Agent William Allen from the American Federal Bureau of Investigation and Francine Vega, a fellow television reporter from New York. As most of you know, Mr. Allen and Ms. Vega are wanted in relation to the nuclear blast that occurred in the Negev earlier this week. They have not only been implicated but have been accused of setting off the blast on behalf of the government of Iran.

"I have just been handed incontrovertible evidence proving that not only are they innocent of these charges but also that they have been framed for a variety of reasons that we will get into shortly. But first, I would like to play a recording made by Mr. Allen earlier today of a conversation he had with Prime Minister Rosen. The first voice you'll hear is that of Special Agent Allen"

Over our earpieces we could hear the recording being played.

"*We were coming to talk you out of war, to tell you that none of what you heard was true. There is no Iran connection. There is no country at all involved. It was all an elaborate scheme concocted by a well-financed rogue American Army officer, abetted by officers within your own military and probably officials in your government as well as our government.*"

"*Yes, I know all that, although I wouldn't refer to Colonel Lawson as a rogue. He's a fine officer and a hero, although he assured me that the launch would not come from inside Israel. That will remain our little secret, one that you will take to your grave,*"

I'm sorry to say."

"I should have known as much. It was way too easy getting to see you. We walked right into your trap."

"Yes, you did, but I do commend your motives. Trying to stop war is a very pure objective, but in this case you are wrong. War is sometimes very necessary. I was supportive of bombing Mecca, but perhaps you did us all a favor. The people will be one hundred percent behind me and, since Iran drew first blood—and a nuclear one at that—we should have strong support throughout much of the civilized world once we respond in kind.

"Unfortunately, in the eyes of the world the three of you are to remain terrorist outlaws who will be hunted down and killed. I will leave it to my security team to decide where your bodies will be found."

Sounds of his security detail walking in could be heard.

"Goodbye, my friends. I will be sure to give Colonel Lawson your regards."

Rachel spoke after this finished.

"We have a call in to the Prime Minister's office. I believe we have his Chief of Staff, Joel Herzog, on the line. Are you there, Mr. Herzog?"

Over our earpieces we heard a cold response.

"Yes, I am here."

"Would you or the Prime Minister like to respond to the recording we just played?"

"I find it to be the ultimate in irresponsible journalism, especially noting that you are sitting with two suspected terrorists."

"I understand that a flash drive containing all the documents exonerating Mr. Allen and Ms. Vega was provided to the Prime Minister. Have you had a chance to review these documents?"

"No, we have not."

"Also on that drive is information proving that Colonel Lawson, an officer in the US Army, purchased the nuclear device from a known illicit arms dealer and that the funds came not from Iran but from lottery winnings. Given this information, the Prime Minister can't be committing our country to war, can he?"

"We are reviewing all information at our disposal."

"Can you describe how the Prime Minister knows Colonel Lawson?"

"You'll have to ask the Prime Minister that question."

"Thank you for your time Mr. Herzog."

The phone line clicked off. We'd finally done it. There was no way the Prime Minister could go ahead with war now. Most likely, he would be ousted from power.

And I was proud of the fact that it was the power of the press that ultimately saved the world.

27

"Miss Vega, all charges against you have been dropped. You are free to go."

I was greatly relieved to hear these words from the Federal Office of the Attorney General. It was especially a relief since these words were delivered to me in jail, where I'd been sitting for the three days since we'd touched down at JFK.

Agents were waiting for Will and me as we deplaned. They had no warrant for Alan; he was still not on anybody's radar screen.

As we were walking through the terminal, our hands cuffed behind our backs, Alan followed along and told Will he wanted to turn himself in for killing Farad Sahari. Will responded that, after all we'd been through together, he was not inclined to arrest him. Furthermore, Will told him we did not see any benefit to throwing him in jail and that Farad Sahari would have believed that he had more than made amends by saving millions of his countrymen from certain death. Justice had already been served, Will advised him. If Alan felt a great desire to get himself arrested, he'd have to go to another law enforcement official. Alan said he'd only turn himself over to Will so he turned to leave.

We said our goodbyes to Alan and he wandered off. To where, I don't know. I wished him happiness, but I somehow doubted he'd find it.

Ever since we sent Frank the files on the flash drive, he'd been hard at work developing a news segment that would tell the entire story. He contacted Rachel and they collaborated on the piece. It was to be the first time Frank had been in front of a camera in nearly fifteen years.

Since the segment was truthful and implicated high government officials in criminal activities and even treason, the station got cold feet and refused to air it. When I was thrown in jail, however, Frank took matters into his own hands.

Waiting until just before the six o'clock news hour, he shooed everybody except his most trusted assistants out of the studio. Jonas, of course, was allowed to stay. Once everyone was gone, he locked each door to the studio with heavy chains and a padlock.

He then sat down in the anchor's seat and signaled for the cameras to roll.

Good evening, I'm Frank McDermott, News Director for Action 6 News. As the world knows, a nuclear device was detonated three days ago in southern Israel. Original reports implicated Francine Vega, a reporter for this station, along with an FBI Special Agent, William Allen, in bringing about this detonation on behalf of the Republic of Iran. As documentation, which will be shown to you in a few minutes, will prove, this is a blatant lie. Furthermore, this lie was perpetrated—and in fact the nuclear blast was condoned—by the highest levels of the United States and Israeli governments.

At this point, the viewers were shown the piece Frank and Rachel had put together that laid out in great detail Lawson's plan to foment war in the Middle East. The video ran about fifteen minutes. I understand that upper management was apoplectic. They were going to pull the plug and throw on a rerun in place of the news but the numbers started to roll in indicating that nearly everyone in New York was switching over to our channel and they let the piece run to its conclusion.

Soon after this, Will and I were released from custody.

In Israel, after Rachel's broadcast the Israeli Parliament went into special session and immediately voted to cease all preparations for war, pending further developments. They also convened a special panel of inquiry to investigate Prime Minister Rosen's activities with the objective of determining whether criminal charges should be filed. Will and I were deposed as witnesses by videoconference. Eventually, the Prime Minister would be removed from office and charged with an assortment of crimes.

Relations between Israel, Iran and the rest of the Muslim

world, which had always been frosty, got no better but also no worse as a result of the resolution of this affair.

Using the information in the flash drive, Captain Fairchild persuaded her superiors to launch an inquiry into Colonel Lawson and any other officers implicated in assisting him. The Army would use this information to court martial Lawson in absentia. Lawson went underground and his whereabouts was unknown. Given that he still had about $200 million of Alan's money at his disposal, I doubt it was the last we've heard of Jacob Lawson.

After we were released, Will and I drove up to Emma's mother's place to pick up the kids. I never witnessed a happier reunion than when Albert and Stella ran into Will's arms. He twirled them around and around as they squealed in delight.

I never felt happier myself than when Will told them that I'd be coming to live with them forever. Albert, while not delighted by the prospect of having me as his step-mother, had been slowly warming up to me and did not appear visibly opposed at the prospect of Will and me marrying. Will asked me if I wanted them to call me Mom or something like that. I told him Fava would be just fine. In fact, it would be perfect.

The FBI was slow in its investigation of its own ranks. The documentation showed that someone within the organization worked with Lawson, but it was unclear as to who it was. I was upset on Will's behalf that his agency was not doing more to ferret out the traitor. Will simply shrugged, chalking it up to the bureaucracy.

We planned our wedding for six months after we returned. Like Reverend McKenzie, we were minor celebrities getting our fifteen minutes. We made the talk show and Sunday talking head tour, but soon we became yesterday's news, which we greatly welcomed. We delayed our wedding thinking that the event, if it were to be too soon, would only regenerate unwanted attention.

I also wanted to delay the wedding so that I could spend some time working to get to know Albert and letting him get to know me. He would definitely be a work in progress over the next few years.

Our wedding was a modest affair; we invited about thirty people. My maid of honor was my college roommate, Zelda, with whom I stayed close over the years. Will's best man was Willoughby. We ended up with an unbalanced entourage as there really weren't many other females I felt close enough to want them represented, but both Will and I agreed that we had to have Frank, Jonas and Agents Fallon and Broderick up there with us.

At my first wedding, I didn't bother with a ring bearer or flower girl, but I sure wanted them this time. Tears of joy streamed down my cheek as Albert and Stella preceded me down the aisle.

As promised, Will paid for Yehuda to come over and partake in the festivities. We wanted to invite all of our newfound acquaintances; we had to do our best to have them there. We'd gotten to know these people so intensely that it wouldn't have been right not to include them. Rachel came as did Captain Fairchild. I invited Inspector Murat, but he graciously declined, as did Edward McKenzie. However, we found his brother not to be of our liking and did not invite him.

I would have liked to invite Alan, but he was nowhere to be found. As he did after his brother was killed, he fell off the face of the earth. He never got a cut of his own winnings as Lawson had commandeered the remainder of the lottery money, leaving Alan destitute. I'd like to think that he's getting along somewhere. His computer skills alone were enough to command top dollar, if he were so inclined.

Will and I, on the other hand, benefited greatly from Alan's fortune. I'd forgotten about the $10 million deposited into each of our accounts as part of the attempt to frame us. It wasn't until I went to check my balance that I realized it was still there. Any freezes that were placed on our accounts had been lifted, but they didn't touch the funds.

"Will, what do we do about the $10 million?" I asked him.

"I checked on it with the bureau and they said that since the money didn't come from illegal activities, they weren't going to touch it. They said it was ours. We just have to be sure to declare it on our taxes."

When the time came to take our vows, the look of love on Will's face as he said 'I do' is something I'll take with me the rest of our lives.

The four of us went to Israel for our honeymoon. This time we finally got to see the sights. Yehuda acted as our tour guide.

After that, we settled into our routine as a modern day family. We both went back to our respective jobs. In many ways, my celebrity status had died down, but the initial surge was enough to lift the station's news program from fourth to second place in New York. Seeking to capitalize on it even more, Frank approached me one day and asked me if I'd like to be co-anchor on the morning news. Willa Banks, one of the current co-anchors, had taken a job with the competition and the Frank thought I'd be perfect for the position.

"Frank, I'd love it, but there is one complication," I responded. "I'm pregnant."

"That's wonderful Francine! We'll work around that, no problem. As a matter of fact, with Will as the father—he is the father, isn't he?"

I shot him a look.

"With Will as the father, we should be able to milk it for a couple more ratings points."

Ah yes, ever the newsman. He then smiled as he made an obvious observation.

"You do realize that this news might be enough to knock you off your perch as New York's hottest reporter."

"The sacrifices we make to perpetuate the species," I responded.

Seven months later, Rosa Vega Allen was born. She was named after my mother.

I was in my hospital bed, sweaty and exhausted from having gone through a protracted labor when the nurse brought little Rosa in after cleaning her up. Will was sitting by my bedside as the nurse handed the baby over to me for the first time. We both stared on her with wonder.

"This is the third time I've gone through this," Will observed, "and I can never get over how utterly amazing it is. Albert and Stella are so excited, waiting for you and Rosa to come home."

We said nothing after that but looked fondly down on her. I was just about to offer Rosa over to Will to hold when both of our phones pinged at the same time, indicating texts had come in. Will was wearing his phone while mine was on the nightstand. He took his phone out and gave it a glance. He put it back in its holster without bothering to read the message.

"I don't know anybody from a 672 area code; probably junk."

I smiled.

"Of course you know someone from the 672 area code."

"I do? Where is that exactly?"

"Antarctica."

Will immediately pulled his phone back out as he handed me mine. We looked at the identical messages on our respective screens:

```
Congratulations on the birth of Rosa.
ASW
```

BLACK ROSE
writing™